UNRAVELED

Published in 2018 by Richard A Gutierrez Holdings, Inc.

Library of Congress Registration Number / Date: TXu001629905 / 2008-04-10

ISBN-13: 978-0692055915 Richard A Gutierrez Holdings, Inc.
ISBN-10: 0692055916

Editor: Emily E. James
Design: Richard A. Gutierrez

This book is dedicated to my Mom, Dad & Sister

With much love and patience: read, write and create!

yarn (yärn) *n.*

- A continuous strand of twisted threads of weaving or knitting.

- *Informal.* A long, complicated story or a tale of real or fictitious adventures, often elaborated upon the teller during the telling.
- *Informal.* To tell a long, complicated story.

> • *The American Heritage Dictionary 1982*

yarn \ yarn\ *n.*

- A continuous often plied strand composed of fibers or filaments and used in weaving and knitting to form cloth.
- A similar strand of metal, glasses, asbestos, paper, or plastic
- Thread
- A narrative of adventures; esp: a tall tale

> • *Webster's New Collegiate Dictionary 1977*

yarn (yärn) *n.* Spun thread for threading or knitting.
yarn (yärn) *n. colloq.* A long tale, esp. an incredible one.
Naut. A tale of adventure, often exaggerated. – *vi.* To spin a yarn.

> • *Webster's New American Dictionary 1966*

TABLE OF CONTENTS

CHAPTER I

As I looked around his brownstone apartment from the living room sofa, I felt the proud heritage of its Puerto Rican occupant. Traditional items like rooster and Coquí figurines, Pilóns, and a small number of Puerto Rican flags were decorated around, but more interestingly was his extensive album and compact disc collection of many of the great salsa bands. This is who he was...his identity. This is what I was missing.

He was taking a long shower to wash away all the dirt and grime from a sewer job, and that was why I decided to watch a video on his television to pass the time. It was labeled "La Promesa", and when I pressed *Play*, it was a group of five jíbaros, which refers to "la gente de la montaña" or "mountain people", in their guayaberas or a traditional button-down shirt with at least four pockets in the front, playing a combination of Spanish musical instruments including Quattros, a guido, and maracas. The lead singer sang soulfully of upcoming promises and I felt my spirit agreeing with him, and although they all appeared to be embraced by the bright and sweltering tropical sun, I was pleased that my body wasn't sticking to any of the plastic covers he had to protect his couch where I was sitting comfortably. The oscillating fan turned left then right and was a nice reminder that too much of anything is no good.

When he came out of the bathroom, he asked me if I wanted a second round of coffee and since the first cup had already wound me up, and if I had taken him up on his offer, my heart would have probably come out of my chest from the embodied caffeine. The coffee was so strong that he had to boil milk and fill the remaining half of my cup, but I just looked at the gold bag of beans sitting open on the counter -

Café Fantástico, which happened to be an accurate name for this espresso.

"No thanks. I'm good," I said, taking a sip, and that's when I started to get up and enter his modest kitchen area.

I then sat at his small wooden breakfast table, located by a window, while he was still getting fully-dressed. A plastic cover helped protect it underneath since he wasn't someone who was in the habit of using a coaster. He had a decent view from the modest third-floor apartment and through the dark-green café curtains, you could see the local tavern at the corner, the NJ Turnpike, and even a crossing guard that helped elementary school children crossing the busy Jersey City streets. Sometimes, we'd go to the roof and feed the pigeons he had caged in a coop.

Mr. Feliciano was a mentor to me, though in reality, I'd been the one to teach him everything I knew about the business and in return he spent more time trying to show me a legal trade. He really knew how to work with his hands, whether it was performing a tune-up on a car or installing new piping for a plumbing project.

"So... Friday's the big night? You ready?" he asked as he was drying his hair with a hand-towel he snatched from the oven door.

"I'm a little nervous, but, uh...what about you?" I countered, trying to divert him away from the subject of my first artist's reception at a gallery in SOHO. "You gonna be able to make it?"

"I don't know. I have a big job to do down the Shore, in Freehold actually, and it'll be all day." he said.

"You always have a job to do." I sneered.

"I've been working since I was thirteen, and no one else is going to take care of my bills, Papi."

"There's more to life than just working. You need to enjoy it." I demanded of him. He put the now-damp cloth back on the oven handle to let it dry then finally sat down to join me. "Yeah. I'll be there."

"You can't wear that though!" I pointed to his blue jeans stained by plumber's putty, different epoxies and who else knows what, but he just laughed it off and showed me his other discolorations as if they were scars and healed wounds of long-ago battles. "Just kiddin'. Just come, all right?"

He picked up his mug and turned to look outside. "I pr....." and before he could take a sip, he had an intense look on his face for the briefest moment, right before the bullet shot through the window and to the side of his face. We looked at each other in a surprised shock before his hot coffee spilled, hitting the table, and then a crashing sound of his mug on the parquet floor.

I pushed off the table with all of my weight to stand back away from this craziness, and the chair beneath me was thrown to the side. Feliciano was shot, and in a slight panic, I took cover and glanced, from a distance, out the window for any signs of the shooter. I could not bear to look over to him because the sight of blood, and even the smell of it, causes me to faint. I crept up towards the lower corner of the window and from a distance, I saw a suited man on an adjacent rooftop, running away but I got up to pick up the receiver of his wall-mounted phone and dialed 911, while I stared at the back of his limp body. His head was slumped over to his right and his chin was resting on his chest. I heard a woman's voice introduce herself as being the 911 Operator and asked me what my emergency was.

"Someone's been shot. Hurry!" but then I left the phone hanging from its cord until it almost touched the ground where there it remained prorogue.

The music video was still playing, adding to the intensity of the situation, but I quickly ran out of the apartment and up to the rooftop. When I opened the heavy-bolted door, sunlight hit my face and then I remembered that I was afraid of heights. I saw someone or something bolt from the corner of my eye two rooftops away and when I reached the edge of the building, I realized that the adjacent building was too far for me to jump, plus it would have been a ten-foot drop on the tarred roof.

The only thing I could do, since I really wasn't sure where the murderer was, was to turn back and hit the street-level in my own efforts to escape. I saw the cooped pigeons, opened the latch and tried to shoo and free as many as I could but then there was Mitch, a white pigeon with some light brown patches on his back who I helped to heal from a broken wing when he was just a squab. He allowed me to pick him up and as I silently said my goodbyes, I threw him, thrusting him high into the sky.

"You're free now." I said to the collective.

I left the coop open as I walked to the rooftop door and bolted it back shut. When I ran down a floor level using the spiral staircase, I couldn't help but peer into his apartment through his opened front door, looked around one more time, and quickly ran to the oven and removed the duffel bag that was inside it.

"La bendición." I said to him as I heard the sirens, from afar.

I cautiously walked out the front door of the apartment building and discreetly got to my car, naturally parked blocks away due to lack of parking spots, and drove off in a panic through the city streets. There were practically STOP signs on every corner, and I'm sure I blew a few of them but I kept looking in the rear-view mirror to see if I was being followed. I had to let someone know what happened other than the 911 operator, but who? I passed an elementary school and noticed a father walking his son up the steps, possibly to his first day of school. I don't know if it was the look on the boy's face, but suddenly I was back over 20 years ago at St. Anthony's Elementary.

CHAPTER II – Happy Birthday (1976)

There are certain decisions in your life which change the course of your history. I remember my first profound moment as I had always been disciplined and obedient. My parents had enrolled me in pre-school a little after registration, and I remembered my first day of school when my father escorted me out of his mint-conditioned orange 1971 Volkswagen Beetle towards a red-bricked building. Ravel's Piano Concerto had been playing from the car radio cassette as I was entranced in its somber feel, and I could only guess that it was Ravel playing because of his unmistakable piano and crescendo. All was quiet in the streets, and I started to open my eyes, I suppose, to life. He escorted me into the building, holding my hand, and into a classroom with kids my age, and as I looked around, I didn't know what to do. It was a large room with a high ceiling, but everything was like that at my age and I wouldn't let go of my father's hand as he spoke with the teacher. She said that everything would be all right, and wistfully took me away towards the other children.

By the time I looked back, I only caught a second glimpse of his back as he turned into the hallway and was gone forever – or so it seemed. I was confused and bewildered for a great part of the day and I didn't know where I was, nor did I know any of these people and although it felt as though an eternity had gone by, I didn't know what to do with myself until the teacher had declared "playtime" and started to open a huge box that may have well been called a treasure chest. It had two hinges in the back and a strong latch in the front and as I stood quietly looking out the window for my father, kids were shouting and running towards the box as she pulled out dolls, action figures and balls, but I didn't pay too much attention because I was just thinking of ways to escape but then I felt something hit my right heel, and as I looked down, I noticed a blue plastic car which someone had rolled over to me. It was my teacher and I didn't move, and as I stood there in silence I leaned over and rolled it back to her and upon further contemplation, I had just discovered the wheel, and found myself sitting and enjoying our interaction. I couldn't stop playing with my new toy. We made contact, and it was good.

Two years later, it was my sixth birthday, and my parents arranged a party at our apartment. They invited some of my classmates from school, my cousins who were all younger than me, and their parents, of course. I was excited as any child would be as they decorated the place with blue and white streamers, and balloons. My parents had bought me the coolest present I could have gotten – a set of Matchbox cars that were these miniature metal cars that I could just roll for hours and I had just put them away in their carrying case when the doorbell rang. My friends had arrived, and I was extremely happy to see them again. I had my birthday party hat on, and soon each of them were wearing cone-shaped decorated hats that you put on with a rubber band strap, under your chin, to hold it in place. Before we all knew it, we had a good crowd and all who were invited were there.

After refreshments were served and we were all more comfortable, I decided to take out my cars and play with a few of my friends in my room while the others gathered in the living room. We lived on the second floor in a two-bedroom apartment, and I didn't have a rug in my room and sometimes I say it is my room, but my sister and I shared it with a bunk-bed in the far-left corner as you walked in.

The original wood parquet flooring helped us roll the cars to wherever we wanted to. After a few races, I started to get a little excited, I suppose, and as I pushed my favorite car, I put a little extra on it and pushed my weight behind it. My knee slid on the floor and I started screaming because a splinter had entered my knee, and I was bleeding. My parents rushed into the room and saw the blood coming from my injury but while my father wanted to see it, I held on to it to dull the pain. I don't know why, but I wouldn't show him because I was afraid to see any sight of blood. My friends and their parents were alarmed and curious to see what had happened as I started to cry.

My father brought me into the parlor and had asked everyone to please go to the other room, while he assessed the damage, but I couldn't stop screaming and crying. My mom had brought in some hydrogen peroxide and I knew what that meant because of some minor cuts I had before, that if it started to bubble after applied, then it was infected. Not only that but when he applied it to my wound, it stung like heck. We were both blowing on it profusely. Like a surgeon, he distracted me, and without warning, he pulled out a pair of tweezers. *Oh, my God*. My mom brought a lamp over, and as we got a better picture, we saw the tip of the huge splinter protruding from my skin. *How could such a joyous occasion be followed by a surprisingly painful event?*

It was pretty quiet in the other rooms and it was probably because I was doing the only screaming around. Because of all my squirming and time consumption, my dad quickly took care of the situation. He pulled it out not for more than a minute's time, and it had to have been about two inches long but I felt better after my mom put an adhesive bandage on it. I was embarrassed, but my parents were great.

Before I knew it, the other kids came into the room and made me feel at ease. It was "Pin the Tail on the Donkey" time and it was as though nothing happened and afterward, we played musical chairs with the music coming from my parents' turntable. Dad would pick up the arm of the needle to randomly stop the album from playing. People were taking pictures, while my father was videotaping me with his 8mm camera.

As I looked into the lens, I professed to everyone who could hear me.

"Today's my birthday . . . February 3rd".

My birthday really fell on the 27th, but I must have forgotten. Everyone sang "Happy Birthday" and after I cut my Beatles-decorated cake, we ate it with ice cream. Despite the great time I had that day, I did not feel like celebrating any more birthdays because of my traumatic experience with the splinter. I held up my favorite car toy and spun the back wheels into the camera.

CHAPTER III

The wheels of my '86 Buick Riviera were spinning. The quickest way uptown was to take the State Highway from the Holland Tunnel area then to hit Route 1&9. I pulled out my cellular phone and dialed.

"Bud, what's up? It's me." I stated.

"Shit, dude. It's been a while. Glad you're alive. What's up?"

"Felix wasn't so lucky. It happened just a while ago."

"What?!" he exclaimed.

"I'm comin' over." I quickly decided.

"Not here you're not. I'm 'hot'. Meet me at Starlight."

"You got it." I affirmed then immediately ended the call.

I was sick to my stomach and due to the shock starting to wear off, my life seemed to fall apart unexpectedly and I was spiraling out of control. I put my hazard lights on, pulled over, opened my door and vomited on the asphalt road and when I finished, I pulled down my driver's side mirror and wiped my mouth with a white monogrammed handkerchief from my leather jacket pocket. I hadn't thrown up my guts like that in a very long time but for an entirely different and innocent reason. After thinking it over a few moments, I put the car in reverse a few feet and hopped out to pop open the truck and reach under the carpeting to slowly pull out a bottle of Felipe II. As I took a swig, I contemplated how I was told never to drink on an empty stomach. *Too late.*

****

When my parents stressed education, and encouraged me to stay close to home I would often read a book or just draw, and sometimes I would do both. Doodling my own

Dungeons & Dragons characters were the beginnings of my own creations. I created my own book, which I drew in pencil in a Composition Book, and the results changed with every decision the player made which was extremely fun and creative! My Renaissance period began when I first caught a glimpse of Da Vinci's Mona Lisa, hanging from the hallway wall.

"Hey, mom, when did dad paint that?"

"He didn't," she said with a half-smile as she walked away. I thought that was the most artistic portrait that I had ever seen. Wherever I went, there she was looking at me with her half-smile, and that was mainly why I thought it was a portrait of my mother.

I was in the third grade when a Chiropractic office held an art contest. First place was awarded $100 and an invitation to meet the Mayor, while the Second and Third-Prize winners also got to meet the Mayor. I was in my class making "fortune cookies" out of paper which I thought was a cool racket. I would take a page out of my notebook and fold it from one corner to the opposite corner only my pages were rectangular, so I tore off the top piece so it would be perfectly square. When I opened the page, I would have two triangles, so I took the adjacent corner and aligned it with the opposite corner leaving me now with four triangles. I turned the piece of paper over so the creases were on the other side, and took each corner and met them in the middle of the page but I had to be careful so the teacher would not see me. I then had four triangles within a smaller square piece of paper, flipped it over and took the new four corners and met them in the middle. I opened the flaps and had my fortune cookie.

It was actually for Bill and he gave me ten cents to make him one. No one knew how to do it, other than Deirdre and myself, and our classmates thought it was cool and so soon they all had one. There were four colors on the outside, eight numbers inside, and depending on what you chose, there was a different fortune message inside. I was on the number "3" of Bill's new origami when the principal and my father came in through the back entrance of the classroom. He brought in the art piece I had worked on and submitted for the Chiropractic contest, of the human spine. I won first place, and now the whole class knew it. They all congratulated me as I got ready to meet the Mayor that same afternoon. My father had come down to congratulate me personally before he had to go to work and I was excused earlier from school along with the other two winners.

We waited on the campus bridge for the school van and driver to transport us to City Hall and during my wait and anticipation, I couldn't help but try to look out the window from the bridge. I wasn't sure if the windows were in the process of being cleaned or if they had condensation, but I started to get dizzy from trying to focus and to make sense of it all and after about ten minutes, needless to say, I developed a severe headache and started to become nauseous but I had to maintain because, after all, I was about to meet the Mayor of our city for an honorary recognition. The van came, and I rode in the passenger seat as I was thinking that this was the first time I ever won first place for anything. We arrived at the City Hall, downtown, and waited in a large courtroom where the lights were dim, and I could hear echoes from the emptiness. Mayor Gerald McCann arrived and shook my hand as he congratulated me. A photographer for the local newspaper was there and took our picture together and when it was all over, I went home and vomited. I felt better after that.

****

Looking back, I could see Hoboken on my left and Jersey City on my right surrounded by old semi-abandoned brick buildings and in the center of it all was one of my favorite main roads into New York City – the Holland Tunnel.

I took the Pike and headed to 14B in silence, thinking about home, Jersey City, from this elevated perspective just passing Dickinson High School and admiring the view. *How did things get so complicated?*

****

Classes were winding down towards the end of my years at my Catholic elementary school, and I had already decided where to go to High School. Lunch was the next period and I loved lunch on Fridays because it was pizza day. They came in squares so I hadn't developed the Jersey-fold yet but they were delicious mini-Sicilian slices to me. We gathered in the cafeteria downstairs, and I had sat close to the girls to see where they would be going next year. Most of them chose really good schools while others were still undecided but overall, I did not want to part with any of my friends because we had grown together and had so much fun. After we ate, we gathered in the schoolyard in the front of the school, and I tried to spend as much time with everyone as possible. My spirits were high, but I knew I may never see any of them again.

Deirdre was talking with her friends about who knows what and while many may have complimented her on her blue eyes and blonde hair, I really enjoyed her smile, smirk really, that came whenever we said something goofy to each other like a silly joke about this or that. We were kids. I knew I liked her, I had a crush on her since third grade, and it was all new to me.

At gym class, we played Dodgeball once in a while and I often found myself sacrificing and taking chances on protecting some of the less-willing or non-performing participants like some of the girls. The goal was to dodge getting hit with the ball but if you caught it, the person who threw it would be out of the game. A few were afraid that the big maroon rubber ball would hit them in their heads or really hurt their legs by an aggressive ball-thrower but in order to participate in the game, contact was necessary just as long as harm wasn't the direct intention in the process. At times I would jump in front of them to catch the ball rendering the thrower "out" and strategically I often attempted throwing the ball at the strongest opponent first to eliminate them right away. Deirdre, although quite athletic, was someone I always looked at and looked after.

My last class was over and school was finished for the week. It was Friday afternoon and there was not a cloud in the sky, except for one that I had noticed in the distance since lunch break in the yard. My sister had already joined her friends and took another route home but I, on the other hand, decided to take a shorter route on my own. It was a crisp, warm afternoon and I enjoyed taking my walk, took my time breathing, soaking in the rays of the bright yellow sun, and allowed the rest of the excited students to pass me by. In the short distance, to my right on the ground, I spotted a small transparent bag with some contents inside and as I approached the fence, which served as a boundary for a paint manufacturing company, an estranged tune by Led Zeppelin was playing from inside of a navy-blue, two-door Firebird, as it slowly rode by. I picked up the bag, curiously, which contained some green leafy material, and put it in my pocket. I ran ahead to a friend of mine.

"Hey, Ron, look at what I found."
I stuck my hand in my pocket and pulled out the bag in the open.

"Dude, hide that. Wait...let me see."

Ronald was a classmate of mine. He had dirty-blond hair parted to the side and green eyes, with a sort of rebellious side to him. He sort of looked like James Dean.

"What is it?" I asked.

"It's a 'nickel' of pot."

"How much is it worth?"

"Three bucks. I'll give you three bucks now."

He reached into his pocket and gave me three singles which I took. It was at that profound moment that I realized I made and could make, a profit from this product. An uncle of mine had a stash of this stuff in a can, wrapped in plastic, in his closet. I found it when I asked to practice with his black acoustic Gibson guitar one day and I accidentally knocked the can over and revealed its contents. I didn't know what it was at the time, but I guess it made sense. Ron asked me to come over later that evening to hear him practice with his electric guitar, so I told him that I would see him later.

As we departed, I headed towards my uncle's place, and to my delight, he was home.

"Yo, Dios te bendiga." I greeted him.

"La bendición. ¿Que paja?"

I entered the cigarette smoke-filled labyrinth in which he called home. An already-lit incense stick failed to freshen up the smell of the cluttered-filled living room.

"How's school? What grade are you in?"

"Eighth. I'm going to my friend's place tonight to jam. Do you have any extra picks I can use?"

"Yeah...check over there."

He pointed to his coffee table in the center of the room and as I stumbled towards the couch, I couldn't quite make where I should start looking. I sifted through store circulars, junk mail and old bills which hadn't been opened. I found a red one and palmed it in my right hand. The dirty ashtray had one of those alligator clips that were used to hang photos. It had a burnt tip.

"No. Nothing here."

I dropped the guitar-pick in my pocket, and I walked back towards the kitchen where he was preparing us glasses of iced tea. There was another pick on the countertop, and he picked it up and handed it to me.

"Yo, here's one. Practice with my guitar. It's in my room in the closet."

I didn't hesitate. I walked into his room which looked like a big hamper and there were dirty clothes everywhere, even ones that were in garbage bags. It was a bit dark inside because he never opened the shades or even cracked a window but when I opened the door to my right, I saw the guitar. It was in great shape, even though it wasn't protected in a carrying case. A black pick was bound-woven through the six-stringed instrument, so it was easy to move the guitar around and not hear a strum. I closed the door, and started to walk back to my refreshing drink, stopped midway and looked to see where he was. I went back and opened the door to his closet while I held the guitar in my right hand. There was the can in the right corner on the floor whereby I opened its yellow top and saw its contents in a sandwich bag so I quickly put the Gibson down and opened the bag. It smelled really green, and it had sort of red hairs on it. I grabbed a small handful and tucked it away and after resealing the bag and closing the lid, the smell of nature permeated for only a few seconds as I closed the door. The odor of the room had dissipated any evidence that I was even there so I grabbed the guitar and immediately went for the iced tea which had two ice cubes, just the way I liked it, and I made myself comfortable on the couch. He had just gotten up from bed an hour before so he was making himself a bowl of cereal. He worked the second shift at a food distribution warehouse, and so he was getting ready to go. I started to tune the Gibson so my chords would sound just right.

"Ready? C...G...D...A... E something or other." I repeated the same chords over again to the tune of *Hey Joe*.

"Well at least it's tuned. I know you have to go so I'm outta here. Thanks for the pick."

"Yeah, anytime. Tell your parents I said hello."

"All right, Tio, La bendición."

"Dios te bendiga, I'll see you later."

I closed the door behind me and headed home.

Our family always ate together around five o'clock. My father, at this time, worked the first shift so he was always home by three-thirty. That night, we had yellow rice with gandules (pigeon peas), with fried pork chops and tostónes (a tropical banana plant or green plantains). *My mom's a great cook*. We ate rice and beans nearly three times a week and I never complained, and after dinner I asked if I could go over to my friend's house but it was unlike me because I usually stayed home, watched television or read a book, but I figured that it was the weekend and that I could indulge myself in something different. They agreed to let me go, but I had to be back before eight and that was plenty of time, considering Ron lived only a few shortcuts away. I put on my denim jacket and had already changed out of my school uniform when I wistfully headed for the unknown.

I had to cut through a gas station and the *Paradise East*, a local Polynesian restaurant, parking lot to get to his place. Ron's mother had answered the door while he ran down the stairs to let me in. I told her that it was nice to meet her, while we went upstairs to his room and while his eyes were bloodshot and couldn't stop smiling, he put on a Zeppelin record and reached for his red electric Strat. I thought the speaker was going to blow up when he connected the cord from his guitar to it because it must have been on high volume plus the humming feedback was a bit loud so he made an adjustment. He was ready but I didn't recognize the tune he was playing as it involved fast notes. It looked complicated but sounded melodious.

"Hey, Lady, you've got to find me. Hey, Lady...oh darling, darling, darling..." I looked around and saw posters of Black Sabbath and Iron Maiden on the wall.

"Dude, that's some wicked weed. Too bad you don't have anymore." I started to realize that he had been under the influence and sat quietly. I was never taught about marijuana or the effects it had. I sure wasn't a user so I didn't need the contents in my pocket. I then pulled out my stash, and his reddish eyes bulged.

"How much can I get for this?"

"Well, you have about two dimes so I'll give you three dollars for each nickel times four...twelve bucks."

"All right."

I didn't know, but I was fifteen dollars richer that day. *What a racket.* I handed him the green-golden treasure he desired while I counted the cash and put it in my pocket. Whoever invented pockets would surely be a millionaire by now. He pulled out some *e-z widers* rolling papers and started to break the buds into shake onto an album fold. It was a very cool cover depicting naked children climbing up some stone stairs, and when he tilted the album the seeds would roll off the creased fold leaving the shake behind. He was very meticulous on removing any seeds plus there were only about four or five and proceeded to roll himself a joint but before he lit it, he pulled an incense stick from his top drawer and lit that. It smelled of strawberries, and the opened window made sure his parents wouldn't smell the joint.

I started to call marijuana, "bunk," because it bunked you out, I suppose. With the incense/punk burning, I referenced the two actions as "bunk punk," and then called any user as a bunk punk. So now I had my own code for pot, weed, herb, and marijuana.

He started to play again, while I looked at my watch. I did not feel comfortable in this environment, primarily because it was new and unnatural to me, so I told him I had to go. It was nearly seven, but I wanted to be home so he walked me out and was sure to close his bedroom door behind him and that was the last time I went to his home, but I would surely see him at school and he knew his secret was safe with me. And that's it. That's how it all started. That would be the beginning day of my corruption, and loss of innocence, but also the day I started my empire.

The next day, Ron called and wanted to introduce me to these guys who hung out around the corner on Starlight Avenue, not so far from my house. I never ventured off that way and hadn't noticed them when I would go down to the corner store and routinely play Galaga Arcade games. It was a small delicatessen that carried bare necessities and I was often sent there by my mom to get milk or orange juice. He told me that some of the guys were looking for bunk and that I could make a lot of money but the only thing was I that I didn't have any.

"Wassup, Max. Where's everybody?"
Max was leaning against the wall with one foot up behind him while he shrugged his shoulders, smoking his cigarette and glanced at me.

"Anyone got anything? This is Corey. He's all right."
"Nah, it's 'dry'. He probably went to the city to 'cop'."

"Corey has Thai."

Max's eyes opened up and started to give me more attention as he stood up straight and asked me how much I had. I asked him how much he wanted. He wanted an 'eighth' so he gave me thirty-five dollars, and I told him that I would be back within the hour. That's when I realized that a nickel was five, and a dime was obviously ten. For him to give me thirty-five meant that mathematically speaking, he wanted an eighth of an ounce which equaled three and a half grams, or three and a half dimes. I soon began to catch on fast, and before I left him, I told him that if he wanted my Thai weed, he was five dollars shy.

"All right, man, it better be good."

He shook my hand and I felt the 'fin' in my palm. This slick move was a handy trick to note in the future, so I used it. I told Ron that I had to get home to do something for my parents, and I would come back so we left it at that. Lastly, I never confronted Ron on how he tried to swindle me out of money and worth, but rather I never allowed him to do it to me again and I kept it in the back of my mind that I would get even with him someday.

The only thing I could have done was to go back to my Uncle's house, but, damn, he was probably working overtime as was his usual Saturday routine. I had to come up with something. I went to his place anyway in hopes that maybe he was too tired and decided to stay home and rest. I rang the doorbell twice. He knew that was my code that it was me so I put my ear to the door in further hopes that I would hear him stumbling to the door. Nothing. I rang the bell twice again and waited and to my luck and surprise, someone opened the door.

"La bendición. ¿Que paja?" I happily greeted him.

"Dios de bendiga."

He was in his boxers and a T-shirt with one eye opened. I must have woken him, but I didn't care. I just walked in and asked him how he was doing.

"All right. I'm gonna jump in the shower. Put the TV on if you want. What time is it?" he asked as he scratched his ass walking towards the refrigerator.

"Twelve-thirty." I sat down on his couch and clicked the remote. "No work today?"

"No. I'm plucky." He grabbed some iced tea that was left over from yesterday and offered me some, but I didn't want any. I just wanted him to take his shower while I borrowed some of his stash, and it couldn't have happened any sooner. I did what I needed to do and slipped ten bucks under his mess he made on his coffee table. He would just think that he found it in luck, or maybe he forgot that he might have put it there. I searched his kitchen cabinets for a sandwich bag to put the bunk in, sealed it, then knocked on the bathroom door and told him that I was going home and that I would see him later.

"All right. Lock the door on your way out, say hello to your parents for me." I certainly lucked out and went back to the spot where Ron and Max were waiting for me. We ditched out of site down a one-way block going up, and I handed him my rough estimate of his product. He looked at me and then the contents of the bag. He opened it to get a better look and stuck his nose right in it. His semi-yellow teeth were exposed as he gave me this big smile. Word of mouth spread like wildfire amongst his crew, so I had to find out where I could get some more without the help of my Uncle. With my new exposure to the guys, I found out who the agents and the heavy-hitters were.

The big guy, Buddy, was picking up a new shipment that day and a certain few knew about it. He was the guy that I had to get a hold of if I wanted anything and it just so happened that he drove by in his brown four-door Dodge and looked at my new face, pulled off a block away from the hangout and called Max over. They were talking to each other, and I noticed both of them looking my way in a manner that perhaps he told him that I sold stuff and that maybe he thought of me as a threat. I didn't know what I was getting myself into when I was called over and hopped into his car.

I agreed to take a ride with Buddy, and he asked me if I needed to be anywhere soon. Buddy was a short stocky fellow with long hair but bald on the top, his car seat was pushed up so he could reach the pedals, and I told him that I had time. He started to ask me how long I knew these guys and that if I wanted to sell for him. We came to the mutual agreement that I would, but that the stuff wasn't supplied by him and so I would make a cut of the profits and report to him once a week. It sounded fair, and throughout all the talking, he paid his four-dollar toll, and we were in New York City. It was rather a nonchalant deal as he took his usual route past China Town, past Mulberry Street, over a bridge and into a busy section of the city which I think was Brooklyn.

As we drove on further, crowds dissipated and we were at a quiet street corner with a lot of Jamaicans with dreadlocks where multiple sneakers of different brand names hung by their laces from the telephone wires above. He got his stash from the Rastafarians, and no one was the wiser. He parked the car two car-lengths from the corner and told me to wait inside the car but I stuck out like a sore thumb, and I was nervous as people walked by every once in a while, and would just look at me but kept going.

"Would you look at this, Mon," one Jamaican guy said to another as he stared at me with his green, yellow and red garb.

Three Jamaican guys walked into the store that only had the cardboard covers of food boxes taped to the windows to advertise the products, and a small girl walked into the store afterward. The girl walked out holding a half-gallon of milk through the small rung of the plastic container then three guys came out with some local soft drinks and bags of chips. I fumbled in the glove compartment to keep my mind occupied, and then I finally saw Buddy walking out of the bodega with a brown paper bag in one hand and a can of iced tea in the other. Iced tea must be the preferred drink of bunk punkers.

He casually walked towards the car in his sweat-suit, hopped in and told me to hold the bag. It reeked of green, fine bud and I noticed he had a big bag of it sealed in a Ziploc. I didn't ask any questions and he told me that once we got back to Jersey, he would break apart the pound and package them as dimes. From his ashtray, he pulled out an already-rolled joint and lit it. *Holy smokes*. I wasn't ready for that and I don't know if it was a contact buzz or the scenario, but I was paranoid because it was daytime and the windows were not tinted to hide the illegality of possessing this marijuana. At a red light he rolled up the windows so no one could whiff in the smell, and on my right, I noticed a crew of businessmen smoking ganja from their car too. He asked me to roll down my window so he could speak to the driver of the blue Ford Taurus.

"Hey, Artie. How 'ya been?"

"Hey, Buddy. What's up?" Artie asked in a surprised but excited manner.

"Broadcast *this* in your news."

Buddy took a long pull and blew out the smoke towards him. Artie worked for one of the special news reports which periodically aired on television once a week and the guys in the back seat were his cameramen since I had seen the huge recorders and the microphones with the fuzzy black ends attached to them. The light turned green and the whole time I just looked straight to avoid any exposure. I rolled up the window.

Although I hadn't seen any cops through this whole ordeal, it was a big deal to me. I just stared out the window and tried to remember the way back there, in case I didn't need him in the future.

"So, where you from?" he asked me.

"From the neighborhood. I'm with Ron."

"Lose Ron. Now you're with me. You're not like the other guys. You look healthy and you're clean cut."

I had always had my straight dark-brown hair parted to the side. I wore a mustache which started to grow since I was in the Second grade, and for most of my youth, I thought that my leaving milk on my upper lip after I drank it, attributed to my hair growth, but everyone thought I was silly to say that. My educational background allowed me to study the arts and formal colloquial of conventional speaking, so I carried myself well. My parents did what they could.

"How long have you been in?" I asked.

"Long enough to know that we're gonna make a lot of money. No 'arms' and no 'shorts'." I thought that was funny since he appeared to be short in height and his arm-reach wasn't longer than mine, but that was his motto and I learned that lesson quickly because it was practical. An "arm" meant lending, while a "short" simply meant not accepting less than the price of the product, or being short of the full amount. Buddy was straightforward and impressionable. It was as though we had known each other for years the way we were addressing each other, but ultimately, it came down to the dollar. In business, there were no playing games and we had to make sure that we were on the "same page" but he didn't see me as a young punk, or some degenerate, but rather as a presentable pawn of a businessman.

Fortunately, we made it back to Jersey and he dropped me off two blocks away from the hangout and told me to meet him at the *Paradise East* restaurant in two hours, and I was there to pick up a hundred and twenty bags. The twenty bags were my cut, but the first thing I had to do was sell the hundred for him bringing in one thousand dollars. If I succeeded, by selling my twenty, I'd make two hundred easy, and *that* I did in two days. I gradually starting selling eighths because the more I stood out there the greater my chances that I would get pinched. Besides, the demand was there for a greater quantity, and after a short month, I graduated to ounces and depending on the quality, it ranged from two hundred to two-hundred sixty for each ounce. By then, I wouldn't waste any more time selling anything less than that, and I needed only a few more days to make twelve thousand, two of which were my cut, and by then I only sold to the guys I knew or friends of the guys whom I've trusted. Unfortunately, one of the drawbacks from selling it to some of these regulars was the word of mouth that connected them to people I knew from elementary school and so I was ousted by the goody two shoes but I couldn't entirely grasp what their gripe was. They obviously knew the difference between good and bad way earlier than I did.

By the end of the week, I had already sold forty-eight ounces and I had three left. Two would put me at my goal, and the other I just gave to Max. I told him that I was out, and that was my going away present and Buddy didn't have a problem with it and besides, I made him a lot of money and never revealed to anyone that he was the head honcho so we shook hands as businessmen and parted. I was only fourteen years old.

CHAPTER IV

I pulled up to Starlight but I hadn't seen Buddy. Instead of lighting up a smoke as I parked, I just opened and closed the top of my silver Zippo because it helped me pass the time and to help distract me from my nerves. I looked down at its engravement: HARD CORE. *A gift from a friend.* I still couldn't believe someone would kill Felix. *What crime did he commit that justified death?* As I sat there, still dazed from his murder, my mind drifted to Big Dave.

****

"Big Dave" worked at the Starlight Laundromat. He was a tall, slim older man with a dirty-blonde mop which came down to his shoulders who resembled Hulk Hogan, the wrestler, but with thicker hair. He worked in his wife's business as the head custodian and enjoyed his work, and the guys in the neighborhood respected him because he was discreet and let us hang around the place. The pay-phone inside was partly the reason why the guys stood around in front of the establishment as it hung to the right of the door as you walked in, and two huge window panes shed light into the Laundromat next to the phone, so it was easy to see who was walking by out front. Transactions mostly took place over the phone: meetings, deals and even calls for the people who did not own a telephone in their homes. Big Dave knew what happened on the phone, but he never said a word because he understood the business and as long as no physical deals took place inside, he would have no problems with his wife, Megan. He also didn't care because he was getting a percentage from the phone company for total monthly usage.

He would normally have *The Daily News* or *The Jersey Journal* on the counter along with his liter of Coke, and the date on those papers, that day, read September 1988. It turned out that he would more than frequently have rum in his soda, but not today. He was drinking a Tom Collins special recipe, or concoction really: part Tom Collins Gin, part bottled-flavored Snapple and part Tropicana banana/orange/strawberry juice. It was his day off and he was spending it downstairs, watching television, along with all the customers that walked in to wash their clothes. Big Dave lived upstairs with Megan, and that was also a matter of convenience.

He usually had a drink in his hand, and with the other, he would tuck in his arm as if his elbow was trying to touch his hip but never quite made it there. This would also follow with a "Yeah". We were all watching the Yankees beating the Orioles 3-2 when Moe walked up behind me and murmured that he needed to talk. Big Dave knew Moe as "Third Base", and it was either because his brother was a pitcher for the Phillies, or because he looked like he was "free-basing". For whatever reason, I knew him as "Malik". "Third Base! This drink is smo-o-o-th...Yeah," Big Dave said out loud. He liked being boisterous and did it often, especially when drinking. I excused myself for a moment and we met at the pay-phone inside because Malik had a plan.

"Hey man, what's up?" I said, offering my palm.

"Hey Corey, not much. Saw you talking to some guys from PA out front. Wanna go for a ride to the feast? Salami's comin'".

"Cool. Give me half an hour." I agreed.

All it took was a mentioning and a handshake. I went back out and wrapped up my dealings with the two guys from Pennsylvania while Malik headed into the neighboring liquor store to prepare for what was going to be an interesting evening. I enjoyed seeing one of my favorite clients drive up in his red van because he normally bought weight and bulk.

From the corner of my eye, coming out of the dark East end of Starlight, was a tall and dark figure, at first shapeless and blurry, but perhaps it was because of the abundance of trees and lack of streetlight near Fuller Avenue that gave in to the illusion of the shadow play. I looked over to Dave who was at the laundromat entrance, and with a shrug with my shoulders and a point to the unknown figure I asked, "Dude, who's that?"

"That's Mr. Belvedere...The Candy Man." He smiled.

Malik walked out of the store with a couple of brown bags and was the next one to see him, and perhaps the first to greet him. He walked right up to him as if they were long-time buddies.

Mr. Belvedere was an interesting character in that he was juxtaposed and yet very accepted here. He was a tall man, at least six feet, a bit overweight and looked jolly however less jolly than Santa Claus although that nickname could have been suitable for him, but more like Benny Hill. He wore a distinguished three-piece black suit with a bowtie, bowler's hat and cane that made him look like an English butler, just like the American sitcom portrayed, hence the name: Mr. Belvedere. He walked rather slow, with a permanent smile, and just looked forward.

Malik put his hand on his shoulder and gave direction. "Hey, Mr. Belvedere. How's it goin'? My car is right around the corner. We'll go there." He didn't say a word. He just walked forward with his cane and kept smiling. It was remarkable to see Mr. Belvedere's expression as if he were communicating without speaking, with a poker face that doesn't change and with the same demeanor as a politician. He looked and reminded me of Winston Churchill. Malik asked me to accompany him.

By now, several of the neighborhood guys already knew he was on the scene and with some chatter amongst them, they knew exactly where they were rendezvousing so everyone was on the lookout for possible police. Like a true gentleman, Malik opened the rear right car door for Mr. Belvedere while he patiently waited for him to get in, and when the door was shut, I leaned against the front passenger door while Malik entered through the rear left side door sitting next to him. I looked to the backseat and liked his black bowtie, and thought only certain people could get away with wearing one handsomely, without possible ridicule. I still had no idea what this was about as Mr. Belvedere stood there motionless, grinning away, and feeling comfortable in this environment.

Then it happened. His right hand let go of his cane and reached into his left suit pocket to pull out a plastic bottle which he held out lap high for Malik to take. Malik took it from his hand and popped the top. There was some dialogue between them and Malik started to count each pill into his ball cap that was positioned between the old man's knees. This was a valium transaction from Mr. Belvedere's prescription bottle and he was selling his pills. I tried not to make it obvious that anything was going on in the back seat, but I couldn't help but looking through the window at random times often noticing that several pills never made it to the cap but rather unto the floor. He was ripping off a guy who was probably on several milligrams of valiums himself.

When the transaction finished, I opened the door and watched him slowly get out before I closed the door behind him. The guys silently cheered Mr. Belvedere's arrival and departure as he walked towards the West end of Starlight, slowly disappearing from his monthly visit. I liked his style. I liked the way he was dressed, his opportunism and his silence. "Later, Candy Man," I said under my breath.

Life on Starlight Avenue was about trying to do something with your time and if there was a plan, there were no surprises. It was very important to know up front who else would be joining us for the nightly excursion. Something simple as seating arrangements, or an annoying conversationalist to one of us would ruin everything. That is understandable in any situation because any surprises in the plan would mean a delay, in response to the confusion, because after all, time is money.

As I walked towards the laundromat, I was cautious not to trip over any rubbish or uneven ground floor cement tiles. Bottles, used napkins and broken glass usually littered the streets waiting for someone else who would be responsible for its cleanup and attention. An older man with dirty clothing was leaning on a fence playing with his red beard and loitering with a look of concern. The only thing that seemed clean on him was his fingernails, as if his hands were rubbed in dirt but still manicured.

Malik and Joshua "Salami" Russo pulled up to the corner, I hopped into the backseat and I preferred it that way because I always wanted to be incognito. By then, they had already mixed their Collins drinks in these tall plastic cups and proceeded to make me one and after a couple of lefts, we were already on the Boulevard. My potion was ready just as we approached the red light behind another vehicle, and as if the car was about to stall right there on the spot, he unexpectedly passes the double-yellow lines on our left, passes the vehicle in front of us and "eats" the red light. I'm freaking out because we have open containers of alcohol, and he pulls a stupid stunt like that.

The gas station is one block ahead to our right, on Communipaw, and we didn't quite make it there because a cop car had immediately pulled us over.

"Holy Schit, dude."

"Salami" had a minor speech impediment. His "S"s come out like "Sh". That's how he got his name. One day we were at a delicatessen and he ordered a ham, salami and cheese sandwich with Mayo. Jimmy, the owner of the deli, asked him what he wanted.

"Gimme a ham, shalami, and cheeshe with a little mayonaishe."

Some of the other guys made fun of him, but I didn't care. To me, he was Joshua and he was hungry. Later on, I realized that there were so many "Joshuas" in the neighborhood that I started to call him "Salami" out of distinction. He knew I meant nothing by it.

We've pulled over about twenty feet away from the driveway to the gas station and Malik is explaining to the officer that he was sorry, but he was afraid his car would stall due to his gas shortage because the "idiot light" was on. That's what we called the gas symbol on the dashboard if it lit up because you had to be an idiot if you let the tank get to that empty point. The cop let us go because Malik was so apologetic and that's one thing I liked about him. He was a smooth talker and a bull-shitter.

We were about to get "gassed up," and leave for the City and even though we lived in a city, New York City was always referred to as the City. Apparently, Jersey is one of those states that doesn't allow you to pump your own gasoline so we waited for an attendant to service the fuel. Malik put in a cassette of Boogie Down Productions and *Criminal Minded* came on, however, I was bewildered by the opening lyrics:

Boogie Down Productions will always get paid
We'll take the wackest song and make it better
Remember to let us into your skin
Cause then you'll begin, to master
Rhymin' rhymin' rhymin'

It sounded like it was in the melody of The Beatles tune *Hey Jude*, but did they consider it to be a wack song to be made better? Either way, *Hey Jude* is not one of my favorite Beatles tunes. Crossover music from hip-hop to rock was being introduced as in Run DMC's *Rock-Box* and the more famous *Walk This Way* with Aerosmith. I was buzzed by the time we hit the Holland Tunnel and by then, we each finished a 24-oz glass. I don't know how Malik does it but he truly drives better than usual when he's buzzed. Some people can just handle it I suppose. My mind drifted into sound.

Music was so influential to me while growing up and during the nineteen-eighties, that I continued buying record vinyl albums so that I could play them on my parents' record player. The first album I owned was Billy Joel's *Glass Houses* and there were so many different artists and great music coming out in the late eighties that I extended my album collection, and organized them in empty plastic milk crates that I borrowed from the front of the local corner grocery store. Some of my prevalent albums were the Beastie Boys *Licensed to Ill*, Run DMC's *Raising Hell* and Eric B & Rakim's *Paid in Full*, although I really enjoyed listening to Whitney Houston, Prince, Peter Gabriel, Madonna, Van Halen, John "Cougar" Mellencamp and so many others on the radio.

The Beatles had already been a staple in my musical repertoire that even after their breakup, whether you blamed Yoko Ono for it or not, I still followed their individual works and as a youth I enjoyed watching the *Yellow Submarine* movie even though none of their actual voices were used in it, so with that my favorite tune was "Nowhere Man". Perhaps it is fitting to begin to rationalize who I was and who I was to become at an early age.

Hip-Hop music was introduced to me through the local radio and I was curious about the style of Break Dancing. I learned many moves, even the courageous Suicide flip where I flip my body and just land on my back, but I could never figure out how to do the Windmill. I saw the film *Breakin'* in the movie theater around 1984 and soon after, starting searching for some good break-dancing music on the radio and cassettes.

I remember asking my father to take me to the Bradlees department store on Route 440 so I could "check out" the music section but there were no samples that I could hear and as I searched individual cassette tapes, I could only guess what they sounded like solely by the title of the song. There were no mainstream artists that I knew that represented the genre, so I picked one that had *Jam on It* by Newcleus, except that when I went home and heard the cassette, I was overly disappointed by the music because the selected songs didn't appeal to me at all. I asked my father to return to the store the following day, but time did not allow it. I insisted that we go the next day because I just needed my music.

We went back to the department store and waited for a very long time on the Customer Service/Returns line as all the other lines were equally slow, and finally, after about thirty minutes we were next. I was thrilled that my dad took me to the store and waited this long for me to rectify this slight injustice, on my behalf. I stood at the end of the cashier's belt where the items are bagged.

"Can I help you?" she asked my dad.

"Hi, yeah. I'd like to return this tape?" my father requested.

"Do you have the receipt?" she responded.

He showed it to her.

"What's wrong with it? Is it broken?" as if the receipt wasn't good enough.

He looked at me down that long cashier bag line and although we never really discussed it prior, I told them that I didn't like the music. I think he expected me to say that it was blank or damaged in some way, but he and the cashier woman looked at each other as if they couldn't believe what I said.

"Sir, you cannot return opened items, especially if they're not broken and especially cassette tapes. They could be copied and recorded."

He was so embarrassed and upset that he grabbed the item and me and we left that store. The ride home was silent but silence was not what I sought.

I started listening more and more to the radio on Friday night. I was hooked on Kool DJ Red Alert "going berserk" on 98.7 Kiss FM and WBLS on 107.5 on the midday mix. I liked how they blended and mixed songs together to make them flow. I emerged into Hip-Hop and early Rap music and music transitioned me from here to there, especially when I headed into New York.

Finally, the gas tank was filled and the front windshield was squeegee cleaned. One thing was for sure...Malik never got lost in the City, and if you think about it, it is difficult to get lost there, as long as you know your bearings. He knew the streets, and before I knew it, we were passing Mulberry St. The only trick now was where to park and it wasn't too bad since we were about three blocks away from the beginning of the San Gennaro Feast when he spotted a parking space on our left. We got out of his four-door, navy blue Ford and he made us another round of drinks. We each had another cup and quickly blended in with the rest of the crowds, and from a distance I could already smell the sausage and peppers.

The San Gennaro Feast, exclusively in Little Italy, is an annual festival with lots of Italian food and while it's obviously about a feast honoring a saint, for me it was about the food. It was just about dusk, in a warm summer's air and as the sky was a grayish blue, there was an occasional gentle breeze. A crowd of people waiting to be served cheesesteaks slowed our forward movement, so we flanked around to the left of the stand and as I slowly passed, there was an open door to an establishment. There were empty cardboard boxes and crates lined against the front wall of the building, it was dimly lit inside, and I could only see towards the back where a hanging lamp illuminated the red and white checkered floors and as I caught myself staring for clues, a husky man appeared in the doorway dressed in a white apron. I kept walking and couldn't stop to further notice the behind-the-scenes of this feast. Perhaps he was a cook, maybe he was a lookout for a potential card game taking place in the back room, or he was just a guy checking out the festivities himself but for whatever the reason, it was an oddly beautiful scene as I was having a good time already.

After halfway through our stroll, I had finished my drink but held on to my cup. Malik spotted a Jell-O shot stand just to our right and by this time, the sky had turned black except for the dark navy blue around the crescent of the bright moon. The woman behind the counter held out a tray of multi-colored cups of Jell-O, but inside, depending on their color, contained a different type of liquor. I stuck with gin, which was the green one.

"Cheers, big ears."

We toasted each other and enjoyed our shots – two each to be exact. We thanked the woman behind the counter as we whistled off towards the other end of the street and Malik took point as I followed behind Salami, who decided to walk around with a Marlboro Light on his ear while smoking one already. The crowd started to pick up, so we did not have too much room to spread out. A couple of Spanish guys ran towards us, and not that they were necessarily from Spain but rather of a Latino ethnicity, and as they ran past me Malik got angry because he knew what was going on. Also, he was the type that became fearless after a couple of drinks. Apparently, a few white guys were chasing these Spanish dudes for whatever reason.

Malik turned around and grabbed one of the last of the fleeing Spaniards that had already run past us.
"What's the matter with you? You're gonna let them do this to you? Let's get these assholes."
Before I knew it, Malik took off running towards the alleged attackers, down Mott Street, and I hauled ass behind him, while Salami tried to keep up. The Spaniards must have been stunned because I noticed they didn't follow until we had a ten-second lead. It was *their* fight but they were probably confused because Malik was a tall white guy with glasses, about six-foot with a slim and muscular build. His Phillies hat was turned backward, as he continued to rant down a dark alleyway.

He was only a block away from Mulberry Street when I realized Malik had picked up an empty beer bottle from the ground and flung it towards the running assailants.

"Get back here. Where ya goin'?"

The bottle had reached the length of the alley and landed on the next main street and luckily no bystander got hurt in the melee as the glass touched the ground and broke into what sounded to be a thousand pieces to me, when we saw blue and red flashing lights. It was time for us to go as we quickly and unnoticeably blended back into the crowded feast, while the Spaniards thanked us for helping them.

The night was young, so we decided to go back home and hang out and unwind. When we got back to the car, there was a couple in their mid-twenties standing along-side the building smoking a joint just starting their journey unto Little Italy, and they asked us if we wanted to finish it but we suggested giving it to the two guys walking towards us.

"Cheers, big ears," I said as we quickly jumped in the car, and rode off towards the Holland. I always enjoyed the return trip from the City, because it was always late in the evening and the city lights just illuminated the surroundings. I would be astounded looking out the window, and in intervals, passing by different types of environments, boroughs and neighborhoods. It mainly took my mind off things and helped me to realize that there was another world out there while *Devil Inside* by

INXS was playing on the radio. I could have been in any of those communities that we were passing through with all their different scenarios, but I felt more secure that I was eventually heading to home base and immediately felt blessed and grateful for being in a loving, caring family.

Back in Jersey, Malik dropped us off around the corner of Starlight while he rode to his house to wash up. Salami and I slowly blended towards the hangout and then I kept walking towards Jimmy's Deli but before I opened his front door, I noticed a pair of Adidas sneakers hanging on one of the corner telephone pole wires. I didn't want anyone knowing what we did, or that we associated with each other that afternoon so I stopped in to say hello and maybe grab some Polish *chrusciki* cookies for my mom. They were sweet and delicate dough, fried to perfect crispiness, then sprinkled with powdered sugar but they weren't made there because Jimmy was Italian and he sold meats and freshly baked bread instead.

Jimmy was bald on top but had a thick mustache and always wore an apron and a smile. He was cutting and weighing up some steaks as he greeted me and I headed towards the back to grab a bottled Iced Tea when a new guy with a full beard wearing an apron and gloves came out of the freezer.

"Hey, Howya doin'?" I asked.

He just nodded and carried over big slabs of meat to the stainless-steel cutting table, and instead of a hairnet he wore a blue toboggan hat that folded up twice above his ears and plastic gloves.

"Hey, Corey, that's 'Chooch'. First day on the job. He's a good worker. He's helped me out all morning'." Jimmy gladly vouched for him. Jimmy most likely paid him in cash and probably didn't even know his real name anyway.

"Oh yeah?" I recognized him from the neighborhood. He appeared to be homeless, sleeping on park benches and sometimes even in the schoolyard grounds and never asked me or anyone for any money, that I knew about. His shoes were really worn, along with his slightly ripped blue jeans and he had an odor about him resembling urine.

"That's good. Hope it works out. Looks like an earner." I said as I grabbed a package of those cookies and placed it on the counter next to my drink. He put the items in a bag for me and I thanked him on the way out.

"Later."

I think Salami just walked around the block and eventually headed back but I don't favor cliques or gangs anyway, plus I would rather have been known as a well-rounded person. It seemed that everyone had side jobs, deals and scams going and I didn't want to be guilty by association. I could and would not trust working with anyone in fear that they, for some chance, would rat or snitch because, for me, if I appealed to the whole group then I could gain the confidence of each member and no one would suspect me being involved in a side deal myself. I think that was the first time I understood politics.

I was happy enough to hang out with and run with these guys, but as sure as hell didn't want anyone else knowing about it. To me, trust was a big deal and the only one I could really trust was myself but that wasn't saying much because I have allowed myself to try new things however misguided it was. I needed a friend. Everyone needs that one friend they can trust and confide in.

Malik also understood that we could make more money by forming a secret alliance. With whatever sound operation he wanted to get into, I funded the money. I didn't ask for much, just the front money and a little extra. It was just better if no one knew that I was involved, from my aspect anyway and I would only suggest patrons going to him if they needed anything. He was the one who was hustling, while I was in the background finagling with my own numbers operation. I would only stay at the Laundromat for about an hour or two a day so I would hardly be noticed. Eighty-five percent of our city was within 1,000 feet of a school and I did not want to be affiliated with the dealers, or agents as I called them, because it was a serious penalty if you got caught. Basically, I was more aware of the risks of getting caught by the law, especially when it deals with the welfare of children.

I was a straight-arrow kid and first got in it for the money and the power that came with it – not the lifestyle. Drugs were a dirty business to get into. I gave up selling bunk a long time ago and felt that being a venture capitalist and an investor would pay off more. I understood how to run a business and applied that to the streets. I was given the nickname, "Cat Man", because I was always quiet and disciplined about my business, and I always stood my ground until it was time to pounce.

One time this neighborhood thief, who was probably in his twenties and strung up on dope, got caught stealing from one of the guys in the neighborhood and they were working him over at the back of Metro Field off Westside Ave. I happened to be walking by with Joshua who was enjoying a joint when I looked over at them for a second, wasn't fazed then continued to walk on through.

"This guy robbed my mother's house yesterday, took her jewelry and says he pawned all of it but when I checked his pockets, I found one of her rings," one of the guys try to explain to me as if he needed to show me the ring and ask permission to kick his ass. Now, I hate theft but to me this was street justice plus it wasn't my business nor my fight so I didn't get involved yet.

"I didn't take shit! Scout's honor!" Mikey yelled.

I turned around and walked straight up to this Mikey, nodding at the guys that it was ok to loosen their grips on his arms. I looked into his eyes. Honor...Scout's honor. That's when I punched him in the nose with a straight left and quickly followed with a right cross. He hit the ground and the guys picked him up while I walked away with Salami.

CHAPTER V

I had been involved in the Boy Scouts of America in my youth, Pack 550, and it first taught me how to learn many aspects of survival as I felt like a young man who was full of self-confidence. My father had helped me construct my wood-carved car for the Pinewood Derby and the wooden block was carved and sculpted into an aerodynamic car, which we spray-painted black, with a LEGO man glue-mounted on top. On each side of my first sculpted piece of art was a stickered number "3", but that day the car won first place. The Boy Scouts allowed my father and me to be closer together and to affirm our father/son relationship as he was always supportive.

That summer I was sent to my first Scout camp. Rock Hill is where I applied everything I learned from the Scouts and on the first day everyone was instructed to meet by the lake with their swim gear and there, we were tested on our swimming abilities and judged accordingly. During the course of my two-week stay, I would wake up as early as I could so I could take advantage of a hot shower and as the saying went – "you snooze you lose". I also signed up for different educational courses, so I would be able to advance in rank with the highest being an Eagle Scout. I must have taken five different classes each week, and they were very exciting and on the first day, after swimming in the lake, I signed up for Astronomy because I had a telescope at home and I was interested in the subject.

"Nine o'clock tomorrow," the instructor said.

It fit into my schedule and I was eager to get to bed early so I could make my first class the next day. Dave and I were from the same troop, and we shared the same tent. He registered for Astronomy too, so I knew I had a study partner and when the next day came, we met at the class location which was about a fifteen-minute walk into the woods. Nine o'clock came and went and we were confused because we were the only ones there.

We waited and finally left to go to the firing range where there was a competition taking place where a Scout Master was there proctoring and making sure everything was safe, and while the two competitors were fairly accurate, there could only be one winner. He was excited he won first place, but I believe his advantage was the type of rifle he used. It was different from the other boy's rifle, and each was issued their firearm from the Scout Master and as I was leaving the event, I heard the Scout Master telling another one of his peers that the gun the winner used was illegal to shoot for the competition. That was pretty rude and unfair, and why did he allow the competition to take place? After that, I started not to trust certain people of authority and guns. Just the night before, the Scout Master who is in charge of our camp had threatened one of the Scouts with an air-powered gun to his head.

It kept all the guys in line, but fear wasn't the answer. I think respect was.

Later that day, Dave and I saw the Astronomy teacher walking down one of the dirt roads heading to the commissary. I couldn't quite excuse myself to get his attention because he was deep in talks with another leader discussing stars. "So binary stars are a system of two stars in which one star revolves around the other or perhaps both revolve around a common center. If components in binary star systems are close enough, they can gravitationally distort their mutual outer stellar atmospheres."

"Excuse me, Professor. We went to the Astronomy class, as scheduled, for nine, but no one was there."

He said, "How can we learn about Astronomy at nine in the morning? It's scheduled for nine at night."

I felt stupid. At this moment I realized I had other things scheduled for that time, so I canceled Astronomy but it would have been a really cool class. Rock Hill is an institution in New York State and I had great learning experiences there, but the best times I had was when it would rain because I would be the only one going into the woods and looking for red efts. They were harmless little orange newts that would only come out when it rained, and they were my little friends. I transported one of the red efts to the movie that was playing that night.

He was hiding in my shirt pocket and popped out when the beginning of Rambo: *First Blood* came on. That was the first time either one of us saw a movie like that. It was a great summer for me, and an interesting learning experience and on the last day at Camp my parents and Gloria were there to pick me up to go home. We packed the car with my gear and I sat behind the passenger's side, as usual. I was very anxious to go but I knew it was about a two-hour drive back home and I still had to unpack. I must have dozed off soon after we traveled through a few scenic hills and valleys because when I awoke that was the last thing I remembered. I enjoy road trips especially when there's a good tune on the radio. *Once in a Lifetime* by Talking Heads was on while I was trying to pull my flashlight out of my jacket pocket. I was trying to be quiet and not attract any attention to myself while I slowly unscrewed the top of it. I already took out the *C* batteries it would need to operate and this was the first time I remember smuggling contents and it was still intact, and judging by where we were on the Jersey Turnpike, we were about forty-five minutes away from home.

When we finally arrived at the house and unpacked the car, I pulled out an empty 20-gallon fish tank that we had stored in a closet in the basement and placed it on the wooden table in the backyard. Using a spade, I scooped some dirt from the yard and also added some rocks and sticks to make a habitat. My mom went outside and confronted me on my little project.

"What are you doing?"

I pointed to the two red-efts I brought back with me inside the flashlight, and explained to her what they were but she crossed her arms and wasn't pleased.

"It's been a long day. Get upstairs, take a shower and change out of those clothes so I can add them to the laundry."

She made sense and it seemed logical, so I did what I was told, and when I finished, I hastened back to the yard only to see that the screen top was moved aside. "No, no, no!" They were gone! The pigeons must have gotten to them. I was upset. I told my mother that the birds must have pushed the top screen off and that they must have been determined because I put two heavy rocks on it so that the wind wouldn't blow it off. She comforted me during my feeling of loss and despair. What an amazing mother.

I suppose when you have a structured organization, rules are set up so no one gets hurt, with structure comes discipline, and with discipline comes order. The leaders of my Scout troop always made everything interesting and fun. There was no reason to doubt them or to assume that they would mislead me in any way. At a rally held at Liberty State Park, Scouts from all troops gathered together to join in on games, festivities, and competitions. Part of being self-sufficient in the outdoors was being able to pitch a camp and when that task was completed, I was asked by my Scout Master, Max, to retrieve a bucket of steam for him from another camp. I did not question him, but I did think about it for the duration of my walk to camp number *five*. Perhaps there was some scientific or practical reason he needed the steam that I had not yet comprehended but

Dave came with me so we could both use this opportunity to scout around and to know who our competitors were.

We discussed our strategies, according to the events, as to "who was the best to participate in the wood-chopping event" and who were to compete in the "fire-starting event", when we approached camp *five* and I confronted the leader.

"We're from 550. Do you have any buckets of steam?" The leader from 245 looked at me and hesitated. "I'm sorry. We lent it to camp 'Nine'. They should have it."

"OK. Thank you."

We were based at camp twenty-seven so it was a bit of a journey for us but we didn't mind because it was a great day in spring with temperatures in the mid-seventies and blue skies that reminded me how great it was to be outdoors. The five-acre lawn had been taken over and based by thirty Boy Scout troops, and it was so organized that everything had been taken care of down to the litter patrol. We walked back towards camp *nine* and we introduced ourselves to its leader and asked for the bucket of steam.

"Do you need the one with the left wind-shifter or the right wind-shifter?" he asked.

I asked him what the difference was and before he could answer, an older leader walked out of a tent and told me that he had lent out the bucket we were looking for to camp twenty-three.

On the way to camp twenty-three, we decided to stop off to our base and ask Max whether he wanted one with a left or right wind-shifter. He sat on his foldable chair with his elbows on the armrest and his hands clasped and started to smile.

"There's no such thing as a bucket of steam."
It was a gag between all the leaders and I did not look at it as falling for it, but rather following a simple request from a man for whom I've learned to respect and trust, but once again that was deteriorating.

The following year, there was a local Scout competition being held at Hudson County Park, also known as Bayonne Park. There were different events such as running to the next hill and collecting three different types of leaves and running back, or being the first person to successfully tie a necktie, in another event, would also win. The first to hammer three nails into a piece of wood would win, and other events took place. It was fun, and this was to test individuality skills. After four fun-filled hours of competition, and my father cheering me on, it was time to announce the winners.

A Scout Master had approached me and told me that I was tied for first place. The other Scout and I had to play a tie-breaker. My competitor and I were the only Scouts there and it was off to the side so there wouldn't be that much pressure from the other Scouts. He handed us each one heavy ball and the object of the competition was to throw your ball as close to a line without going over it. The other Scout went first and I was a little nervous because this was for first place amongst three-hundred other Scouts who competed. The other Scout went first and he threw it too hard, so it went over the line. This was too easy. I hesitated. I wanted to just drop the ball. I looked up at the Master and my father because I was a bit confused and only wanted to know if I could just drop the ball, or did it have to officially roll?

"Can I just..."

"Will you just go!" my father said as if I were just soaking up the victory. I rolled it so hard so it went over the line that was about twenty feet away. I couldn't believe it...we had to do it again. The other Scout got close to the target line but not over. I didn't have the confidence at this point to roll the ball closer, so I aimed to hit his ball over the line. I missed and my ball was over. It was all over. The moment I realized I was second place, the other Scout was already jumping and cheering.

I had lost confidence in myself, let myself down, but worst of all, let my father down. He always told me that I was smart, but lacked common sense. That was one of my downfalls that will have changed my life forever.

Basketball was my favorite sport. Ever since I bounced the ball in my backyard, and practiced dribbling, I knew it was going to be lots of fun. I joined the Pee-Wee Basketball League at my Grade School, but I never played because the older players were the starters, while I was a substitute. My teammates did not even know my name. I was a "nobody", but I never gave up. My father and I would practice at the park after school, on weekends, whenever he had the time. Every game, I watched and learned a new move. It wasn't before long that I was playing amongst them but I didn't score any points because no one passed me the ball but I did get to play. I may as well have joined track with all the running I did.

Our team was the "Braves" and we hadn't won first place in the two years I played with them. That was all right because I had school and Scouts to worry about. "Winning wasn't everything. It was how you played the game". I knew how to play the game, but I did not have the chance to prove it until that one season when all the starters got too old for Pee-Wees, and I became the starter. I couldn't believe it because now this was my chance. From the moment of my first "jump ball", I knew I had to lead the "Braves" to victory. Not only did I have my most-scoring game, but I used a very fundamental rule of the game – teamwork. My teammates scored, especially the substitutes, and I felt invincible until I was tripped and fell to the ground. I stayed motionless on the ground, for what had to have been a whole minute, and waited for someone to help me up. I just stayed there and wanted someone to come to my rescue.

All was quiet and I suppose they wanted me to gain my own composure and when Mr. Soto, the referee, picked me up, I was crying from the pain and humility. After a few minutes on the sidelines, because we did not have any benches, the coach asked me how I felt, and needless to say, I was ready to finish the game. We won, and I headlined the newspaper the following day. I learned a lot from that one game. Do your job right...always. Never give up. It was enough for me to play in the big leagues – sixth grade.

When I reached the sixth grade, my parents bought their first house. It was about seven or eight blocks north of the apartment and it was a great improvement but they hadn't asked me for my approval, or suggestion, they purchased it, did some minor repairs and that was that. It had two floors, a basement and an attic, and a sizable backyard and ultimately it was a great improvement and investment on their part.

My sister agreed to take care of a mixed-breed puppy which she called Brutus, who was half Benji and half German Shephard. He was playful and even had his own dog house in the yard but one day, on a fourth of July, he was so terrified of the neighborhood fireworks that he jumped over the metal garbage can, which served to block him from leaving the yard in the first place, and we never saw him again. I saw the time, patience and the care my father and sister put in to take care of Brutus, and that was too much for me to handle. I would rather stick with a bowl of fish, but even then, I'd have to clean the bowl.

I still remember when my mother dropped me off at my first big-league basketball practice. I sat in the car, while she got out and asked the coach if I was too late and the whole team just looked in amazement as I hopped out the passenger side and ran in excitement towards them. Despite me being the shortest, they accepted me.

I loved practicing the game as we would run all these drills for hours at a time. It was part endurance, and conditioning your body because we mostly ran. I was a guard, because I ran really fast, and I had plenty of practice at it and besides, I was too short for the other positions, but my best skill was defense and I would either be so fast and short to steal the ball, or I was the greatest at drawing "charging" fouls. I was just glad that my teammates ran the score so high that I had the chance to play. I learned a lot from them and although I didn't play with them much, I practiced with them. I was so ambitious during one practice that I accidentally hurt the star player as he went up for a lay-up and landed on me. I was just going for the rebound but he hurt his leg in the process.

"Sorry, Bobby," I said, "I didn't mean to."
I sensed that some of the guys blamed me because they all looked at me but it didn't stop Jamie from coming over to me and saying, "Don't worry about it, Corey". I felt guilty because we all played our hearts out that season enough to make it to the State Championships. Bobby made it to all the future practices but sat out on all of them so that his leg could fully heal but he never blamed me or said that it was my fault. A couple of weeks later, the Championship game was upon us and we were losing considerably during the second quarter. I was surely going to sit on the bench

this game because I wasn't a strong scorer or player so I knew there was no chance for me to play meanwhile I sat next to the guy who could have pulled us out of this defeat and I knew he wanted to play. Besides, at this point, his leg had gotten better, but the coach would not allow him to play. Bobby didn't even bring his uniform in protest even though it was in his blood to go out there and perform.

There was a huge crowd in the Home team's school auditorium. People, kids, and everyone else were roaring for the excitement of the game, and as I looked around, I wished there was something that I could do. I took off my uniform top and gave it to Bob. I felt that we all had something to prove that day, so he finally decided to put on my shirt and checked in. There was redemption for both him and me. We won the Championships and, ironically, his father later became coach of the losing team. The last I heard from Bobby was that he was playing for some University, and later ended his Basketball playing career in a driving accident but luckily, he survived the crash.

The following season, I went out to try for the Baseball team. I had a lot of practice playing with my cousins at their local parks, and I had a really good swing. My hand and eye coordination were good enough so I didn't strike out as much. Father Mueller was my coach and we practiced on Metro Field which had only been a few-minutes-walk from the house but I hadn't been given the same attention as the rest of the team because this was my first year, and the coach didn't know what I could do, but I hung in there. It was Spring, and it was good exercise. My first game was pretty exciting, and my family had been there to cheer me on as I looked official in my red and white uniform, cleats and the "cup" that my mom and I had bought together weeks before, and I felt ready and invincible. I batted sixth, and when I stepped up to the plate, I looked for a spot to hit the ball.

The first pitch was a little high, but after the second strike, I heard the opposing coach tell his pitcher to throw it down the middle while I thought they were both high and should have been counted as "balls". Wouldn't you know that I was called out, and had never even swung the bat?

"Can of corn," Father Mueller said as I walked back to the dugout. I didn't even know what that meant.

I was robbed, swindled and cheated but I would get them next time, I thought, but there was never a next time because I had been replaced by another player. When the game was immediately over, I walked off with my parents, and by the time we made it to the car, the coach yelled out to me telling me to stay with the rest of the team. I ran back to the dugout only to have him scold me for leaving without regrouping with the team after the game. I didn't need that. My team was waiting for me in the car.

CHAPTER VI

I made everyone money, I never betrayed anyone, and I was always low-key about everything. In fact, Malik was in for some guy for three hundred bucks, and he didn't have it. He lost a "sixty-time" bet with his bookie, and it was pay-up time, but had he won, he would have been given three-hundred dollars. If he didn't have it by noon tomorrow, his ass would have been kicked. If it weren't for Salami, I would not have known.

Malik probably did not tell me because, for one, it did not concern me, and two, he had a lot of pride. Nonetheless, I paid his bookie, Mark, out, plus the thirty-dollar vig, and told him to cut him off. That was my way of flaunting my power and letting it be known that Malik was with me. After all, one thing you don't do is welch on a bet because that was up there with being a rat. Malik eventually found out and thanked me for bailing him out.

"Don't thank me...just give me my three-hundred thirty back."

Within a week, he paid me what he owed, and was never late with any future payments. It's a great feeling knowing that you're needed and that you have gained someone's respect. It was a simple operation and it quickly became a routine, fixed income, but with capitalism comes a dangerous and infectious disease – greed.

****

Out of concerned fear and self-defense, I tucked my 9mm Ruger under my thigh while I sat, loosely, so that if I needed to use it, I'd probably lose a half of a second pulling it out in the draw. I saw him pull up behind me, get out of his white Yugo, and walk towards my unlocked passenger side door to get in.

"What's up, brotha? How you've been?" he asked.

"Seen better days. What's up? What's goin 'on?!" I loosened up some tension because if I were the next target it would have happened in those first moments, plus his fingers were so pudgy he wouldn't be able to retrieve a pistol then allow his finger to pull the trigger in time enough, but also, he has enough strength to pull out a shank. I believe knives used in weaponry are more of an intimate and close-ranged means of harm, almost personal and one-on-one. We might have been on that level, although a heart-attack might beat him to his demise.

He looked tired, lost most of his long hair although I'm not sure he spends time washing it, and he put on a lot of weight. He wore a faded grey sweatshirt and because it was unzipped, I could see that bald spot on his head got bigger when the hood slid off his head as he slid unto the passenger side.

"Let's get out of here." He insisted.

"Where to?" as I drove off.

"Some Chinese joint. I'm in the mood for chicken wings."

"Which one? Mike's, the one on Neptune or the one at City Line?" I asked.

"Yeah, the one on Greenville. The one on the corner. I like their Spareribs." He was rather specific about it.

I drove the side streets from Starlight to McAdoo then to Fowler where I back-doored and parked on Greenville Ave.

As we got out of the car and started crossing the street an older guy with a slight limp came out and asked us for change. I kept walking and paid him no mind. I opened the door and walked into the Chinese food place first. Mike was the head chef and proprietor there and always recognized me no matter how busy it got.

"Oh hello, Eggroll!"

I wasn't sure if he was asking me or if that was the name he gave me because on any given day I would eat here as my "go-to" place and whenever I was tired of deciding on food choices and couldn't think of what to eat next, an eggroll was a definite constant hence the name. Buddy grabbed a menu, as if it changed since the past fifty years, and knew exactly what he wanted.

"I'd like a *Sweet and Sour Chicken* with pork fried rice and a fried egg on top. A quart of shrimp fried rice and a small order of ribs." he requested, then looked at me. "What are you having? What do you want?"

"I'm good. I can't eat right now. It doesn't feel good," as I held and rubbed my belly. "Maybe a soup? *Wonton*." I added.

"And a small Wonton soup." He added for me.

I think anything over fifteen dollars included a free soda but they hadn't asked him yet. Instead the clanking of pots and pans, industrial forks and other utensils were busy moving as if I were in a mechanic's shop or some sort of an assembly line. We stood at the counter for a brief moment, just enough time for me to witness the raw marinated meat and already fried chicken wings being taken out of the refrigerator and into the hot grease pits. Even though I couldn't understand what they were saying, mainly because I never learned how to speak Cantonese, they were pretty transparent with how they cooked their food. Their open-kitchen concept is something I had always admired, as I witnessed flames rise whenever another chef squirted liquid from a clear bottle into a wok stirring feverishly with just simple flicks of the wrists.

We sat by the window and looked at passerby traffic of the busy Boulevard. The same panhandler approached random victims, asking for change, as if they owed him compassion or something. Seldom were the sounds of horns or yelling because of the quick light changes and convenient hurriedness around this area, but as engaging as it was out there, we were coming to a slow halt as to the main issue at hand. Buddy looked at me.

"Sorry about Felix. We made a lot of money together! Nobody knows who did it, but you might wanna ask Juju. He's been dealing with him the last couple of months." He explained. I had just realized that he wore a wife-beater shirt and smelled like weed.

"Juju," I said under my breath.

"Wonton soup, Eggroll." Mike called out to me.

"Listen, I'll keep an ear out and let you know if anything comes up. We'll grab a drink when you're up for it plus Mark's been asking about you. Get with him before you leave us again."

"Yeah, dude." I nodded my head as I began to stand up to get my soup and leave. With his left hand, he lightly hit my right shoulder and neutralized my personal space.

"Don't forget."

"Yeah, Dude. Thanks!" I said as I raised up the soup, walked out and avoided being asked for change on the way to my car as I was listening to Zeppelin's *Wanton Song*, in my head.

****

I met Jerome "Juju" Jacquet a long time ago in 1987. It was in my Freshman year of high school. I remember that because of the circumstances in which we met. I was way too shy or comfortable to ask Deirdre out on a dinner date, not with the impression that it was called a date anyway, so I asked a couple of our Elementary School friends to join us, and so the six of us had dinner at an Italian restaurant on Avenue C in Bayonne close to the border of Jersey City.

I remember it being a nice and fun evening and afterward, the young ladies were picked up and the three of us guys walked over to Marist High School so Haasan could show us his new school when a white two-door Camaro pulled up next to us and parked with the engine and loud rock music still on. The driver got out first and unexpectedly got in our faces about some crap or another. He wore a blue and gold colored Letterman jacket, which I assumed was the Marist colors and jacket. He also wore a gold chain with a big "F" pendant around his neck.

Two other guys came out of the car. I didn't recognize the passenger in the front but did recognize the guy coming out of the back seat as a fellow graduate of OLM, perhaps a couple of years older than us. He wore a mullet and I told him I knew him from our Elementary School whereby he toned down any attitude he was about to have because I identified him. While I focused on him, the leader was getting in Haasan's face about why he was there.

"He goes to school here," I interjected.

"Shut up! I'm not talking to you." He said to me as he looked over at me, but then looked back over to my friend.

"I'm talking to you, black boy. We don't like your kind around here."

That was the very first time I experienced someone disliking another because of the color of their skin. To me, some innocence was lost at that moment, as Jersey City is well-diversified and perhaps Bayonne was slightly different and tainted in this guy's eyes. I knew Haasan since second or third grade and he was who he was without any negative connotation. He was probably one of the very few black students we had at our school but it was never a bad thing.

"Frankie, let's leave them alone," the guy I recognized said.

"Yeah! Leave us alone!" I said and with that, Frankie took a swing at my face but I ducked down to avoid it. He tried to punch me three more times but I happen to dodge and avoid any contact. Instead of the three of us engaging in physical contact or violence with the three assailants, I pushed Frankie until he fell off-balance on his car and we quickly ran away, along JFK Blvd, for help. I must have been the fastest or more determined to get away because I ran into a corner store asking the workers inside to help because we were being "jumped" by three white guys. And so, the racial divide continued.

Maybe it was because they saw two out of the three young kids: a Puerto Rican and a black guy they wanted nothing to do with the altercation so they told us to get out of their store before they called the cops on us. That's exactly what I wanted to happen. I wanted the police to come and help us but no help came as we were thrown out of the store and I don't even know what happened to our mutual Irish friend. Haasan said that he was going to call a cab from there, which he did. When I opened the door, I looked to my left then right then left again, and when I saw that it was safe, I ran back towards the restaurant towards Ave C.

When I reached the restaurant, it had already closed for the night and the streets were empty and instead of waiting at a bus stop I decided that I was going to walk one and a half miles back home and do it discreetly. As I walked along towards Jersey City I turned around and saw headlights about two or three blocks away and it high-beamed me. It came towards me at an accelerated rate, and I don't know how they knew it was me, but it was them. I walked faster towards the city line crossing and when I reached close enough, I heard doors opening and closing. They parked in the middle of the street, got out and started to chase me.

"There he is! After him!" I heard someone yell.
I stopped in my tracks and looked over to the Jersey City side and saw the five high-leveled bricked buildings known as the Currie's Woods housing projects. It is the southernmost part of Jersey City's Greenville section, named after James Currie. I had only been there once or twice when my uncle took me with him to visit some guys. I remember going into one building that had spray paint on its front doors and the elevator smelled like urine, and the

guys that hung out there smoked cigarettes and drank in public. When I out-weighed my current situation I decided that the projects were my safer bet.

I ran so fast towards Currie's Woods, past the overhead 14A Turnpike and Route 440 bridges, that I could not even slow myself down, and before I knew it, I was quickly approaching a big group of guys who were hanging out at their bench amenities. A few of them quickly stood up in fear that I was going to run into them or assault them. I slowed down enough to convey a message to the pack.

"I got a bunch of white boys jumpin' me!" then I stopped to breathe.

"Oh, hell no!" one of them shouted as he threw his cigarette on the floor. "Let's get these mutha fuckers!" At that point, about ten of them ran towards the city boundary line and ran after my attackers.

When I finished catching my breath and removed my hands from my knees I stood up and thanked him. He wore a small black Fedora with a red feather on its side.

"Yeah, man. No problem. Shit has been going on for years. I'm JJ."

"Corey. JJ? I've been through some bad juju up until now, Juju. I've been here a few times with my uncle. Thanks again, bro." We shook hands and that was the beginning of my connection with Juju. I left Starlight and rode up Van Nostrand Ave. to the Boulevard. Jerome moved his operation from the Woods to Duncan, years ago.

CHAPTER VII

Sometimes you are so far in the forest you cannot see amongst the trees, and so I decided to leave Jersey City and head to Bayonne Park to be one with nature and get some air. I needed a different perspective. Maybe I just needed a Strawberry Shortcake from the ice cream food truck vendor there, after I finished my soup. Perhaps I needed to prioritize and value what was important in life. *Values*. *Family*.

****

When my father was finishing his Bachelor's Degree in the Arts at the city college part-time, he worked full-time at the Main Post Office. Classes would begin rather early in the morning, and he would help to support his family working the "graveyard" shift. He was rarely home, or rather, awake enough to spend time with his two children – myself and my younger sister, except for lunchtime, where he would take us to a fast-food joint or an occasional deli to get ham and cheese sandwiches on an Italian roll with Cheez Doodles and a Pepsi.

Afterwards, it was quality time at Hudson County Park, or Bayonne Park. My sister and I had great times there being pushed on the swings, and playing with the monkey-bars and the see-saw. I wore my blue, zippered-down sweatshirt and had taken the string off the neck area which tightened the hood plus I had a dual pocket on my front waist so I could put my hands inside if I had gotten cold. It was December 8th, 1980, but it didn't feel much like a cold, wintry day. The big top-tinted sunglasses covered any glares from the sun, and my black denim pants protected my backsides from sitting on a possible dirty swing seat. My sister had pretty much worn the same except she wore more layers of clothing than me.

I could never forget the look on her face when we played on the see-saw. She had the biggest smile, and the face she would make as she tightly gripped the front handle when she either went up or down was as though she had butterflies in her stomach every time, and after we had exercised our legs for a while, we decided to go on the big slides. We had to be careful getting off the see-saw first. Since I was taller and heavier, I slowly got off my seat and held down the weight of the bar, then slowly raised it so she could at least touch the ground with her feet. It was another successful adventure as we ran to the slide to my left, her right, and each climbed ten steps. Our mom waited behind us in case we fell off the stairs but we made it to the top and posed as our father took a snapshot of the three of us. We were high off the ground, but we managed to sit on our slides and let ourselves go and sometimes we went down so fast that we learned to hold on to the side rails and to slow down by pressing our feet against them.

We would always wind down our excitement on the playground by going on this spinning carousel-like ride. I've forgotten the name of it right now, but it had a circular base and is divided into six sections and each section had a color and was divided by metal rails that you could hang on to. My sister would sit in a section, while I spun it around to get more speed and, at that point, I would jump on and enjoy the ride. As I looked over, she was clinging on to the bar for her dear life, because if she hadn't, she probably would have flown off. We laughed and enjoyed ourselves. My parents, who looked comfortable in jeans and loose shirts, lounging against the green wooden slats of a nearby bench, made sure we had fun. What we loved most was feeding the squirrels some shelled peanuts which our dad always had ready in a brown paper bag. It was just nature, the serenity, and togetherness which brought the family closer together and it was these quality times we shared, the two hours a day during lunch that would be the foundation of our growing bond. Gloria and I knew them as mom and dad.

After we had left the playground, we were surprisingly off to New York City. I had been there a couple of times before, mainly to join my father on his art excursions for school. I loved the architecture of many of the older buildings, Washington Square Park for its diversity of people, but most of all, Central Park for its beautiful landscape. They were taking us to Central Park and it hadn't even been a half an hour ride from Jersey before I saw the stone wall which bordered a section of the grounds. We found a parking spot but had not entered the Park just yet. Dad had noticed a horse-drawn carriage in the near distance and propositioned the driver for a ride through the square.

As the ladies entered first, sitting behind the driver facing the rear, my father made sure I also safely entered the carriage. It had a white convertible top, which was down in case of bad weather and cushioned by its burgundy leather seats. I felt completely comfortable knowing we were all there as a family. With the ladies on one side and the gentlemen on the other, we were facing each other. My parents were wearing their "Beatle-Mania" T-shirts with a jacket, and my father had his 35mm Canon camera in hand taking photographs.

The driver had a black top hat and wore a black wool coat. His white shirt brought out the black bow tie as well, and his mustache seemed to be a straight line because he was always smiling. The carriage was drawn by a properly harnessed and magnificently groomed dark brown horse with white on the bottom of each of his legs, and a white diamond shape on his forehead. Our tour was nearly over, and very inspiring, yet before us lay a great open field of green and brown earth tones while the background, streaked with vertically-towering and overwhelmingly busy skyscrapers, distracted me so much so that I needed to quickly stare at a nearby tree just to rest my eyes. We wondered if we could stay here longer, but we knew that it was getting late and that we had to begin our journey home and since the day had been so eventful, I wondered when I would return again.

Later that night, a tear or three ran down my eye when I heard the news that John Lennon had been shot in front of the hotel he was staying in. It was not too far from where we were in New York that day. Somehow sadness fell upon me once again, as I heard his Double Fantasy album being played on the record my parents had owned.

****

I knew Mark from Starlight Avenue. He used to buy bunk to entertain his heavy betters and he liked my style and my product, so I became his agent. He would page me, or even drop by every once in a while, to see if I was around, but he never stuck around for more than five minutes. He also realized the lack of potential that existed in that section of our city and it was not so bad compared to some areas but nonetheless, if he was going to get caught, he'd rather do so in other parts of town, just for reputation sake. I felt the same way, but in the meantime, I did what I wanted to do. He beeped my pager, and I used the phone in the laundromat to call him back. By then, his needs were steady and often I would walk the three blocks to his house.

"Mook, what's up?"

"Bring a couple of movies over, and stop for some food. I'll have a quarter-pounder with cheese, no pickles, and an iced tea."

"On my way." I hung up the phone and went to the grocery store to pick up a newspaper and a loaf of bread. Rather than placing my goods in my duffel bag, the grocer placed my items in a black plastic bag and I was off to his house. I decided to cut through the public schoolyard where a few kids were playing Wiffle ball, and beyond some tall grass, there was a hole in the fence. I went through and started to follow the trail up to the Blvd. I made it there in no time and rang his second-floor bell which was located on the side of the house whereby he came down to let me in and invited me to come up. The stairs lead up into a spiral, and I became a little dizzy. His apartment was also occupied by Izzy, his pet iguana and every time I saw her, she would stick out her tongue at me very quickly. She had a quick-draw and I imagined what Izzy would look like in a gun belt toting a firearm. There was a guy in a suit in the living room, but we walked into the bedroom to take care of business first. I opened the duffel bag and started pulling out the items he wanted.

"Two movies" (two ounces), "a quarter-pound of ever-so-green bud – hold the seeds."

"What, no iced tea?" he joked but I didn't say anything about my iced tea theory.

It was a beautiful thing making an even thousand in ten minutes' time, but the guy in the other room, his collector, just handed him forty-five thousand in profits for one football game.

"'Lexy here is moving to Chicago and doin' his own thing over there. I'm gonna be short one guy. You want in?"

I saw the money I was making and the money Mark was making, and there really was no thought process except for my payroll amount. Besides, I was looking to get out from the business and to work with numbers. As if it were an interview, I asked him when I could start and as we walked into the living room, and he introduced me to Lexy. "Hey. How's it goin'?" I asked him as we shook hands. I wished him well on his trip, said adios to Izzy, and left shortly after.

Within the first month working with Mark, I met and learned all of his players and became more familiar with the daily operations. I was a very eager student listening and copying the developed methods he already had in place and built enough of his trust and confidence in me that I could make some serious money. Before long, I had my own route, Lexy's old one, and began maintaining the tight rapport I had established with all of the gamblers. Most of the guys that I dealt with were veterans, guys who had been testing their luck for years and had developed their own patterns, methods, and superstitious rituals. Most of them had used mascots, from the traditional team mascots but with beads around their necks and maybe a cigar attached to its hand, to a troll doll, I saw wrapped in a suit Elvis would have worn. There were a group of guys who would burn incense, give the sign of the cross certain number of times while saying a prayer, while this one guy would kiss a real egg throughout the game. All of their attention to detail believed them to have special and divine luck.

I wasn't much of a follower of sports except for the casual Yankees games that were on the tube, but besides that, I hadn't been much into statistics. Statistics were for fanatics or the gamblers who truly believed that the odds were in their favor. I first started watching baseball when the Yanks came to my hometown in the seventies at Roosevelt Stadium. My father took me there a few times, and so I began cheering for the home team. I started getting involved in football, and that was the season that brought in the dough.

The whole operation was simple and quite mathematical really. I knew what all my possible outcomes were before the games even started. If a bet was lost, the penalty would be the actual bet plus the *vig*. That's what you call the interest given to the bookie for covering your bet when you lost, and the minimum bet I covered was a "five-time" bet. The winner of this bet would receive twenty-five dollars, but if they lost, the cost would be thirty dollars. A "ten-time" would give out 55:60 odds, but a "twenty-time" would pay out 100:110 odds. Now, if Mr. X placed a "twenty-time" bet for the home team, and Mr. Y placed a "twenty-time" bet for the visiting team, how much had I won? A ten-dollar profit was mine just for finding two opposing bettors. When you added three hundred bettors on my payroll for the week, the numbers were astonishing. It got to the point where I couldn't continue traveling everywhere to place these bets.

Mark and I found a stash house, my new playground, where we could set up shop and receive the bets over the phone. He had a neighbor on Third Street, downtown, who didn't mind that we had crossed his telephone wires with the house next door and that we used his place to run our new operation. We paid him off for the racket, and we only maintained it every other week for three months, or just in time for the football season to be over. Mark also had a guy who worked for the phone company who deliberately switched phone lines with neighboring houses so that if there was a wire-tap from the feds that gave them enough evidence to raid the place, they would be rushing to the wrong house and in turn gave us time to bail. Also, if the feds knew what building we were in they wouldn't hear any illegal activity over the phones because they were the neighbor's phone line. Our gig brought in about three million a year and helped feed my account plenty.

We had another stash house in Hoboken, and this one was more user-friendly. It was located on top of an old bookstore, and the building looked old enough that you wouldn't suspect anyone coming in or out to see us. The front door leads into a vestibule and another door guarded passage to a flight of stairs up. A small but noticeable camera gazed down from the second-floor landing at all patrons, or possible intruders, as a sensor on the front door triggered a silent bell each time it opened. Only the guys on the listening end upstairs could hear the door chime. Patrons came upstairs and through another protected door into smoke-filled rooms filled with "gentlemen" of all ages. Then there was Joe, an older Italian man in his sixties who always had the corner table seat and was always reading a newspaper. He hardly said a word but seemed to listen really well.

One afternoon during lunch I went straight from school up to the second floor to the stash house and on this day, there were three students with their school jackets contemplating "round-robin" options, and once in a while they would win, but most times than not, everyone lost. A "round robin" was a bet which entailed three different bets in one. You could either bet on three teams and their outcomes or just bet on three possible outcomes in a game and if one of the outcomes lost, the entire bet was lost, but if all three won, the odds were favored considerably. I had tables, chairs, four television screens to view live games, pencils, ashtrays and even a large board with all the posted odds. It looked a like a regular Bingo night, but I knew this wouldn't last forever because although the odds were always stacked towards the favor of the House, Lady Luck would soon run out and there weren't enough insurance policies on the payroll to protect us forever so after a year and $200,000 later, I told Mark that this operation was too big for me and that I was more comfortable running the street numbers for him.

The street numbers were an entire game altogether. It coincided with the horse track and its total haul. Whatever the Meadowlands Racetrack in Secaucus took in for the entire bets for the day, that number was reported and the local newspapers would include that figure in their papers the following day, up to the penny. Bets opened midday and results would be posted the following day, but the results that were of only true importance to the gambler were the last three-dollar amounts of the total take. If the Track collected $1,234,567.89 on a Wednesday and you bet, on Wednesday, that 567 would come out, you would find out on Thursday, preferably by way of The Daily News newspaper. This New York paper somehow had this daily result highlighted and made it easier for those who were looking for it to see. For a mere fifty cents, you could pick a three-digit number to come out "straight", or exactly the way you called it, and for another fifty cents, you could pick it so that your three-digit number comes out "boxed", or in any combination. Say the number was 418, as was mine, and one dollar was paid for that number to come out straight, the payout was one thousand bucks. If 148 or any other combination, but 418, comes out, for that same dollar, the payout was two hundred bucks. It was pretty enticing, and many people have been playing for years, and before long I memorized about two hundred number combinations and who played each.

The bet had to be placed before noon each day. That was my cut-off point because I had to drop off the loot and many times I would visit the track myself. Most of the time I wouldn't even know who was racing. Programs at the racetrack were about ten bucks, but one of the best things about the racetrack is walking into the joint, and having someone who is walking out, handing you their paid program book instead of just tossing it in the trash. What were they going to do with it anyway, and besides, when I left, I always returned the favor. It was probably one of the most honorable deeds amongst gamblers that I could think of.

CHAPTER VIII

When I worked in the Spanish communities, I was known as the "Bolitero," or the guy who collected the boletas, or lottery tickets. Although I was of Spanish descent, I had not truly learned the entire language, but I knew enough to get by and I believe with every new language I attempted to learn, for some reason I seemed to learn the bad words first.

Today, I walked toward my favorite barbershop. He was the first Puerto Rican barber to open in the Jersey City Downtown area, plus he gave me my very first haircut. I also liked it because it had that red–white–blue striped spinning cylinder as you reached the front entrance and a tiny bell above the door rang as I opened it and walked in.

"Buenas. Saludos."

There were a few guys sitting patiently to get their haircuts. There were always five barbers snipping hair away, and the Hispanic authenticity was obvious in the Coquí figurines hanging above the front mirrors, a few hand–made carvings of musical instruments, and myriad tropical plants. The floor had black and white checkered tiles and was always clean from hair since the barbers swept every time one of them took a break.

"Hola, Coronado."

The head barber, Indio, always collected the number selections and their bets for me and placed them in a sealed envelope near the register. I usually used the restroom first, and on the way out he would hand it to me, but things changed for me on this day.

While I was in the four-by-four-foot room that is small enough to probably only serve as a utility closet but was really the bathroom, I overheard the bell chime followed by a loud demanding harsh deep voice.

"Where is he?!"

I could only hear the Daniel Santos music, the type that my grandmother would play in her kitchen every morning as she made breakfast, playing in the background, followed by a radio transmission coming from what sounded like a police frequency but I didn't understand the jargon.

"I know he's in here." The chime sounded again and I could sense that other officers had entered. It was at this moment that I felt that I would be arrested and that it was over for me, but how did they know I was here? How long were they following and surveilling me? What if they find all the things I have on me? Names...numbers...weapons. I looked around quickly. Other than the porcelain toilet and sink there was a mop in its yellow bucket, a couple of wooden brooms, paper napkins on a wooden shelf and some white aprons on a hook on one of the walls. I scanned some more. The shadow on the bottom of the floor near the door alerted me that someone was drawing near. I didn't move nor did I have time to shut off the light. It was so silent, *En El Juego De La Vida* was playing on the radio and the brass instruments sounded really clear.

The policeman reached for his service weapon with his right hand while he slowly reached for the door handle with his left as some of the patrons watched in anticipation. He slowly turned the knob. Indio snipped his scissors one last time and put them in his apron pocket. His customer sat there quietly until the radio silence was interrupted by a voice stating that they had caught the suspect on the corner of Newark and Barrow. The officer slowly released his grip and started to turn around now noticing the Spanish-themed business he was in and only took one step before he turned back around and thrust opened the door anyway. The only disturbing view he had inside the closet-sized restroom was that the toilet seat was up and it hadn't been flushed.

While quickly searching the room in a slight panic, I noticed that the white aprons on the wall were actually hanging on a hook to a door that led to the hallway of the old brownstone building. The knob was covered at first by the lambskin woolen aprons and luckily it had been unlocked. When I entered the hallway, I locked it on the other side and quickly walked down the hallway and looked out through the curtain side window of the front door. When I was satisfied that the police had all gone, I walked out the front to the next entry of the shop and opened it. Indio reached over to the register and handed me the envelope.

"Gracias," I said as I walked out and heard the bell tinker.

Who they were looking for was a teenage punk who punched an old lady in the face and stole her purse. They chased him from Van Vorst Park down Jersey Avenue to Barrow, where the barber shop was located. The kid ran towards the Police Station on Erie, between Newark Ave. and Bay Street and got him because he ran right into them, but better him than me. I wasn't a juvenile delinquent. I was better than that. I had class.

There are two kinds of crooks I can't stand the most and they are thieves and rat bastards and so by that classification I was better than that delinquent kid, but if it weren't for him, I wouldn't have been faced with the possibility that I could get popped by the police, or worse Federal Agents, for things that were deemed illegal and wrong by their standards, at any time. I was alone in that closet, faced with the impending fear that by some random reason I had been sloppy or not careful enough to take care of business. Things were done because that's how things were done and taught. There was no prior morality class between right and wrong. It was a way of life and the unspoken dichotomy of the streets.

I walked to the corner of Newark and Barrow in front of a furniture store and just had to stop and get a couple of "dirty-water" dogs from the corner Sabrett hot dog vendor. A Canary-yellow Toyota low-rider drove by and was playing El Gran Combo's *El Barbero Loco*, and only lowered it when he pulled a U-turn in the middle of Newark Ave and pulled up in front of the Sabrett guy. Coney Island can have their Nathan's franks but whenever I saw the blue and yellow umbrella covering up the corner stand, I was all ready for at least one with mustard and sauerkraut and the other with onions and they tasted great with a cold can of Welsh's Grape soda. I'm pretty sure they sell the same frankfurters at Boulevard Drinks at Journal Square, just to the left of the Loew's Jersey Theatre, across the street from the Stanley Theater. Sometimes I just needed a break from the hustle and bustle.

In between jobs, I try to take advantage of the locales that I'm in so running my personal errands was a bit easy for me. Being in that barber shop's utility closet reminded me that I may have needed some items for my place like a utility broom and maybe a box of rags, so while I was somewhat close, I went around the corner on Jersey Ave and saw the logo of an Indian, with feathers in their hair, above the front doors of Borinquen Hardware. It was partly-owned by a Puerto Rican woman who always knew where everything was, no matter how small or obscure, and always pointed me in the right direction. She ran the cash register that day and greeted me when I walked in.

The place looked like a huge warehouse with so many aisles of products. They met your hardware and contractor accommodations for practically any project you were working on, but I was so curious about all the things they carried, I just took my time to look at them all from keys to be made or boards of wood to be cut, for all of your one-stop home improvement shopping needs. Time was fleeting and I had to continue my rounds but, although I enjoy window shopping, I do not like leaving stores empty-handed so I quickly scanned the bodega and quickly purchased a utility broom, an inexpensive yet functional garden shovel, and she sold me on an Artist Paint Set that was on sale by the register. I was pleased but I had to go and thanked her on the way out.

Other than barber shops, I inconspicuously walked into bars, candy stores and even backroom card-playing operations to see my clientele, but my favorite spots were the warehouse union workers who loved the game. Often, they waited for me to show up around their break time, just when the lunch truck would appear outside their doors. I had my notepad and pencil ready in my coat pocket and waited for Tommy to come out those doors and into the sunlight.

"What's up, Corey?"

"What is it, Wizard?"

I had known Tommy for the past couple of years since he started popping over onto Starlight from his house on Fuller Avenue to buy liquor, and he had been working at this food distribution warehouse for three years now. We shook hands, and I casually slipped him his six hundred bucks minus my ten percent, or sixty dollars, for hitting 880 straight and box, and he gave me an additional forty bucks to make it an even one hundred. It wasn't bad for investing a mere dollar. I hung around the place so many times, I should have gotten a paycheck from the company, and each time I was there I noticed how easy the guys made their job seem and how much money they were making, and with medical benefits. I often thought about having a part-time job, so I could at least claim an income and pay my taxes like any other American, but what did I know about warehousing?

The time had come when Mark reached his limit and felt that it was time for him to take a break, or retire, so he closed up shop and I was unemployed. I had made tons of cash, and experienced the adrenaline that came with the chance of being caught, but it was time to start looking for a real job and to use the skills and smarts to make it on my own, the legal way. Mark just wanted a break and to enjoy the spoils that came with all the risk and hard work. It was an early retirement and until he calls again, I will be doing the same, however, that idea taunts and haunts me because I know that I could not go back, and should not go back because I love the free air and value my freedom in the US. I am at a time when I am safe - home base.

CHAPTER IX

Back at Starlight, where my underground process began, some of the older crowd were now into a heavier drug. Thank goodness they weren't into heroin because that was killer and, in my books, a pretty heavy addiction. Nearly twice a day, Donny and Joe would go up the hill to cop some coke from the shady characters across the Boulevard. The Boulevard separated the good neighborhood from the bad, depending on how you looked at it and which side you were on. They usually met guys, who hung out at their corners, and bought jugs (vials) of rock from them. Typically, five vials were a called a "clip". There was no telling how good the stuff was until they reached Starlight because they did not want to expose and spend too much time verifying the product, which was aggravating and seemed, to me, to be a sloppy way to do business.

Donny was in his late twenties, skinny, semi-bald man who had his own game, or style, of dealing with people. His slick reputation got him practically anything he wanted, so he was the leader who bought clips for everyone else. He and Joe spotted their regular seller and always proceeded with caution.

The drug dealer was wearing a thick gold chain which gradually turned into status symbols in the streets. Women started wearing big gold hoop earrings. It was the style, and many of the thieves were snatching gold chains like it was going out of style.

"What's up? You got anything?" Donny asked.

"Whatcha need?"

"Gimme a clip."

"Twenty-five." The dealer demanded.

Donny handed him the twenty-five dollars needed for the trade, and he always made sure that he had correct change. It wasn't good to over-tender, because most of the time the sellers would say they don't have the change just to possibly make the buyer purchase more, and because you did not want to let the ever-watching neighborhood know that you were conducting a money transaction in public. Besides, Donny knew that five jugs came in a clip, and most of the time there were six just for a play. He would keep the sixth one, and that would be another of his incentives for going up "the hill". Joe was the lookout and he also made sure that there was no foul play. Although no one from Starlight packed any firearms, they never feared that things would go wrong from those dealers, but rather what came from the police, because the Starlight boys all felt they were invincible and could physically crush their opponents if it came to a fight. Joe was a short and stocky ex-Navy man who could win any brawl, and he and Donny lived in their old-school ways of settling disputes like men—with their fists. They never showed any fear, and because of this, many of their dealings went smoothly.

"All right, man. See ya," Donny said as he walked away with Joe by his side.

They went back down the hill and into the schoolyard where they took some of the rocks from the other vials and distributed it amongst themselves. The other jugs were for two other guys, and they probably would not have noticed that their supply was just a tad bit light. That's what this drug did to them. It turned them against each other so they would have more of it for themselves.

I was in the corner pizza parlor, playing an arcade game with Malik when Jay came in looking for Donny or Joe. My hand was firmly gripped on the joystick maneuvering my starship around when I told him that I hadn't seen them. He walked out of the parlor in a huff and headed towards the schoolyard, but by that time the two of them were walking back. My game was over, so I walked over to the counter and ordered a slice from Stan, the owner, and then I looked out the windows and saw the three of them heading down the block—probably to go to Jeremy's house to indulge.

A couple of Malik's buddies came into the parlor and started talking to him while he played his game. I knew who they were and without anyone else knowing, they made a bunk deal. While one of the guys kept talking to Malik, the other went over to Stan and ordered two Cokes. It was a business casual day, and everyone got what they wanted, except for Jay who came back into the store whining and complaining that his drug stash was a bit short.

That was Jeremy's style. I called him Jay for short and I could always tell what was on his mind by his body language and his verbiage by the way he always vented and blew off steam by telling everyone his business, and luckily Malik's buddies had already left the place. I didn't want anyone to think that anything was wrong in our places of business because it would make the patrons nervous about coming back. My slice of pizza was ready, and I sprinkled some garlic powder on it.

"What's up, Jay?"

His hands were in his pockets and he kept pacing around.

"Nothing, Corey."

He was a tall Irishman who always wore a cap. He sort of looked like "Jughead" from the Archie comics, and I thought it was funny that he was a jug-head. He walked out of the parlor and walked across the street where his German shepherd was chained to a capped gas pipe in front of the Laundromat. That was when Malik walked over and suggested to me that Jay should get his stuff from someone else. I hadn't realized it then, but it sounded like the best idea for him. Cocaine was becoming a serious business, and I also despised the idea because I considered it to be an addictive killer and dirty racket. From a distance I saw Ron walking quickly towards the schoolyard but he didn't look good, or as healthy as I once knew him, as he scurried along as if he needed to be somewhere or to evade being chased or captured. A few days later, the word was out that the guys up "the hill" were robbed and some of them killed for their stashes, by the gangs from Newark.

Newark was a neighboring city of ours and was nicknamed Brick-Town because of all the buildings constructed of brick, while Jersey City had been donned as Chill-Town because that is where you went to relax and chill after you finished partying. Every year the boys from Newark would hit the Chill-Town hot spots and rob them of their cash and loot, and it was a bit peculiar that none of them guys had realized that these gangs would always come out a couple of weeks before Christmas with their posse. Things were getting hot up there, but Donny and his clan needed their fixes so they were forced to go up there to cop again and they figured that if they could round up a bunch of cash together, they would only have to go up there this once and it would last them for a couple of days. Anyone who knows about this drug knows that it is hard to not keep dipping into the bag, especially when there is an ample supply around.

They bought five clips, Donny kept five jugs for himself, and it was a bad batch. Half of it wasn't even coke, but probably soap or detergent, and all who were involved took the loss. The dealers were probably hit so hard by the Newark gangs that the former tried to rip everyone off for some cash. No one was hurt on Starlight, except for their feelings and their pockets, but they contemplated on their next score.

Malik told me that he knew a couple of players from mid-town who had a good supply. I told him that I didn't want to get involved, and I suggested to him to stay out of it as well, but he looked at it from a business perspective.

"C'mon, Core. Think about it, cuz."

I noticed the look in his eye like he was on to something. His smile was trying to lure me into his grand scheme and he was on to something all right, because the following day I spotted Jeremy sporadically moving his jaw, and his tongue came out like a slithering snake in the hot sun.

"What's up, Jay? Chewing invisible gum?"

"Hey, what's.... up...Corey?"

He could hardly speak, but from what I could understand, it seemed that he got some good stuff from Malik and took a "freeze" first. A freeze was when cocaine was rubbed on the teeth, and I suppose it was to taste the product to see if it would numb the gums.

Basically, any type of drug ending with the word "Caine" was specified to act as a numbing ingredient. Drugs like lidocaine and benzocaine are prescribed to numb. Cocaine is even used in hospitals and it's legal but the fact that it is a controlled substance in hospitals made it legal, and the illegal aspect comes when entrepreneurs take it upon themselves to try to make their own buck from it. Besides, the abuse of cocaine is a great reason why it should be illegal to distribute.

Malik had delved into a new realm, and because I didn't admire it, I had to slowly back away from his endeavors.

That was a great time for me to also dissipate from the whole Starlight scene, but as I did, I craved and hungered for the next score. Like the drugs, I was addicted to the action and I couldn't find it in myself to leave, so I thought about the new circumstances and opportunities immensely.

A couple of days later, I went back to the pizza parlor to keep up with current events, and the place was a ghost town. The only person I recognized was Big Dave, from across the street, and he was tending to his regular laundry customers.

"Hey, Stan, where is everybody? Was the pizza bad?"

"I don't know, you know," he wittingly said.

"I'll take a slice," I responded.

He sliced a piece off of an already-made pie and stuck it in the oven. I went towards the arcade game and inserted a quarter. A few minutes later, Salami walked in with his usual casual look, a cigarette on his right ear and said hello.

"Whashup, Core?"

"Hey, Josh. Where is everybody?"

"They're on a misshion. They've been gone for two daysh without shleeping and eating."

"Where's Malik?"

"He sshould be home shleeping shtill."

"Cool. Wanna slice or something? Stan's got mine in the oven." I asked him.

"Yeah, dude." He ordered it himself.

"A shlice, Shtan."

"One slice coming up."

I kept playing my game until my starship crashed into an asteroid, but it was just in time for me to grab my already-heated slice and sprinkle it with garlic powder. By the time Joshua got his, mine had just cooled off enough so that I wouldn't burn the roof of my mouth then we grabbed a booth and sat across from each other.

"Dude, check thish out."

He pulled, from his back jeans pocket, a folded Daily News clipping of the hierarchy of the Italian Mob that was featured in that day's paper. Paul Castellano was in there, and so was Josh's new boy, John Gotti. Josh was fascinated with the Mob and hoped that one day he would be down with their crew, in whatever capacity.

"That's a cool chart, man."

"Yeah, dude. It sshows all the playersh and Gotti'sh right here at the bottom."

"That was a sweet move on how Gotti and Gravano whacked Castellano."

"Right in front of Shpark'sh Shteak Houshe."

"Oh, yeah, man. And how his boys dressed in Russian hats and coats threw everyone off for a bit. Slick, dude." The happened mid–December in 1985.

Joshua was truly fascinated with that life, and somehow wanted to live it himself, and it was partly the reason why he hung out with Malik and me. Although by no means did I consider myself part of the Italian Mob, or any other organized crime faction, even though we admired and respected such a powerful organization. Besides, there was no honor and complete secrecy amongst this crew. Most, if not all, of these guys, were for themselves and that was the biggest part of not being organized. The Starlight faction was organized on being disorganized, and a free-for-all.

Across the street, towards the end of the block near a public elementary school, was a quiet little restaurant and bar named Grieco's. I was only in there a couple of times, once out of curiosity, and it was a bit dark for me. It was a central location to where Deirdre and I lived and so we also met up there one evening long ago with mutual friends for dinner. The dim lighting and smoky atmosphere didn't make it suitable for me to want to sit in and have a quick lunch. There was no advertising other than the sign above the door, and you had to park on the street. None of us went towards that block and it was off the beaten path for a reason. Just then, we saw Salvatore "Sonny" Grieco come out the door of his place with another guy and lit a cigarette with a zippo. He wore sharp-pressed olive color pants, a white shirt and colored tie, and a jacket that had a burgundy flower on its lapel. He reached into his coat pocket and put the cigarette case back.

"Waddya think they're up to?"

"Holy sschit, dude, that's Sshonny. Whatever it ish, he's living largse." *Living large*. I wondered what "living large" meant. With it, must come sacrifices.

Malik came into the parlor and saw Josh and me talking our Ying-Yang when he came over and asked us if we wanted to go for a ride.

"What's on your mind?"

"Let's go into the City."

"Schit yeah."

"Shotgun," I called.

We got there in less than an hour.

"Spanish Harlem. This is where my boys from mid-town go to cop."

"You know where to go?" I asked.

"I was there yesterday with them. We're almost there."

He made a right onto a narrow one-way street, and it was unlike any place that I had ever seen, except for maybe in the movies. The street was lined with huge apartment buildings, and when we stopped behind a car at the red light, I noticed a few guys hanging out sitting and playing dominoes on some chairs and a foldable table that studied the action. I don't know if it was because they never saw us before, or because they read our Jersey license plates, but most of them stared at us as if we were outsiders and not welcomed in their realm of the living.

He made a right unto a wider street, and for some reason, a group of five guys came right up to the car. Malik pulled over, with the car still running, and listened as they pulled out their clips, in broad daylight, and started propositioning him with their stuff.

"Yo, man, I got the good shit."

"Check it out, bro. I got rocks."

I cautiously watched as they seemed like they were practically inside the car but Malik was calm through the whole ordeal. Salami lit up a cigarette, anticipating any moves, and their hands were so much inside the car that I could almost see how many rocks were in each vial.

"Gimme two, man." Malik said with no fear.
One of the guys tried to stick his hand inside the car to turn off the ignition as if we were there to rip them off and speed away, but Malik held his ground and convinced them that there was no foul play. There were about six of them hovering the driver-side window, rather aggressive and drawing attention to us, and I started to become anxious and nervous.

"If it's that good, we'll come back and get a lot more." I involved myself and stated.

That sounded like a sweet deal to them. If they would come out alright on this deal, there was no telling how much they could make on their next one with us. It was business, and in the beginning, it had to be done right if it's to last again, and gratefully they understood that. It was because of that, we got a play.
He gave Malik two extra vials to turn us on.

I just wanted to get the hell out of there in one piece because I didn't feel good about the whole thing at all. When the transaction ended, he sped off down the street and I wondered if anyone else noticed us. When I rolled down my window, I noticed that there was a guy standing in the front of an apartment building looking at us.

"You just bought garbage. You should come see me next time."

I thought that was rather odd about how flagrant his opinion was. Salami held the stash, cracked one open and took a freeze to see how it was.

"It'sh good, dude."

"Of course, man. They're our boys." Malik confirmed.

I just let things happen and I played it cool because I was more concerned about not getting stopped by the police, and I knew that we wouldn't be in the clear unless we were on the other side of the Hudson. I asked Malik to play some tunes to help myself calm down while Salami had been puffing away at his smokes.

When we got back to Starlight, we were dropped off a block away from the pizza parlor, because we didn't want to be associated with Malik, or rather, let anyone know that we took the ride with him.

"I'll see you in a few," he said as we shut the doors and walked off.

The whole thing seemed surreal. Malik bought each clip for twenty-five and they looked like dimes, so he easily sold them for fifty times two, making himself a hundred bucks, or fifty dollars profit plus the two extras which he gave Salami to get rid of.

I was indirectly involved in some master scheme, and I was somehow cut out of the action. If I could in some way be a part of it and ensure my own safety, that was all right by me, I thought. *Damnit.* I had to see what the reaction was from the users first before I did anything. If favorable, I would need to go with Malik a couple of more times after that, before I go on my own and get comfortable with the idea of solo expansion.

I took a stroll through the school #38 courtyard because it was quiet when the children weren't around, and to think about my next moves. I sat on some steps that probably needed to be pressure-washed, along with the entire school grounds, years ago but I was used to the urban grime and grit. I rested my eyes and lowered my head into my supporting hands, elbows on the top of my legs, relaxing and unwinding from the bustle and hustle, only for a brief minute until the crescendo of chaos slowly ensued.

A small group of five guys were walking into the school's enclosure, one carrying a boom box loudly playing a taped mix of rap music, and there was no doubt our paths were about to meet because of the sharp looks I was getting from a couple, if not all, of them.

"Sup, yo?!" one said or asked. The guy holding the radio lowered it maybe just a couple of decibels when I nodded my head to acknowledge. I remained sitting as not to show signs of aggression or fear but they halted by me and decided to carry on their objective. I carried nothing of value on me. There was no flaunting of expensive jewelry, no name brand clothes and I probably only had about fifty dollars cash on me so I was unsure what they were looking for.

"I said sup, yo!"

"What's up?" I got up and extended my hand to shake but the front man slapped it out of his way. I sat back down and just looked around at them. Run–DMC's *Run's House* began to mix into their music selection. That's when the instigator hit me with a right to my left forearm that instinctively raised up to protect myself, but it still made contact enough to razzle me a bit. Two others joined in on punching me and while I was trying to protect my head and face, I kicked one of them really hard in their leg enough that I think I broke his bone while he fell to the ground screaming in agony. What was up with my space being violated today? Every so often I tried to push an assailant off and I might have connected on a punch to a jaw but they were relentless. I was being smothered while one guy tried to go into my pockets but then a loud crashing noise suddenly stopped everything.

The radio had been destroyed with one quick swing of a baseball bat and while the four of them looked up to see what happened, the quick distraction allowed me to throat punch the main guy and for me to quickly angle myself to hit another in the chest so hard that he couldn't breathe right away. Silence took over except for the guy screaming and holding his shattered kneecap. The owner of the radio was in so much shock that after he stood motionless for those crucial seconds he ran away.

It was Chooch. I didn't know where he came from and I didn't really care at the time, but there he was standing with a wooden Rawlings baseball bat in his hand, his grip tight around the handle of it that it was as if it were an appendage. I couldn't help but notice how filthy and dirty his hands appeared, as if he were overhauling and rebuilding engines but couldn't avoid handling the oil, grease and soot. His fingernails were jagged and he may even have lost one or two but those hands were crafty and ultimately saved me out of a possible good beating.

He noticed my extended stare and without feeling affronted, began to tell me how his hands were a true indicator that he was indeed destitute and not just a panhandler pretending to be homeless. Some will occasionally hang around the front of the same stores asking for change but will already have housing, are on government assistance, or even have another job but still have the audacity to pretend to have nothing, not even shelter, or even a basic need for survival. I don't know where he came from. He may as well have come from up above.

"Thanks, bro!" We all need a friend from time to time.

CHAPTER X

Stanley's paint store was my first "on the books" real job and it was just minutes away from my high school. It had a huge paint can on top of the building so that the drivers on the NJ Turnpike could also see it, and it was a warehouse clerk position which meant I stocked the shelves, pulled merchandise for customers from our inventory and loaded and unloaded freight from delivering trucks. I learned how to drive a fork-lift and work the pallet jack while John Kaminski was my supervisor and he showed me the ropes until I became really good at it. He was a young stocky fellow with a wife and two young daughters for whom he loved dearly. He also bore a mustache which hung slightly over his upper lip, and I always thought it was a bit funny when his coffee would hang or be absorbed by it whenever he drank a cup. He managed the five of us, two of whom were Portuguese and didn't speak a word of English at first, me, Eddie and Sam.

Sapo and Gerald lived in Newark and commuted every day to start their "8 to 5" jobs. Sapo was a bit slinky looking and at five foot five, one hundred and twenty pounds wet, he did not look like he could carry heavy boxes at all. He was in his mid-forties and periodically dyed his hair black to get rid of the greys, to look younger. He was very ambitious and knew all the hiding spots, but he felt that because I was new on the job that I might have been replacing him, so he tried to look busy and avoided contact as possible. Gerald, on the other hand, was very happy to meet me as he tried to speak the little English he knew, and I helped him learn the language as much as I could. He looked more Australian than Portuguese because he always wore a casual, yellow-straw safari hat, and wore a mustache like Yosemite Sam. He was very handy and a hard worker. Often, on Saturdays, he would take the electric mower around the perimeter and work on the landscape and even if he wasn't busy, he always looked it.

The store had seven aisles with the main one in the middle that either lead to the warehouse in the east direction, or the wallpaper department in the westward direction. The front counter had nine salesmen who somewhat knew the business, and were constantly busy greeting customers, mainly contractors, or keeping inventory.

John had asked me to help Sam with the inventory upstairs and prior to obliging, we put our gloves in our lockers and exchanged them for writing utensils and notepaper. He asked me if I wanted to call the numbers out or take the notes, but I figured it was rhetorical when he said that he would call them out because he had sloppy handwriting.

"You should be a doctor," I told him as we ran up twenty-five steps using the back stairwell up to the second warehouse floor. This place had a rack system where all the freight was stored on racks and built upwards to consolidate space and as we passed all the handy tools like sheetrock hammers, screwdrivers, and mop heads then walking through a narrow aisle, I approached the end and saw the mega supply that I had to count. The first door to the right was a restroom and so I decided to make a pit stop first, while Sam turned on the lights located on a column near the center of the room.

When I finished, I tried to find him but I couldn't even hear him past a large constant humming noise. To my right was a huge fan connected to the wall and it served to release the hot air that was present up there.

"Let me give you a quick tour. We have different size paint brushes to our left, canvas drops, paint grids, gloves, painter suits, paint trays, and rollers. Over to our right, we have more trays, more rollers, different sizes of tape, and over here we have our extension ladders. Along these walls, we have wooden and aluminum ladders – 2ft., 3 and so forth. Where do you want to start?"

"Let's start with the boxes of brushes and work our way up to the bigger things."

This was going to be an all-day event, and that was a good thing. What it did was show me where everything was and what we had in stock. We were halfway completed when we heard the freight elevator making its way up. The doors opened manually by stepping on a latch and pulling on a thick, sturdy rope downward. It was John and when he found us, he told us to come on down and take lunch. He walked towards the extension ladders and behind a six-foot wooden ladder was a door, which I hadn't seen before, and it leads to the room that stored office supplies. He led us through the door and at the end of the room was another door and that door led us into a narrow corridor with filing cabinets lined up on our lefts and as he opened the final door, I was feeling the gradual process which led us away from the dirty, hot warehouse into the air-conditioned offices that were occupied by ten women and a receptionist. Before we went down the stairs which lead to the front counter, he introduced me to some of the ladies, and just quickly showed me the offices of the owners. It was a pretty big operation. The chain had fifteen other stores throughout Jersey, and this one was the main one.

We made our way downstairs and Sam and I walked out the doors which lead into the huge parking lot and towards Ruggiero's Deli around the corner, while John went back to the warehouse checking up on the other guys. It was Saturday, and Gerald was whacking his weeds and trimming the hedges. I asked him if he wanted anything from the deli, but he just shook his head. Sam was a year or two younger than me, but you couldn't tell with his physique and focused attitude. He worked out at a gym, took good care of himself and exercised as much as he could plus he didn't smoke or drink.

A couple of truck drivers and one of the ladies from upstairs were on the line ready to place their orders while Sam asked me to tell him a bit about myself while we waited on line. I mainly told him about school, and how I was a freshman, and where I was from. There was no need to talk about anything illegal I did since this was an opportunity for me to start brand new with a whole new set of friends and coworkers, and it just wasn't glamorous. *We were next.* I was a bit surprised when he ordered a hot pastrami and cheese with mustard on a roll and a bottle of water. I ordered a ham, Swiss with mustard on a long roll – no lettuce or tomatoes with a Pepsi. We sat after we placed our orders, and then I told him that I was only working part-time after school, until closing which was about five.

"Don't let that 'Macaco' Sapo bother you. He'll do anything to keep his job." A macaco, he told me, was a monkey, in Portuguese. He learned a few words from them, but I guess with any language, you learn the bad words first.

Our sandwiches were ready and as we were going back to the store, I noticed several car mechanic shops lined up all along York and Colgate St. I recognized one of the guys from one of the gambling dens in Hoboken. He would just drop off loot, have a drink and leave.

"Oye, Nelson." A worker called out to him.

Tinkering and cranking sounds from wrenches and drills were constant as they were busy fixing and repairing cars from Toyota low-riders, applying and sanding Bondo to a quarter-panel and a dented door, and replacing all four tires on an old Pontiac. Now I don't know much about different cars and not really up on all different types of models but the red Ford Mustang, with its logo on the front grill and chrome trimmings, caught my attention. Too bad it had a busted windshield.

We passed the front counter when Chris, the star salesman, introduced himself and asked Sam and me to come to his house to play some cards or Chess later that night. He looked more like Yosemite Sam than Gerald did with his handlebar mustache. His straight thin brown hair hung down to about his shoulders, and his thin fragile body had a slight slouch. I told him that it sounded like a good idea and that I would see him later after I had my lunch. The entrance to the back was separated by a plastic poly-sheeting so the customers couldn't see what was behind in the busy dungeon. We pushed the plastic door to the side and walked down a ramp which led past water-pressure machines and caulking supplies.

"Let's find a spot down one of the aisles. The kitchen area is too small, plus there aren't any chairs."
On the first floor, that's where all the paints, lacquers, varnishes and spray paints were. There was nothing better than eating a nice meal next to any one of those things. We went down the paint aisle where there were gallons and gallons of it in cardboard boxes. They were fully stocked, six high, from the Wednesday before, so Sam and I just took three off each and made ourselves seats. I had just opened my can of soda when I suddenly smelled Chinese food.

"Damn, Sapo, *me sustáste*. You scared me. How long have you been there?" He just smiled and continued to eat his half chicken and pork fried rice with mounds of hot sauce. He built a fort from cardboard boxes and was hidden underneath one of the racks with cases of paint around him. He must have put the cases back enclosing himself within but I didn't mind. He was quiet, and perhaps he could learn some English while Sam and I spoke, but also, I thought, I should be careful about what I spoke about.

The *Howard Stern* show was always on the morning radio station. I thought it was brilliant stuff, but that was an hour ago when one of the others changed the station. De La Soul's *The Magic Number* was now playing on the radio, which I not only thought was pretty cool since they were originally from Jersey City but because we listened to the Classic Rock station on the radio about five days a week, and change was good. Lunch would be over in about fifteen minutes, and I did not mind going back upstairs. We wrapped up our garbage, took our empty containers and placed the cases back to where they originally were. As I walked by Sapo's mini castle, I saw a couple of chicken bones on top of a cardboard case and the grease that left a permanent stain on it.

It wasn't until a few days later that I met a guy by the name of Eddie. He had just come back from vacation, and we hadn't had the chance to meet yet since it had been so busy. John and I were in the kitchen area when Eddie came out of the bathroom.

"Hey, Ed, this is Coronado. He's the new part-timer."

"Hey, Core, what's up?"

We shook hands hoping that he had at least washed his hands from exiting the restroom, and John left the area to take care of some errands for the Manager. Sam walked in from punching his card, since he was a part-timer too, and started to put his belongings in his locker. Seven lockers were joined together several feet from the kitchen sink and the water cooler, and in front of the warehouse restroom and another set of lockers, although smaller, was located inside the restroom itself. Eddie's was in the bathroom.

"Hey, guys, what's up? What's up, *Bunda*?" he asked Eddie. That was Ed's nickname in Portuguese, and it meant "ass".

"Vitamanakoo, Fash Azul," he responded. After a while, I started to pick up more bad words and names, and everyone was in on it.

"How was your vacation?" Sam asked as he finished putting his things away and slammed the locker door shut.

"All right. I got hammered the whole week."

Sam and I left to go see what John wanted us to do, while Eddie went back into the bathroom. I asked Sam if it was normal that he was in the bathroom a lot, and he told me that Eddie was a big drinker and that he was probably feeling the effects. John had us pull a few orders for the other stores, and while I was retrieving seventeen cases of flat black spray paint, Eddie was adjusting the radio to the classic rock station.

I woke up this morning and I got myself a beer. He asked me if I liked *The Doors*.

"Yeah, they're all right. I like this station, but my favorite group has to be *The Beatles*."

"The Beatles are cool..."

"Yo, Macaco, turn it up," Sam exclaimed as he carried four gallons of paint thinner to the front counter for a customer.

"What are we doin' for lunch? Wanna take a walk for some pizza?" I was asked.

"I don't see why not. Let's tell John that we're both goin'."

Ed and I hit it off rather well from the beginning. John approved of our lunch disappearance and when lunch time came, we hurried to know we only had an hour to return.

When we approached Third Street, I could not help but notice the apartment building in which Mark and I ran the gambling operation from. A young boy was riding his bicycle towards the corner of the block, and I noticed that an elderly woman was walking towards the same corner but neither of them knew that either was coming until it was too late. He had run over her foot and almost knocked her over, and although he was very apologetic, he explained to her that he would be right back to treat her wounds. We were in front of a pizza parlor and I started to walk in.

"Not that one. This way."

I took a step back and saw the sign for Ray's Pizza, and looked to my right and, lo and behold, was another pizza place owned by someone else. I followed Ed to Leo's Place and ordered two slices. There were two pizza establishments right next door to each other, and I hadn't noticed it when I worked around the corner. They had been competing for years and I also hadn't known that each slice was only a dollar.

"You're gonna be able to eat two slices?"

"Yeah, sure." I could eat, and I knew one slice wouldn't hold me over. The slices were ready and because of the competition, a pie was cut into four slices instead of eight, so I really got two slices in one. We took it to go, and when I looked across the street, the boy had come back and tried to apply adhesive bandages on the lady's foot. I'm sure he meant well but the elderly woman insisted that she meet his guardian. We walked as far as the corner and into a bar.

The bar was on Monmouth and Third St. and was really dark and rather small. A pair of Converse sneakers were hanging on the electrical wires in front of the place, by their laces. There was a pinball game to our right as we walked in, and further towards the right was an open door which led to the only toilet in the place, but at least it had a light bulb. To the left and center was the counter which was L-shaped, and the two black lights illuminated a shorter, Italian fellow scribbling some information in a spiral notebook, from behind the counter.

"Hey, Ant'ny...this is my friend Corey. He's with me."

"Hey, Eddie, haven't seen you in a week. How've you been?"

"Little Anthony" was the owner of this corner bar, and it primarily helped to quench the thirsts of some of the neighborhood wise-guys. It was a little after noon, and one guy sat at the bar looking up at the television broadcast of the daily horse races. Eddie leaned over and softly told Anthony that a guy was bothering him and that he needed someone whacked.

"What are you talking about? What?" he asked as if he didn't know what he was talking about and maybe, perhaps, it should not have been said in front of me, because Anthony just played "dumb".

"I need your help. Someone's messing with me."

"Who?"

"The 'Slasher'," Eddie said as he pointed at me. I just looked at Anthony, not knowing what to expect, and he finally looked my way and looked back at Eddie smiling.

"Ant'ny, give me a Bud, and the 'Slasher' will have a..."

"Seltzer with lemon."

"You don't mind if we eat here, do you?"

"Go right ahead. Just don't make a mess."

I pulled my slices out of the brown paper bag and made sure the dripping grease didn't land on the bar top. A statue of the Madonna stood behind the bar and against the wall with dollar bills attached to it.

"Ed, what's with the statue?"

"Oh, that's for the feast we have here once a year. Say, Ant, you still need me to work a stand?"

"Yeah, I could always use a couple of guys."

Little Anthony and some of the other businesses along the way contributed to having a feast with food, games, and raffles right there on their block. Eddie then looked at me.

"How 'bout it?"

"Sure, when is it?" I gladly volunteered.

"This weekend, and don't worry, you'll be working with me."

As I ate my lunch, I wondered what the difference was between the two establishments. I used two hands to place the triangular slice in my mouth, and then took a refreshing gulp of my seltzer. Grease was pouring down my wrist and I made sure that none of it hit the counter, although it was so dark, I hadn't seen how anyone would have noticed.

"Hey, Ed, why don't you buy from Ray's?"

"Why don't I buy from Ray's?" he repeated as he turned to Anthony. I was seventeen when I fell in love with this girl. Anyway, we hung out together all the time, and this one time she was waiting for me across the street, in front of Gino's bar, when a black Caddy drove by and slowed down when another guy was approaching her, but I guess he was just walking by. A couple of guys from inside the car shot a few clips and killed that guy."

"What? He ordered from Ray's?"

"My girlfriend was shot eleven times, even after she hit the ground, and Ray was the only one around who saw it happen, but he didn't say shit to the cops, and well..."

"Sorry, man..."

"No. That's all right. I'm getting married in two months to my future wife, Maria, and that's all behind me, except that the people around here knew her too and we just deal with it."

He finished his second mug and asked Anthony for another.

"One of the guys from my wedding party is moving to Michigan. You mind being in my wedding party? I mean, you're a cool guy...yeah, I'd like for you to be in the party, but first, you have to help me this weekend at one of the stands at the feast."

"No problem, dude. What's Maria like?"

"I'll tell you about her on the way back to work."

We finished our lunch and he had already drunk three drafts. Before we left, he grabbed an eight-pack to go and concealed it in another brown paper bag. Anthony then continued to scribble in his notebook and as I opened the door to leave, I looked back towards Eddie to make sure he was behind me, and I noticed that Anthony had shielded his eyes from the bright sun.

We returned back to work with seven minutes to spare, and while I listened to the radio that was playing *The Sound of Silence* in the back of the warehouse, Eddie headed straight for the bathroom to put his belongings in his locker. Sam was eating his lunch around that area, so he could be closer to the radio, and told me that it was from Simon and Garfunkel's concert in Central Park in '82.

I was at that concert and was probably the best one I've ever attended.

The Feast that weekend started late afternoon, and by the time Eddie and I showed up after work, there was already a good size crowd walking around and trying their chances at some of the booths. He grabbed the key from Anthony and opened our stand, which was really a small trailer, and inside it were the prizes to be won if the patron knocked over all the pins by rolling a heavy ball towards them.

Somehow, I was reminded of my past Scout experience, and on how I let my father down, but all the patrons who stepped up and took their chances looked as though they were having a lot of fun.

I heard minor chatter that sounded like it was coming over a CB radio. It mentioned something about a fire on Bright St.

"You hear that? Where's that coming from?" I asked Ed.

"Sounded like a fire call. It's from my mobile scanner." He pulled it from his pants pocket clip and showed it to me. As I was checking it out, he was telling me how he listens to it during the night when he's alone and it's very quiet. It let him know what was stirring in the streets while everyone was asleep. I remember having a base station scanner at one of our stash houses but I kept that to myself. I admired its purpose and the condition it was in. It looked like something out of a military movie but more compact.

"I brought it, in case something happens out here. I'll sell it to you for forty bucks," he asked me.

"Yeah. Here." I pulled out two twenties.

I thought it was really cool that he let me have it for cheap, so I shut it off to hear and absorb the sounds of the sirens, bells, and whistles of the current festivities.

"I'll have my Maria at night so I won't be needing it anymore. I'll give you a code book when I see you next so you know what the hell they're talking about."

"Nice! Thanks, bro!"

Parents brought their children over, and even young couples took this time out to enjoy some fun together. It was getting a bit dark and in the near distance, I noticed two guys in fancy suits walking towards Anthony's bar. One of them was Mark and the other I later confirmed to be Sonny Grieco. I was still in my semi-dirty work clothes and missed wearing my clean shirts and jackets when I used to work the street. I snapped out of my daze and continued my feast rhetoric.

"Win a prize...Only a buck...Step right up and test your skill."

A little girl had already spent five dollars trying to win a stuffed, white unicorn.

Ed knocked over the pins.

"Another winner," I shouted. Ed smiled as he handed her prize to her. Her father appreciated the gesture and they walked away towards the cotton-candy booth.

"Ed, 'ja see those two guys before?"

"I didn't see anyone." I dropped the subject.

"Step right up...Only one dollar," I demanded.

John and Sam had stopped by to check us out and had already purchased an Italian hotdog and a Sausage and Peppers sandwich. That was another beauty about this city. It was so diverse and big that I don't know why I even bothered to realize that those two guys were Polish because it didn't matter. They came by to support the Feast and have fun.

"Hey, guys, what's going on?"

John was just stopping by for a moment but he had to get home to his family soon. Sam had invited us to hang out at his house later on, but Eddie said that he had to take care of a few things with Maria in preparation for the wedding.

"You're 'whipped', Macaco, but that's all right, man. Next time," Sam teased.

"I'm there. Just wait up for me. I'll be outta here soon. Hey, grab me a bag of zeppoles before they close. Here...here's five bucks!" I iterated in excitement. John and Sam took a walk toward the other end while finishing their food, where there were a few kiddie rides. I had only minutes before we would be finished working the booth, and so far, the evening wasn't dull at all. Sam came by, without John, and waited while I helped Ed close shop.

"Later, dude. Tell Maria I said hello, and I'll see you tomorrow."

"Thanks, Core, man. Later, Sammy."

CHAPTER XI

Sam lived in Bayonne, by the park and the water, and it had only taken us about twenty minutes to get there. His parents were already sleeping even when his two Great Danes were barking really loud when they saw me. We hung out in his room and it was covered with body-builder posters in the front and a couple of Stones posters above his stereo system.

"Make yourself comfortable. I'm gonna get something to drink. You want anything? Juice? Water?"

"No, thanks."

His room had a dim, over-hung lamp over his CD collection and stereo. I crouched down to peruse through his selection and recognized many of the artists. I sat on his futon which was under the window, and before long he reentered his cozy room with two bottles of water.

"I'm going to throw on some tunes. What do you want to hear?"

"Something new. Something cool." I eagerly responded.

He looked through his collection of three-hundred some-odd CDs and pressed play on one that was already cued in the player. He hopped on his top bunk-bed and lifted a tile from his drop-ceiling, reached in and grabbed a stash bag of bunk and also grabbed a "chillum" pipe. When he climbed down, the first song started to play and I heard the song before, and it sounded really tight.

"Who's this?"

"CSN with Neil Young."

He packed the pipe, and with his lighter, he took a pull and held his breath until he couldn't breathe anymore. He had a smile on his face and started to get into the music. He took another pull, grabbed the remote control and skipped the selection to another song when the first one finished. He handed me the pipe and I took it to see what all the hype was about. I took my first pull, and I choked almost spilling its contents.

All this time having handled these goods I had never tried it, even from the first time hanging out at Ron's place up until now. I had seen the many joyous effects it had on its many different users, but not once had I inhaled.

"Do it slow. It's pretty strong."

My eyes were watery from choking, but I decided to give it another try. I took my time, and I was light-headed from holding my breath for as long as I could. When I finally let my breath out, an enormous cloud came out, and then I passed it back to him.

"Try to breathe it out the window."

"I'll concentrate on breathing first." I joked.

Before long, he passed it back to me and showed me his technique of covering the pipe with a match-cover while I pulled and as I tried it, I felt the effects of my throat burning but I was starting to catch a buzz.

I didn't know what he was talking about for the next few minutes. Somebody spoke and I went into a dream because he turned me on. I was too involved in a daze, and perhaps even day–dreaming, and when I snapped out of it, I asked him to play the song that was playing again because I missed it the first time.

"Deja 'Vu?"

"No. I never did this before."

"No. The song is called *Deja 'Vu*," he laughed.

"That song's kickin', especially the beginning. Their vocals are tight."

He played the song again, and I had on a permanent "Kool-Aid" smile. He reloaded his chillum and started talking about some girl he had been seeing. He was probably talking about her for a few minutes, and I suppose I kept nodding my head as if I was really listening, but I was in such an altered state of consciousness that everything was just beautiful. After the album finished, he played some melodic Simon and Garfunkel tunes which appealed to me.

After a couple of hours, and in time for my bunk experience to wear off, I was able to drive back home and get some sleep. Although I had a million things on my mind, I hadn't felt paranoid nor had I ever told Sam about what I used to do.

That was in the past as far as I was concerned.

The following day, I went to Eddie's Bachelor party, and it was held at a Polish hall in the late afternoon, near the Hamilton Park area. I had the day off, and I rested for this occasion. This was to be my first Bachelor's party, and I did not know what to expect. Rumors of strippers showing up intrigued me but when I did arrive Wayne, his best man and brother, Tommy, and myself were the only ones there. *Crucified* by Army of Lovers was playing as I walked in.

"Hey, Coronado. That'll be forty bucks," Tommy requested.

I took out my wad of twenties from my right pocket and kept my wad of singles in my left for the girls later on. The floor had red and white checkered floor tile and the gray columns supported the ceilings from falling down. A couple of guys soon entered after me and they paid the required admission. Eddie and his brother had already started drinking, and Ed sat on a metal folded chair next to the stereo system.

"Eddie, what's up, buddy? Cool times, man."
He was on his fourth shot of Vodka, and his cigarette hung from the left side of his mouth. He couldn't stop smiling, and he moderately swayed back and forth in his chair.

"Slasher, where's your drink?"
I turned around to find the bar, mostly to indulge his desire for me to have a drink with him. There was the vodka bottle on top of the bar, but it was too early for me to get trashed so I looked for the beer. Tommy pointed to the corner where the beer selection was, and the cold ones were stashed in the refrigerator. I quickly opened the door and grabbed a Coors Light bottle while Eddie started to sing to the tune on the CD, and before I could join in Tommy started to croon with him. We tapped glasses and I walked off to get to know the other guys.

"What's up? So, how do you know Eddie?" I asked Robert.

Robert was a biker who wore a leather vest and boots. He was smoking a cigarette and held his pack in his hand.

"Ed and I hang out at the bar whenever I ride in. He can drink."

I looked over at the brothers and they had their arms on each other, singing and just being happy. I didn't smoke cigarettes, and I didn't mind the second-hand smoke, but it does leave a certain aura about itself. The smoke filled the room until a gleam of light came in from someone walking into the basement hall.

Robert knew him and when he greeted him, I introduced myself to John.

"What's up? Where are the chicks?"

"They aren't coming, man, but Eddie still thinks they are. Maria's a good girl and Tommy's not gonna let him screw it up."

While Rob and John caught up with conversation, I walked over to the fridge and got myself a beer.

"Hey, hey. The Doors. One of your favorites."

Riders on the Storm was playing and they knew every word of it. Ed tapped my beer bottle again with his vodka shot glass, and would just not stop smiling. He was in good spirits indeed. He was amongst friends a week before he was to be wed, and it was a shame that I couldn't have witnessed this much fun every day. Tommy gave his brother a kiss on his cheek, and then a great tune came on for the first time to my ears. When the others heard it, they came towards us and gathered around. With drinks in hand, they raised their glasses and saluted my friend, Eddie.

This is the end...my only friend, the end...It hurts to set you free.

Eddie had the following week off from work, and the next time I saw him was on his wedding day. Sam told me the night before, on Friday, that John didn't know I was taking that Saturday off and that if I did that I wouldn't bother coming back to work. I understood that Saturdays were very busy, but thought he also understood that I was in the wedding party. Needless to say, I attended Eddie and Maria's great day and I had a stellar time, but when I did report to work on Monday, I was warned not to take another day off unless it was previously excused. I understood from that point on that communication is always the key to move forward and John and I respected each other even more on that level. The best part was the personalized monogrammed Zippo lighter Eddie gave me as a gift for being in his wedding party: *Hard Core.*

CHAPTER XII – (1989)

ANGLES & ANGELS

The beginning of my junior year of high school was upon me, and I started to get more into music so I decided to become a disc jockey and host events at my school. I became so engulfed in mixing records that I began to invest in professional equipment and it felt great. That was a fulfilling entertaining business, and it was generated through my talents and self-motivation. I mixed two, sometimes three records together and would record them on tape, and upon selling each tape for five dollars, the word was out. It reminded me of the fortune cookies I used to sell back in the third grade. That was a great medium of art, and everyone loved to share in it.

I bought so many records that by the time high school came around I was ready to really showcase my musical-mixing talents and it was a fabulous time to get into the club scene, but more importantly, the high school dances, even Marist in Bayonne. I immediately registered for the Dance Club my freshman year, along with many other clubs and after working house parties during my freshman and sophomore years and networking throughout, I wanted to appeal to a larger audience. Junior year was when my life began to take a more active role in the social scene. I was very active throughout my four years of Prep School and for me I found it to be classier and more dignified every morning when I put on an ironed buttoned-down shirt, jacket, and tie, and I had incidentally acquired a nice tie collection. I think it was because the only times I dressed in a suit was for formal occasions like weddings, funerals and even flying in an airplane on *Eastern* or *American*. Prep was an all-boys Jesuit institution, with a rich history, and one that I was very proud to be associated with because I felt like I belonged.

I presented a demo tape to the director of the Dance Committee, and they approved it. Fliers were distributed throughout the whole school, and it was a great sensation for me because for once my job would require that I would be a focus in an event, instead of working in the shadows on the streets removing myself from any notoriety. I didn't start getting nervous until they told me that the same fliers were distributed throughout our "sister" school – it was an all-girl school about two miles away on the Blvd. It was one thing to throw on some tunes for the guys and hang out, but I forgot about their dates or even the girls they would try to impress, on the dance floor, if they were single. This was perfect. I was single. I could probably give them the old "I'm the DJ" routine. Whatever the situation, the event was next week.

I teamed up with my cousin Angel, and with this three or four-hour gig, one of us would take a break while the other made sure the music kept going, and it did. Most of the time, we would grab a drink, and mingle with the crowd. With songs like *Running*, *You Used to Hold Me*, and Adonis's *No Way Back*, we kept the rhythm and mood goin'. He was excited about the event, as I most certainly was, and so we practiced new mixes, cuts, bought more records, made more demos and breathed House and Club music all night long.

Showtime was upon us. I waited for Angel and his father to come and bring the equipment from the studio as it was heavy and filled the entire van during transport and it wasn't every day I got to see the two of them together, except for some of our previous gigs, but I think it had to do more with investments and money. I didn't remember the last time I spent a father and son moment, but I nonetheless felt secure in our relationship. School was out for the day and we had about two hours to set everything up.

We had home-made speakers, "towers" really that stood about six and a half feet tall with a 24" bass-bottom Pyle Drivers and a 10" bass-bottom MTX's on top of that. The highs consisted of a horn and six tweeters which were at ear level and two towers that were heavy with the inch-thick wood as its body. The both of them arrived and everyone on the Dance Committee was very helpful in making sure our paths were clear as it was very expensive and delicate equipment, and we were on in less than two hours. *Oh, man! We've got no time to lose* I thought to myself. The rest of the equipment consisted of three Tehnic 1200s, two mixers – one Gemini and the other was a Numark, a monitor speaker so we wouldn't hear any echoes as we listened for the next record, about eight crates of records, a couple of fans to keep everything cool, a microphone and tons of wires to connect it all together.

It only took an hour for "systems go" so we put a record on to check the audio, and I felt more comfortable after a couple of guys came over and were impressed with the setup. Since I was still with the Dance Club, I figured I could also help to host the guests as they arrived through the door as a few proctors were ready and checking school IDs. A good friend of mine, Joey Casanova, was also on the Dance Committee and helped promote the event and he knew a lot of people who liked to party but only guys from the Prep school were allowed at the dance, while all the girls were more than welcome. I knew all the guys and even one who didn't belong to our school and he almost made it inside, but a Jesuit priest stopped him. As soon as he turned his back, I immediately escorted him in as a guest of mine.

My intention was to get the dance floor as packed as we could and to do that, we played all the greatest club hits and even an obscure song for my friend Charlie. He was part of a small clique which consisted mainly of skinheads and radicals who wore Doc Martin boots and preferred to stray from the norm of our fine Prep school but they were all normal to me and were cool. Charlie, our mutual pal, Yoshie, and the rest of the gang walked in fashionably late and saw that there was a kickin' party going on. He came up to the booth and asked me if I could play a song for him.

"Sure, man, whatcha got?" I asked him.

"Cool. I'll be back in ten minutes, and bring you the record."

He came back and handed me a *Misfits* album which I've never seen before. He asked me to play number five and thanked me as he anxiously anticipated the first notes. I slowly faded the last record and began my introduction.

"Hope everyone's having a good time. We're taking special requests starting with this one for a good friend of mine." I put his record on, and he and his cohorts started moshing towards the center of the floor. It might have been death metal and I couldn't understand the words but I let the song play out in its entirety. The others might have been too shocked because they really didn't move from their spots. I wanted to please everyone, in every clique, in every way so I had no regrets and soon after, girls were coming up to us requesting special songs, and for one of them, I played When in Rome's *The Promise*. It was my pleasure to play it for her because I enjoyed it as well, and I wanted people to be happy.

As she walked away, I noticed one of my sister's friends from her high school in the distance. She had long brown hair, wore a burgundy dress and a nice sweater. I think her name was Alicia. She came to the house once to visit my sister for something, and when she left, I asked my sister who she was. She told me that she had a boyfriend and that she wouldn't be interested in me. I professed to Gloria that she was the one I was going to marry. Music tends to soothe people, whichever genre they listened too. Alicia brought music to my eyes and ears.

I immediately noticed Deirdre walking in with some of her girlfriends. They were all from the local all-girl prep school located towards Greenville. She looked the same except with make-up on which accented her blue eyes and a great smile. I approached her, asked her how she was doing and how her family was. Everyone was fine and told me she enjoyed the music. When we parted I looked for a song that I could play for her. I skipped over the R.E.M. *The One I Love* track but instead played a more suitable tune. I changed the pace of the music and queued in U2's *With or Without You*. She looked back towards me when she heard The Edge's guitar intro and scanned my area until our eyes met. I smiled while she held her grin that I appreciated so much and we met up with each other near the center of the dance floor. I grabbed her hand and slowly gestured to dance. It was the dance I longed to have with her since the eighth grade, but was too nervous to ask her for and was horribly discouraged by possible ridicule by some of the "others" in our grade. No words were spoken. We held each other and slowly danced while Bono and the boys did their thing. *Go Ireland!*

We might have stepped over our bounds when we neglected to play certain songs. I managed to make my way to the soda stand in the back of the cafeteria where the towers were, and a girl came up to me with a concerned look on her face.

"Why is the beat the same? You haven't skipped a beat yet."

I looked at her and wanted to thank her. Mixing records took a certain skill, and if it wasn't done right it would sound horrible, but I know she didn't mean it in that way. She wanted some more slow songs and love ballads because she was tired of the club music. I paid for my can of soda and walked back to the right side where I would catch a nice breeze from the opened windows. It was time for Angel and me to change the pace, so we grabbed a record and slowly faded the one that was playing.

"And now, by special request, a song for the beautiful girl way in the back there."

Of course, she thought she knew who we were talking about, but I couldn't help but notice a lot of guys turning around to see who we were talking about. We played one of the traditional tunes, and everyone's favorite – *Shout*, by the Isley Brothers, and proceeded with *Bully, Bully*. It was time for the Prepsters to take their dates and to start to boogey. The only regret I had that night was to have to play a song twice. It was like a magician showing the same trick twice. It was taboo, but the majority liked it so, what the heck, we played it.

Angel and I triumphantly finished for the night and decided to go to my Cousin Mike's house in Stanhope. His friend was having a huge party at his house plus it was only about a forty-five-minute drive from Route 280 to 80 to the exit. If you asked anyone from Jersey where they lived, they would tell you which exit it was off of. It was 11:40 pm and we were listening to Snoop Dog on Compact Disc on the way there. We were still adrenalized from the successful party we threw at Prep, but we had to creep into the town so we wouldn't attract attention towards ourselves because it was a quiet town, and it only had two police cars.

We passed the Blue Woods Inn on our right and we were only a few minutes away. Mike met us at the front of his mom's house and jumped in the back seat of Angel's blue CJ-7 jeep and a couple of winding roads and hills later, we arrived at his friend, Michael's, house. An exterior house light shed light onto the parked driveway but the way was luminous enough that we hopped out and entered the garage. Three Sharpei show-dogs were in the garage as we walked towards the basement and there was some music playing from a portable CD player on the mantle behind the bar. There were about thirty people with about a 2 to 3 girl/guy ratio which seemed to be good odds for a successful mixer. It did not take long before we were offered cold beers. I was introduced to everyone there and some of them I had already known.

I don't know if any of them had seen a live Puerto Rican before, either because we were new to the crowd or because Angel looked more Hispanic than me, but I found most of them staring. We had no problems mingling or conversing with our peers and it was getting pretty late so I decided to call home and ask my parents if I could stay at

Mike's house. My father answered the phone, close to 12:30 am, and quickly hung up as he denied me. One problem...we were having a good time, and Angel was driving. We would just stay for another hour or so and head back to my parent's house where we would part and I would crash. I didn't want to sit down on the couch because I would probably mellow out and never get back up, but behind the couch was a weight room, and behind *that* was a sauna where a few people were just drinking and smoking.

Behind the bar, on the mantle, was an urn with Michael's grandfather's ashes. He took it and placed it on a coffee table. As I peered over curiously, I noticed that he had placed it on one of the corners of a Ouija board. *What a crock*. I hated the board because it seemed too creepy and evil, but I couldn't help to get closer and somewhat participate because I was curious. Michael then brought over a candle, and with the flick of his lighter, it was lit. Now all he needed was one more person to join. *Oh, what the hell*. I indulged him. Besides, Angel and Mike were in on it too. The two Mikes each held a piece of the directional gadget, and Angel and I watched tentatively.

"All right, Angel. Think of a person and only tell Corey the name."

He leaned over to me and said the name "Michael". That was too easy I thought so I told him to think of another. He said "Candi," and we sat back.

"Oh, Spirit, I summon thee and ask for your identity."

The thing moved. I always think that someone moves it. *What a farce*.

"Wait," I said, "let Angel do it with you."

Angel and Mike switched places, and I still held the secret name to myself.

"Spirit, who are you?"

After a few seconds, it moved again to the letter "G". I did not believe it when the word spelled "grandfather". Michael freaked out in either fear or jubilation. He got up and said that it was his grandfather summoned through the ashes from the urn.

"He always comes through." Michael stated.

"Did you move it, Ange?" I asked

"No, man." Mike said in disbelief.

"I swear I didn't move it." Angel again claimed.

The crowd was just going about their own business as if this was a normal occurrence, and Rocco even asked Michael if he had any more beer.

"All right, you two guys switch. Let Mike give it a try."

"Spirit, what was the name that was whispered in Corey's ear?"

And just as the board spelled the last letter of Candi's fictitious name, the candle's flame flickered so high, that I even took cover.

"Nah, man, this isn't happening," Angel said as he walked away to grab another beer.

My mood had changed, and luckily some of the others wanted to bring the party to another house, and while they all thought that was a great idea, I needed to get home. The two of us had gotten comfortable with the others, and decided we would stay at the other party for a short while and leave from there.

Rocco's parents had been gone on vacation, and wouldn't return for another couple of days so we headed out there through more hills and winding roads and quickly adjusted to our newer surroundings. We parked the jeep on the side of the road and we went through the rear entrance so we wouldn't attract the neighbor's attention, and so we wouldn't have to go through the living room area to get to the basement. How would the neighbors not have known we were there from all the cars and traffic that came through the street that night? Nevertheless, we were quiet and respected the noise level of squirrels running across trees. Going down the basement, the music became louder. At the bottom, to my right, was a bar with about six stools. It was pretty long, and the barkeep asked if we wanted anything. I only wanted a cold bottled beer. I think they taste better than the canned ones because you don't taste the aluminum. Next to the bar was a great-size pool table.

"Hit the switch above the table. The triangle is over there, and, well, you can't miss the cues. Feel free. Is everyone all right?"

Rocco was originally from Brooklyn, but his parents moved out West a few years ago. Angel and Mike decided to start a game while I just hung at the bar drinking my brew and as I finished my first long-neck and placed the empty on the bar, the Gaston had quickly given me another one, uncapped. Angel broke the rack and the loud crack of the balls attracted the attention of competitors. Unfortunately, he hit the cue ball so hard that it flew off the table and knowing that he had scratched, it was Mike's turn so Angel came over to the bar, as I was focusing more on the angles as to where the balls needed to be hit to fall.

"Bro, how are you feeling?"

"I'm not even buzzed," I said.

"Yeah, me either."

I reached into my pocket and pulled out a napkin that I had rolled into a ball. I opened it up and took out five "biscuits". They were valiums, 10mgs each, that I bought from Mr. Belvedere the last time he visited Starlight. I had about thirty of them on me, and I took one while Angel took two. As Mike missed and forfeited his turn, I called him over to the bar.

"How you feelin'?"

"I'm ready for another beer."

"Here... take two of these." He grabbed them then looked at me and washed it down with the cold beer, my new friend, the bartender, had just given him.

The girls tended to be a bit cold and distant so far, so I mainly hung out with the guys. I switched to seltzer and lime and tried to mellow out but the pills had no effect so I gave Angel and Mike two more because they hadn't felt the effects of coming down and relaxing even after an hour from taking the first doses. The party was winding down so

Rocco and all his guests decided to stop off at the local diner for some food. I felt that Angel was a little too tipsy from the alcohol so I came over to him, and without me asking him, he handed me the keys to his jeep. I knew that I had to drive because I was barely the only one all right to do so. We made it outside to the crisp, cool air when three girls waited for me to open the door. Mike and Angel escorted them, and the six of us were set to go. There was one problem, well…several.

I didn't know how to drive a stick-shift, for one, and it started to drizzle. Kelly was sitting on Angel's lap while Mike and Michael each had one girl on their laps in the back seat. They brought their nearly-finished beers with them, and I had about twenty valiums in my pocket. In a drunken state, he tried to guide me through the driving process while Mike gave me the directions. It was sloppy at first but I got the hang of it as soon as we got to the main road. The rain started to get a little heavier, and I was mainly driving in second gear because of the hills and the slippery roads and as I came to a stop sign, I stalled. *Oh, boy.* I turned the car back on, slowly let go of the emergency brake, looked both ways before I crossed the intersection, and popped it into first gear. The close was clear and we were only two miles away from the diner when I noticed that Kelly and Angel were passed out. The two Mikes were barely awake and the girl on the right took over and became my co-pilot. I could do this, I said to myself, right before the police lights signaled on right behind us. I pulled over, but it was me he was after.

"Yo, Ange, it's the cops. Where's your paperwork?"

"Huh? In there."

He pointed to his glove compartment and I quickly searched for his registration and insurance cards. I pulled out my driver's license anticipating the initial questioning and as I looked out the side view mirror, he was making his way towards the vehicle with his yellow poncho and a long, black flashlight.

"Mike, hide the beers. He's comin'".

My heart was racing. I was in a strange town, with a strange face, not to mention the precarious situation we were in but I rolled down the window, and without question, handed him the necessary paperwork I needed to survive. He shined his flashlight inside the vehicle and did a spot check.

"Having trouble driving in the rain?"

"Yes, sir, I can hardly see so I'm just taking my time dropping everyone home." He took the credentials and walked back to his patrol car. He must have been checking everything out and running the plates. I wondered what was taking too long for the officer to return. *Was there something wrong?* Was he calling in for "back-up"? I was in fear of losing my license or worse getting arrested for anything illegal I was doing. I kept looking at the rearview mirror, the side mirrors and to the party-goers, peripherally, all without looking too fidgety and nervous.

Keep calm, keep calm. I should have listened to my father. I should have quit while I was ahead with the Prep Dance. What was I thinking?

I saw movement coming from his vehicle. It had to have been all right because he came and handed back my papers, and told me to drive safely. Two police cars in the whole damn town and I get pulled over by one. I counted my blessings, and slowly put the gear in first and drove off. Only the two girls in the back seat and I witnessed the whole thing while the others were passed out cold. It was a good thing I had everything under control.

We met up with the rest of the gang at the local diner and we were seated at a table for thirteen which was pretty ironic because, for most, that is superstitiously an unlucky number. Everyone looked like zombies as the patient waitress handed out the menus. Angel was sitting across from me at the oval table, and my last co-pilot was sitting in between Mike and me. There was a light conversation, we were too young to order any beers, and the mood was dying down but Angel ordered the roast beef dinner, and Mike and I had ordered the French toast with cinnamon. After I gave the waitress my order I glanced over and saw Angel resting his head on the table. As she was walking away, she noticed him too and just nodded her head in an unsatisfied manner. He fell asleep. Nobody really cared as they just went along with their business and carried on. After twenty minutes, our waitress had come with all the food and didn't know what to with his meal. Rocco, who was sitting next to his right, not paying any attention to him, just asked her to put it in front of him. He just laid there fast asleep while anyone who wanted his roast beef and fries helped themselves. When we all finished, we asked for the check and that's when he woke up. He must have been hungry and wanted his dinner as he thought that it had just been served.

"You ate it already. It's time to go," I said to relieve any tension.

He chipped in for his bill and we soon scurried off to drop the girls back to their homes. One by one, they made it home safely, but we had to drop Michael back home for our last stop.

I made it back to Michael's and he asked us to come in. I had to be home a long time ago, but for whatever reason, we obliged to stay a while. We were talking "ying–yang" for a duration, and I was raring to go but Angel and Mike were passed out on the couch and I could see the sun slowly coming up.

"You guys can crash here if you want. I'm turning in myself."

You've got to be kiddin' me. My ass was grass if I didn't make it home before my father woke up. I tried to wake them up but to no avail. I paced back and forth calling their names, but the valiums and the booze did numbers on them and as the sun was getting brighter and brighter, I was getting frantically impatient trying to get their attention. On the table was a water gun. I don't know how it got there, but there was water in it and I was shooting at their faces. *Wake up. Wake up.* I shot them some more but that wasn't working. I sprayed their pants and their crotch area so if they did wake up, they would think they wet their pants. It was pretty silly of me but I had to make light of the situation because I was stressing and when they eventually awoke, I started to pick Mike up and tell him that we had to go. Angel got up, on his own, and my mission was accomplished. I helped them to the car, and we drove off to drop Mike at his place, while Angel and I sped off into the sunrise.

I turned the radio on and kept it at a moderate volume, but not too low or else I probably would have fallen asleep at the wheel. I followed the signs for 80East, but I must have missed the turn to 280East because the freeway suddenly didn't look familiar to me. I woke him up to ask him where we were, and we figured that if we don't catch the Turnpike soon, we would head straight for the George Washington Bridge into New York. We kept our eyes open, mine more than his, and we spotted a young blonde woman up ahead pulled over on the left shoulder.

We had never even considered helping someone on the road if they had car trouble or needed assistance. I didn't want to be a victim of an ambush, like the ones in movies, or having to really go out of my way for a stranger especially when I was pressed for time. I slowly passed her vehicle which had its hazard lights turned on, and she was pacing back and forth, crying as if the world were coming to an end. He briefly mentioned that maybe we should take a look and help her. She was a damsel in distress and chances were that if it were a mechanical problem, we would most likely be able to fix it quicker than when a tow truck would arrive.

I signaled my left blinker and pulled over. I put the hazard lights on, shut the car off and took the keys in case someone was in the back-seat conniving to carjack us. There was a moderate flow of traffic and in case something happened that we couldn't handle, one of us could have easily flagged down another vehicle, that is if they were silly or daring enough to help someone along the side of the road. We approached the woman who was in her late twenties, and she had a note in her hand.

She was in a frantic, hysterical state and she tried to control her speech as she was fighting back her tears. She wiped her eyes with her left hand, and that's when I noticed that the note in her right hand had blood on it.

"Car troubles?" I looked at her four-door Mazda RX-7 and the car was running fine. Her windows were opened and on the front seat, I could see traces of blood. She turned to me and desperately wanted me to take the note and to give it to her boyfriend. She obviously did not know what she was talking about.

"He broke up with me, and well..." she fidgeted back and forth, and I noticed that she was missing a digit of her ring finger, "...it's over." I almost fainted at the sight and smell of the blood. Had I never discovered the negative effects blood had over me I may have decided to become a doctor, however seeing that she was missing a limb concerned me to the point that I could hardly focus on anything else. I took a subtle step back and I had Angel grab a small towel from his jeep so we could place the note in it without us touching the blood spots. On his way over he must have picked up a rock or nail.

"Don't worry, we'll make sure he gets this note. In the meanwhile, wait in the car and we'll go get help for you. OK? Everything will be all right. Just stay put. Don't go anywhere."

He came back with the towel and I allowed her to place the note for me in the center. We went back to the jeep and he sat behind the wheel and I rode shotgun thinking that we were probably sleeping and that all of this was just a dream.

I figured that we missed our exit for a purpose and that maybe we should see where it leads us. We took the next exit off the freeway, which was less than a half of a mile away. The plan was to go into town and find the nearest police station or a hospital. The towel was wrapped up in a ball on the floor behind my seat, and we hadn't read what the note said. Perhaps it was a requiem for her attempted suicide, or maybe a sonnet of how things were between the both of them. A volunteer fire department was just at the end of the turn.

We were in uncharted territory, and I was hoping that when all this was over that I would be able to find the quickest way back to my bed. The white, clean building looked uninhabited. We pulled up to the front door and tried to look presentable in case they thought this was just a big prank on our part. We had to present the facts, and convince them that this woman needed immediate assistance. Two men presented themselves to the door as I rung the bell. I told them the whole story, and they had a few guys go there to check it out. They wanted to get some information about ourselves, and we obliged. We handed over the piece of the puzzle that would unveil what this psycho bitch was talking about. The commander put on his set of gloves and opened the note. Apparently, she was distraught over her losses and wanted to take off her engagement ring, but when she couldn't for whatever reason, she just cut off her finger with a knife and threw her ring out the window.

"I want to thank you guys for all your help. We'll contact you if we need any further assistance." He pulled off his plastic gloves and threw them in a trash receptacle. I again thought about the missing finger and what would compel someone to desperately take it that far, while Angel looked restless and wanted to continue on our journey home.

We asked him for the quickest way back to 280East, and he eagerly and readily gave us our escape plan as if he didn't appreciate us giving him work at six-thirty in the morning. I don't even know the town we left from, but I hoped that she would overcome her fears from leaving him, and was able to start a newer and better life. We were back on track and he dropped me off at the corner of my parent's house and from there, Angel would have to drive back home, to Elizabeth. "Good luck," I told him as I walked up my block, quietly opened the front door and slipped into bed. Midway home, Angel reached deep into his pocket and pulled out a shiny object. As he closely inspected the merchandise, he hadn't quite realized that he was holding a possible ½ carat diamond ring which he found as he walked to the jeep to grab the towel for the bloodied note. Good luck was what he found.

A GREAT ADVENTURE

Junior year was almost over and everyone sensed that summer was coming. Angel had called me and said that "Senior Cut Day" was this upcoming Friday at his high school and even though we were only juniors, he wanted to hang out with the guys he had known. I told him that I couldn't get off from school and that it was nearly impossible to hide it from my parents. I had to come up with a plan as to how this was all going to transpire. We had a gig that night at a club at ten o'clock, and I had to work at Stanley's from three to five, classes from eight fifteen to two-eighteen and if I didn't go to the school that day, I surely had to be back by two-thirty.

"I'll be by your school at eight on Friday." I said confidently.

"You won't get in trouble?"

"I'll be there." I said.

Friday morning came and I woke up the same time as usual. My father had already left for work and my mom was making sure that we were getting ready and off to school. Before I left the house to take the bus, I secretly made the call to my school and told them that my son, myself, would not be attending classes that day. The secretary took the message, and the first step was accomplished. I hoped to take the earlier bus so none of the other students would see me, and so I would not have to explain to them as to why I didn't get off the second to last stop, which was where Prep was located according to the bus route.

Midway through the journey, Matthew and Scott boarded and they saw me. It was a pretty diverse crowd, and I always sat in the back corner of the bus next to the window in case the other rowdy students wanted to throw stuff at the people in front of them, and besides that, I had a great view of anyone who boarded and of the crowds who waited on the bus stops. Sitting with my back to the wall was reassurance that nothing unexpected would happen to me behind my back.

The bus was diverse with students from public schools, a rival private school, college students and the adults who were on their way to the City, but since it was too crowded in the back, Matthew and Scott were forced to stand and cling on to the strap irons. Although we hadn't spoken, I knew they saw me and that wasn't good if I wanted to make a clean getaway from classes that day because they would surely be looking for me in one of our classes.

After about twenty minutes into the ride, three-quarters of the passengers had already disembarked and the two of them found seats way up in the front. The next stop would be mine, and I had to quickly exit through the back door if I wanted to catch the subway to Elizabeth. We had just passed City Hall, and I rang the bell signaling my stop when I looked at my watch and noticed that I was making good time. When the bus stopped, I hid behind another passenger who was also leaving and I made it off without being noticed.

I thought about changing my mind. I mean, *what was I thinking? Was I that deviant to stray from what was right? What the hell?* I walked towards the steps of the entrance of the subway and proceeded downwards into the humid, pasty underground and the PATH train just pulled in. The cars were filled with business class people with their collared shirts, jackets, shoes and briefcases sort of like me, but with a duffle bag. There were no truant officers or Gestapo, but just me and my will to complete the mission, and I think I did it to see if it could be done and so far, I had no worries.

The passenger car was crowded and I was standing for most of the time and I was careful not to stare at anyone at any time or to talk to anyone because to me impersonality was just the way of the subway as if no one had the time to associate anyway. A few stops later I arrived at the last stop in Newark and with the flow of people traffic, I hurried to my next transfer station. I went downstairs to purchase a round–trip ticket, but the line was a bit slow so I used the time to gather correct change for the fare to hurry my process and to find out which track the train left from and with the tickets in hand, I walked quickly to Track Four, where I was to await the North Corridor train headed towards North Elizabeth, then Elizabeth being the second stop.

I boarded the scheduled train and decided that I would stand near the door so I could be one of the first to exit at the stop, plus again I didn't want to be noticed by any of the other passengers. I heard the clicking from the hole-puncher that the ticket collector was carrying, and when he approached me, I just handed him my ticket to Elizabeth and kept the returning voucher in my pocket. The ride only took about ten minutes and after I exited the train, I hurried past the other passengers, and derelicts who were begging for money on the platform.

His high school was about ten blocks away from the station, but I was vaguely familiar with the route so after a few shortcuts, I made it to the front of the steps two minutes to eight. The school bell rang and all the senior students left the building in one fell swoop. I saw Angel walking out with a guy and two ugly girls.

"What up?" he asked me.

"What's up, man? What's the plan?"

"This is George."

"Hey, what's up?"

"They're goin' to Great Adventure...let's go. He's driving."

"We're gonna be back in time?" I asked.

"Yeah. No problem. We'll come back early."

"All right...let's go."

We walked to a nearby parking lot, and the five of us fit into his small "hooptie". I tried not to talk to the girls, especially when one of them was probably with George. I just sat quietly until our hour ride on the Turnpike lead us to the amusement park. No one from Jersey knew it as Six Flags, rather it was always termed Great Adventure, exit 7A, and it had a Safari next to it.

The parking facility was a bit crowded at that particular time of the day, but when George parked his car, I made note of where it was parked in case he tried to ditch us. I never went to a place I didn't know how to get out of. That was just a rule of survival. We paid our admissions and decided to split up, mainly because I wanted to hang out with Angel and also to get away from the ugly hags, but before that, we had agreed to meet near the entrance by the water fountain at one o'clock. We had better chances of meeting "good-looking girls" without them by our sides.

Angel and I went for the adrenaline rides such as the roller-coaster and the fast-thrill-seeking rides. We were lucky because the park wasn't really crowded inside, and sometimes we even rode the same rides twice.

The park was fairly large and had an immense number of rides so we found ourselves walking here and there, and after a couple of hours, we became thirsty. I saw a soda vending machine in the near distance, and when I walked over to it, I noticed that a can of soda was a whopping three dollars.

"Three bucks for a soda? What a rip-off, but they got us by the balls. I hate being put in a position like that," he stated in frustration.

"There should be a stand somewhere else. Let's get some lunch."

"Bet."

We scurried off further and found a burger stand, so we ordered and sat under an umbrella that shielded us from the rays of the sun. I periodically looked around to see if I could spot the other three and thought to myself that at that time, I would have been in Latin class with Father Olivero.

*

Father Olivero was great. He was a short stocky Jesuit priest who periodically smoked a cigarette in between classes. One day in class, we had an exercise in which each student had to read a sentence in Latin and translate it into English, and luckily, he didn't randomly choose students, but rather we went up and down the rows so it gave me ample time to count off which sentence would be mine and translate it. I was extremely nervous, because the first three guys translated their sentences without a problem, and when I saw my long sentence, I became anxious. I recognized some of the words but somehow could not figure out the conjugations. I sat towards the back row, and if someone was stuck, another guy would whisper the correct answer.

Charlie was next. He was the guy for whom I played the song for at the school dance, and when he was called on, Ed, his buddy, started to help him out with his whispers. Although these guys were social deviants, they were extremely smart and always helped each other. I was still in panic mode and knew that if I was in a jam that they would help me out.

The subject was about Hercules and the Olympics, and I recognized some of the words to be: "thrown," "Queen," and "lap". I was nearly next, and I was sweating. Ken, who was in front of me, made a flawless effort and it was my turn.

"Will you please just go? Will you please?"

Father Olivero always said that mainly because he didn't want to waste too much time on an exercise and because calling on names wasn't necessary since we knew who was next anyway.

"Hercules began to..." I started.

I shrugged my shoulders. My sentence was three lines long, and I needed help already.

"Will you please...Hercules began to what? Will you please...Hercules started what?"

"Hercules started to run the race...no... run a lap...then throw...um...the Queen."
Charlie whispered over to me his interpretation and I repeated it aloud.

"Hercules sat on the lap of the Queen on the throne and broke her disc." The classroom held back their laughter, but a few couldn't control themselves, like Charlie and Ed in the back.

"Will you please...Hercules ran a lap, and afterward threw a disc, and the Queen, who was sitting on the throne, was content with his performance. Will you please? Ken, finish the sentence."

I was relieved that I didn't have to go through that again but I had started studying Latin even more and understood it even though it was a dead language. Anyway, I missed Latin class, and when I thought about that day I chuckled.

*

"What's so funny, man?"
"I can't believe a can of soda is three bucks."
"Yeah, I know. That's 'shot out'."
When we finished our lunch, we became a little relaxed and lazy so we decided to take the sky-ride over to the other side of the park. We were about fifty feet from the ground, and I had asked Angel not to rock it because we had just eaten. I think it was mainly because my father,

whenever he took my mother, my sister and myself on the Ferris-Wheel, rocked it and we were all petrified. I tried to see if I saw the others from this height but I couldn't.

I started to think about some rides that James J. Ferris High School had funded in the past, and I remembered riding the *Spider* with my uncle and almost fell out. The ride had a metal bar that was pushed against my lap and the bar acted as my grip stabilizer because when that ride took off, it spun around, up and down, really fast. It was so out of control and crazy that I started to feel myself slide away from my seat. I might have been too short to ride the ride or something, but I closed my eyes and held on for my dear life, and my hands started to get numb. I couldn't hold on any longer and I so wished for the ride to be over. I screamed, but not for the thrill, but out of fear that I would fly out and probably die. My body wasn't even touching the seat, or even strapped in by a seat belt, but I knew I had to hold on just a little longer. I made it and vowed never to ride the *Spider* again.

When we disembarked from the sky-ride, we walked towards another rollercoaster, and we only waited about fifteen minutes to get on. It was pretty cool and fast and lasted about two minutes and as we were walking through the turnstiles to ride it again, amidst all the other high-schoolers, I spotted George and his beasts.

"Dude, they're over there."

I pointed towards the refreshment stand.

"Let's go over to him," he said.

We walked over and he assured us that we had ample time to enjoy more rides and to meet up at the fountain at three.

"All right, man. Don't 'dis'." That was slang for disrespect.

We jumped on a line for the roller-coaster again, and it was better than the first time because at least, by then, I had some reassurance that I would make responsibilities. I enjoyed amusement parks, just as much as the next person, but more so because it relieved me of my worries, anxieties, and pressures, and all of that was left the minute I entered the front gates. Angel enjoyed the stands, and I knew he couldn't wait to shoot some hoops for prizes, and so that was our next stop.

He played ball a lot in the schoolyards back home. He was a great ball handler, but somehow, I felt he was wasting his talent on unfruitful things such as hanging out late with street punks, and not being able to maintain a steady careered path. He slapped his dollar on the counter and demanded his chance of glory. He stepped back and dribbled the ball a few times and positioned himself and with his flare he released his shot, and like butter, it smoothly entered the rim and all I heard was the distinct sound of the net. He wasn't much of a small-gift earner, so he slapped another buck on the counter and made the second shot. *Swish.*

I looked around but didn't see any girls that were that attractive. I kept my cool about the whole thing, and nonchalantly scoped the surroundings. I still hadn't seen anything that I liked. When I was finished sweeping the perimeter, I turned around and he had an enormous blue stuffed animal – a thing, really.

"C'mon, man. Let's go." He stated.

"Is that gonna fit in the car?" I asked.

"It better."

I suggested that we wander off into the arcade, in some air-conditioning, and play some devious "shoot'em-up / bang-bang" games. I enjoyed video games, and my favorite was Asteroids, but it was outdated and it was rare that anyone carried it. I slipped my five dollars into the change machine and was excited to hear the change drop unto the dispenser, so I quickly grasped the twenty quarters and looked around in search of games that I already knew how to play, and for some cool ones that I had never heard of.

It was then I was reminded on how when my father took us here, he would enjoy his time in the neighboring music studio that shared the same space with the arcade, and he would record his vocals over The Police song *Every Breath You Take*. He loved singing and I enjoyed his voice. When he would finish his track, he would come out of the booth and await the cassette recording of it. He was so proud he would sometimes play it on the ride home.

Angel deposited his cash, and he was not too far behind me. We must have zapped, killed and destroyed enemies in our quest for Arcadia glory when I noticed that it was nearly one in the afternoon so I suggested that we finish our game, and meet the others by the fountain.

We sat by our rendezvous point until one–thirty, waiting and contemplating their next move. I started to get a little worried, and by one forty–five I decided to call John to tell him that I would be running a little late.

"Good afternoon. *Stanley's*. How can I help you?" the receptionist asked.

"Good afternoon. John Kaminski, please."

"Please hold."

I waited for nearly a minute when he answered the call.

"John speaking. How can I help you?"

"John, this is Coronado. I'll be a little late. I'm here at Great Adventure, and I'm waiting for my ride."

"It's almost two. If you're not gonna make it on time, then don't come in at all. You might as well have some more fun."

"Well...I'll try to be there before then."

"All right, kiddo."

We hung up, and I desperately tried to look for those wise–asses for being late. Angel and I decided to get our hands stamped, for a return entry, and to see if George's car was still there. In the parking lot, we could see the parked car, but there was no sight of them anywhere. Well, I was excused from work, but I still had obligations to the club to disc jockey for the night. Angel and I went back to the amusement park to locate them but there was still no sign of them. We figured that if we rode the Ferris wheel, we would have an advantage from spotting them from a great height.

We waited on the line for about ten minutes, and even then, we had to routinely stop to let the other passengers behind us board, so we hadn't reached the top or ran a full cycle until twenty minutes had passed.

"Do you see them?" I asked.

"No, but his car is still there."

That was a good sign. We randomly searched for them amongst the crowds, and I hadn't had time to notice if Angel was rocking the car. I was already feeling sick from the nervousness and anxiety placed on me and my responsibilities, or thereof and when the ride was over, I started to become angry while we walked back to the fountain, and then, suddenly, they appeared.

"What's up, man? Are you ready to go?" Angel asked.

"We haven't hit this ride yet, Yo," George said as he had his arms around both of the witches. "Right after the ride, we'll go." George had tickets to the TKA concert that night so he was managing his time.

"All right, man," Angel said as he held onto his enormous blue animal. He and I just noticed how long the line had become, but what could we have done? We weren't going anywhere without George, and I had already gotten permission from John to have some fun, so we decided to walk off to another attraction while they had their fun waiting on the long line.

Practically, an hour had passed and we hadn't seen them. We must have been busy scoping for chicks, or whatever, but we decided to take another look for them by the immediate exit. We found none of them, and in a temporary state of panic, we thought the worst and felt that they had ditched us. Angel felt a tap on his shoulder and when he turned around, it was George.

"How was it?"

"It was phat. We're gonna grab something to eat over here."

"All right. We'll meet you at the fountain in about an hour. We have to get back."

"No problem. Five o'clock." We looked at our watches.

"Five o'clock," Angel confirmed.

At this point, I had definitely played hooky from school and work, but it was still important to go to the club that night. It wasn't until five o'clock went and six o'clock came, that we decided to check the parking lot to see if the car was there. After we got our hands re-stamped, we went to where we thought the car was parked.

"3E, right?"

"Yeah. The car was here. He left us here, Yo."

I was still in shock because it didn't really dawn on me that we didn't have a ride to get back. When I did realize what had just happened, I didn't know what to do. I couldn't call my father to pick us up because he would have known that I wasn't at school or work, and Angel couldn't call his father because he probably would not have come anyway.

We didn't have anyone else to call. We had to figure out who would be all so kind to pick us up, but we were limited on funds which meant that we were subjected to only make two or three calls from the payphone. One thing was for sure, we had to call Rick and to let him know so he could cover for us at the club in case we didn't make it in time. Rick agreed to that, and in that sense, we were fortunate.

It was getting dark, and we were frustrated.

"How could your boy do this to us?"

"I'll fix him when I see him, bro. Don't worry about that."

We had no other choice but to report to Security, and to admit to them that we were stranded. It was embarrassing but it had to be done.

"Sir, are there any buses that go to New York?"

"Only private ones and those left about an hour ago. Are you two stranded?"

"I suppose we are."

"Well, you two can follow me into the offices and call whoever you need to call."

That was great but no one had come to our minds.

"All right."

When we got to the security station, we were interviewed on what actually happened and afterward, we were placed in a room to use the phone, but we sat on the desk pensively thinking about the whole thing. We were staring at it so hard that I thought it was going to ring, and it would be someone to rescue us. The room was very cold from the air conditioner and we had been on some water rides, but we felt no comfort while there.

An officer walked into the room.

"Did you make the call?" Head of Security asked me.

"No. My father would kill me."

"My father would too. We don't know who to call."

"Well, you can't stay here. Let me get this straight..." He opened a folder which contained our statements and tried to understand the scenario.

"You cut school because it was Senior Cut Day, and you didn't go to work, as scheduled, and you missed a DJ gig at a club so you could come here and enjoy the park."

"Yes. That's basically it."

"Who do you think you are? Ferris Bueller?" I smiled, but he didn't think it was funny at all.

"Call your father." He demanded.

I was afraid to, but I knew that it was the only solution for this nonsensical situation, and when I did, he wasn't too thrilled. By the time he reached the already closed park, Angel and I hadn't said a word. We didn't so much as breathe wrong during the whole hour-plus ride back home, and when I was safely back in my bedroom, I just wanted to curl up under the covers and sleep.

I heard my parents talking behind the closed bedroom door while I was getting undressed, and when he opened the door, I just looked at him while he closed the door behind him.

"I want you to write a thousand-word composition as to why you were suspended from school, a thousand words on why you were fired from your job, and a thousand words why you are being punished for two weeks. All before you go to bed."

He slapped a notebook on the dresser, along with an already sharpened pencil, and closed the door behind him. *Wow*, I thought to myself. *Did John fire me? Did the school call my parents? Had I to write all of this before I went to bed?* I wrote for hours, and with every page, I reflected on how deviant I had become to neglect my responsibilities. What kind of person was I becoming? I had to prioritize my life and shape up because the last thing I had ever wanted to do was to let my parents down.

That's when I started to trace back on everything that shaped my life, and I thought of my father. I thought about all the stages, phases and every-day life in which my parents taught and inspired me. I started to think about the Scouts, sports, Ron and bunk, Starlight Ave., San Genera, Mark, but mostly about myself.

To this, I am grateful to understand me, and now I must move forward.

My mother told me the next morning that Fr. Olivero inquired on my whereabouts to the other students, then to the other professors, and it trickled down to the principal. The principal checked with the secretary to see if I had called out sick, and the secretary made the routine call to the house. *I was caught*. John called to see if I had gotten home yet, and when he realized that I wouldn't really be at work he told my father that I needn't come back. I didn't know John really meant that if I hadn't shown for work, that I shouldn't even come. Apparently, Stanley, the owner, just wanted to teach me a lesson about responsibility so he made the ultimate decision to let me go.

That was a pivotal point in my life and was one that shaped me up to become better and more responsible for myself and for the people directly involved. I could have ultimately blamed it on Angel, who was turning out to be a very bad influence in my life, but I felt that I was the only one to blame for my actions. I was becoming more aware of my latest decisions and how they were taking a turn for the worse. I cared about those things and that's why I had become more serious in what I did and had less fun in daily activities. I had become a serious loner and I needed to do something with my life to keep me busy. Perhaps I needed a better job.

CHAPTER XIII

I responded to an ad at a refrigerated warehouse and about twenty guys showed up for the interview process while nearly half of them worked in a refrigerated environment before. After all the tedious paperwork of application forms, there was a test which included the mathematical skills portion and I thought it was a big joke because it had simple and basic adding and subtracting problems. I thought it was a trick, but lacking these fundamentals was a big macro matter. Familiarity with fork-lifts which I learned at Stanley's, and driving a "double-reach", or "cherry-picker", were also primary functions and if you didn't know how to, and they liked you, they would teach you how which is what happened to me. Downstairs on the front dock, Mr. Fritz had my resume in hand and noticed that I wasn't too far off from getting my college degree. He wore glasses and a college baseball cap and never smiled. He pushed his glasses close to his face with his left hand and held my background in his right.

"You went to Prep, huh? What are you doing here?"

"I'm making enough money to pay my remaining tuition through college. But it won't affect my job," I said as though he would not pass me because I was over-qualified to wind up in this sort of environment. He didn't take his eyes off my resume as he asked me how many cases were on the skid we were a foot from. Without hesitation, I told him "seventy–two." It was a "twelve–block" meaning there were twelve on a layer, and it was six high. Then I walked around the pallet to make sure, again that it wasn't a trick and checked for any missing cases on any other sides.

"It says you know how to drive a fork–lift. Get on and pick up this pallet and bring it closer to the loading door."

I jumped on, turned the ignition key, strapped on the seatbelt, popped the emergency brake and hit the gear lever forward. I was sure only to lift the forks no more than six inches off the ground and inserted the blades into the skid and when I finished looking around and placing the freight where he wanted, I went in reverse, looked back for any passerby's, parked the vehicle with the blades touching the ground and turned off the ignition before I stepped on the emergency brake. It was Fork–Lift 101 all over again, but I knew what the safety precautions were then, finally, I looked at the double–reach. He asked me if I had ever ridden one before and I replied with a "no". He demonstrated first and told me to give it a try.

The concept was since the aisles inside the freezer were narrower, it wouldn't be as effective with a forklift to bring down freight from the racks, so it was designed for drivers to stand. With my left hand, I grabbed a mini steering wheel and with my right, I grabbed on to this joystick which enabled me to move forward or backward. There were two buttons on the joystick which were responsible for extending the blades out or in. The top button was positioned where the index finger was, and to retract the blades I had to use my middle finger and lastly, there was a cone-shaped mechanism, by the thumb area, which was responsible for moving the blades up or down. It was quite perplexing considering that the electric power was controlled by stepping on a pedal with the left foot. I gave it a whirl, but it would take a while before I got used to it considering I was not a quitter.

"I see you're not dressed for the freezer but let me show you how to get in."

He pulled on a rope that was suspended nearly seven feet from the front of two heavy, metal doors. I guessed that the smoke mist resulting from the cold air hitting the hot air from the front dock was a sign of the elements within.

"I'm ready."

Mr. Fritz pulled the rope again and the doors closed. It was refreshing to have that cool air hit me on this hot day and with that, he approved me and told me that I should do what I had to do and get out before it was too late for me. I understood and tried to learn every aspect of the job so I could use it to grow and better myself.

So my head wouldn't get cold, especially my ears, I bought a new blue cotton Toboggan hat that I could fold up or down depending on the temperature. It definitely reminded me of the one my parents used to make me wear in elementary school during the Winter months. One day, my sister and I were walking home from school and by the time we reached home I realized that I had lost my hat because it wasn't on my head or in my pockets, and so to avoid my parents getting upset or concerned about it I decided to retrace my steps back towards school. In front of an apartment building, sitting on the bottom step, was a man with worn and torn pants, had a slight unshaven beard, and looked and smelled like he urinated on himself but most importantly, he was wearing my hat. I asked him if he found it and he said that he did, so it had to be mine.

When I got back home, I told my father and he was so upset that he first called the police and then took me to the spot where that guy was. He was still there and an officer questioned him but by the time it was all through, the policeman told me that I didn't want that hat anyway because it looked like it already had lice or bugs in it. *Perhaps it was a case of mistaken identity?*

The job at Port Newark only needed thirteen of us for full-time positions and we were asked to report that following Monday. I used the weekend to my advantage by gathering old work clothes, ones that I wouldn't mind if they got dirty, buying a new pair of warm gloves, and packing some sandwiches for lunch. I walked to Exchange Place, took the Path to Newark/Penn Station, and then took another bus which took me to the industrial company that was responsible for storing perishable goods and for supplying my weekly paycheck. The back doors of the bus opened and only a few of us disembarked. I noticed a couple of guys from our preliminary day on Friday, but I kept to myself and across the street was an empty burnt sienna color container that was used to store and ship freight on ships. There were nearly twenty guys standing to the right of it, directly across from the building, hollering and screaming at us but I stood my ground and walked into the hot vestibule and checked in at the dispatch office. The girl standing behind the glass window asked for my name and, upon verification, issued me a time card then told me to punch in on the gray clock next to the manual pencil sharpener. I punched it, put the card in a slotted organizer, drew a smiley face on it so I would immediately know which was mine, and walked to where the other guys were on the front dock.

It was seven in the morning and the entire new warehouse crew was present. It was said that we would be issued new gloves and freezer uniforms, and some of the guys brought their own, but I was nearly sweating with my thermals and jeans, and my blue and white checkered-flannel shirt. Two foremen approached us issuing new white cotton gloves. Lenny was a short and an average-sized man from Brooklyn. He wore a gray Gumbalini. It was one of those Italian caps that had a short brim in the front. He was married with two children, and I sensed that he was a good family man and had strong leadership skills. As we met, I think we might have had an understanding, or rather a clue, of who we both were. This wasn't a case of stereotyping but rather more like a mirror image in which, in those two seconds, I knew everything about him and he knew everything about me. Frankie was a heavier-set fellow who made it through the ranks of working in the freezer and making it to being a second-shift warehouse supervisor along with Lenny. He commuted from Teaneck in his Harley Davidson motorcycle. He wore a goat-tee and was looking and analyzing us behind the clouds of his Cuban cigar. Within that brief moment, the two of them decided where everyone was to be placed.

I was told to walk across the adjacent dock and to report to Dave and between the two docks was an old railyard where railcars were placed and unloaded. Rather than walking the U-shaped dock which was past the engineer's office and would have taken about five minutes, I listened to Lenny and climbed down the five-step ladder and walked directly across to a stoop on the other side. Their front dock was loaded with beef from Argentina which had to be inspected by USDA. The Department of Agriculture's facility was located about one hundred feet from where I was standing, but first I had to walk past twelve hundred cases of beef to meet Dave.

Dave was a tall, white, skinny fellow with a mustache which added to his character. He wore a black, Russian hat to cover his bald top, and walked over to introduce himself with a slight limp. He smiled and laughed to himself while he checked out his new freshman crew.

"I'm Da-a-ve. I'm in charge here, and this is Fra-a-nk." He dragged his words when he spoke, but I was just hoping to get everyone's name right. There were two Franks, Lenny, Da-a-ve, and his brother Billy. Billy was a quiet guy. In fact, you hardly ever saw his lips move. If he was older than his brother and had more seniority, Dave could have been his ventriloquist dummy. Dave pointed to Frank, and he wasn't amused as he sat on his wooden stool in the heater room.

"Let's take a quick walk into the freezer, so I can show you the freight."

I started to walk with the rest of them, but Dave told me to stay behind along with another guy and handed me a clipboard. He tugged on the rope and the heavy doors opened. When the doors closed behind them, Frank got off his stool and approached us with a snide look. It didn't look like he wanted this new five-man crew, but he was stuck with us. One of the truck doors was open and I heard more screaming from across the street by the container. The other guy, Mike, asked Frank what all the fuss was about.

"Oh, them? That's the old crew you guys are replacing. They're striking, but you don't have to worry about them."

The Daily News strike occurred a while back, and well, I didn't want to be a scab. My new employer hadn't told any of us about the strike and I was curious about my job security. *Why were they striking, what hardships were they experiencing and what was I doing here?*

"You'll be counting the inbound freight from now on, but first start counting the different lots of beef. It's been inspected and just needs to be separated and stored. Got a pen?" he asked me as I pulled one out of the two I had in my shirt pocket. He told Mike to mark each pallet according to its lot number, which I had the manifest for, with a piece of white chalk he handed him. We both walked over and started with our duties. We made it out of doing freezer work, and I held the prestigious position of being the "checker".

I heard the doors open as the chain and the mechanisms made a chilling noise. The other guys spotted us working, while Dave issued guys to drive the machines to carry the already marked freight into the freezer. It was a slow day, partially from the union-run truckers who also boycotted the facility, but also because upper management knew it was going to take a while to get back to business. The job was completed and we were sent to lunch. The five of us left and walked back over to "Cell Block B", as I called it, and the other eight were already purchasing their goodies from the "roach coach". A lunch truck had pulled over to our side after it met the needs of their old customers across the street. It carried the usual stuff: your juices, milk, pastries and hot food, but all I cared for was a nice hot cup of coffee light and sweet. I went inside to avoid any trouble, and to get to know some of the other guys, and in the process, some introduced themselves to me with Muslim names and at that moment I became "Faruq".

Sports was the topic in the locker/break room. I was just listening to some of the guys talking about Ewing and Jordan. I was more of a college basketball fan because those guys played their hearts out and didn't get paid the salaries the pros did. I waited for the conversation to die down and started to let these guys know what I was about.

"Those guys across the street are striking. We have to stick together if we're gonna make it here. I take the bus in, and I don't know who drives here, but keep an eye on your cars in case your tires are flat or you have broken windows." I walked into the bathroom to wash my hands and to also leave them thinking about what I said. When I entered back into the room, they've either listened to me or changed the subject back to basketball. While I grabbed a towel from the dispenser, a young Hispanic man walked in and nodded a hello to me as he turned the water on to wash his hands. I exited and proceeded to the front dock to see if Lenny was around. He had made an impression on me, and I just wanted to see what this company was all about. He wasn't there but I stood there waiting for something. The door opened to the dock area and it was Lenny with a coffee, from the food vendor truck, in hand, and Nelson, the guy who entered the restroom following behind him.

"How are you?"

"All right. How's Dave treating you over there?"

"OK. I'm more worried about the tough crowd outside."

"Don't worry about them. Their contract's up, and they want more money." A few other guys walked in and asked Lenny about the guys across the street. It was like we were organizing a peaceful rally, trying to understand what we should do to secure our own jobs.

A few weeks had passed and only one guy was left striking outside. The union had placed the others in other warehouse outfits, but he refused to let go. He had been with the company for eleven years and didn't know what else to do with his life between the hours of the second shift. I didn't want to end up like that man because it seemed that he was abandoned and alone and had lost his heart. He was a "lifer" and his life as he knew it was over.

They hired a couple of new guys, and one of them I swore I knew already. He wore a black cap, wore a mustache and a goat tee. He had a small tattooed–cross on his right hand, between his thumb and index finger that I noticed when I shook it, and he said his name was Freddy. Freddy worked the front dock on Lenny's side and was really good at it, and as each day passed I knew I had seen him in my youth, but never said anything to him until I was certain.

It was when I was talking to Joe, one of the engineers who also bartended in the City as a side job, in his shop, over a cup of coffee from the lunch truck, that it hit me. Joe and I were talking about his new–born son when one of the other guys, Charlie, came in to get help on one of the forklifts that weren't working. Joe left to go check it out and I thought about Charlie, then my uncle Charlie. Freddy was my uncle's friend and they hung out often. That night I asked my aunt Carmen for a picture of Freddy so that I could bring it in and shock him. After all, I was accustomed to finding out who people were in the most peculiar ways.

The next day, I brought in some flash paper that my father used with his Magic illusions and placed it on top of the picture.

"Hey, Freddy," I called him over to the side dock. When he got close to me, I lit the flash paper and as it disappeared, it revealed his semi-youthful photo. "You recognize this guy?" He just looked at me in amazement and he waited for me to explain myself.

"My father...he's my uncle Charlie's brother." He took a step back as if he hadn't ever thought he would hear my uncle's name again, and surprised to be working with someone he had already met.

"Corey, I haven't seen you since you were this small. How's your father?"
"He's great...yeah." I shook my head in affirmation.

"And your mom? Wow, I haven't seen your family in years. How's your grandmother?"

"Good. I spoke to her about two weeks ago."

"God. She blames me for Charlie's death. She said that I was a bad influence and that I always got him in trouble. After that, I left him alone and let him do what whatever the hell he wanted. We were wild in those days."

I suppose he was seeking closure for what happened to my uncle, and perhaps even trying to apologize for all the bad things he had done in the past, but as far as I knew, they were friends and I was fully unaware of the wild and crazy life of my father's brother's past.

"You know, one time Charlie and I were hanging out at this bar with Manfredo. I don't know if you know him, but we were at Gino's, downtown where we used to live, and we were having a good time."

"Yeah, I know Manfredo from the barber shop."

"Yeah, yeah, the barber shop. Back then there were gangs. You had the Italians versus the Puerto Ricans, and I had parked my car in the front when he noticed this huge black Cadillac try to park in front of my car. I don't know. He told me that some car was trying to park there but that they wouldn't fit, and they tapped, I mean tapped, my car and we were furious. He came out telling his guy that he wouldn't fit and the driver stepped out talking shit. Before we knew it, there were guys everywhere and a fight broke out. He came out swinging the cue stick and even Manfredo got into it. Manfredo grabbed this guy while Charlie whacked his hand with the stick. Someone yelled, 'call the cops', and the guy with the broken hand said, 'the cops are here.' With his other hand he pulled out his badge and we split. We left, man. We left the car and ran to my place a few blocks away. The next day, one of the big boss's guys came to the house and we had a meeting."

"They came to the house? Was my uncle there?" I curiously asked.

"Yeah, Corey, we just had to apologize to the cop and everything was fine. He had been mixed up with them and he couldn't get caught up with that, so that was that. We never went back to that bar, and it was a good thing because a week later, we heard that some guy and this teenage girl were shot right in front of the bar. Things were crazy back then."

I thought about Eddie. Break time was over, and we had to go, but before we parted to our workstations, we shook hands and were glad to have met again. Things were looking up at the job. Max, the USDA inspector had seen my ambitions and tried to show me a few things about what he did. I started off by stamping the freight with the rubber-stamped seal after it was inspected and cleared.

Before long, I ran the entire front dock and didn't have to step into the freezer except to notify the others when it was time for lunch. The freezer was set at an even zero degrees Fahrenheit because thirty-two degrees was not enough for management to be convinced that the freight was frozen. It was very quiet inside except for the humming of the air generators, and maybe a horn from a passing double-reach. The air was so still that often guys would get tired and fall asleep. *Imagine falling asleep in a freezer.* It was one of the only places you could escape from the hustle and bustle of the front dock and halfway through lunch, I noticed Sammy wasn't around. I asked around but no one saw him, so I went to check the freezer in "Cell Block A," but first I wanted to check the cooler area.

I quickly walked over to the cooler, which stored our Krakus ham from Poland and the drums of concentrated juices of Snapple or Tropicana, and looked down the three long aisles for Sammy but he wasn't in there. I was hoping he was because I did not want to venture into the cold abyss. There was nothing else I could do but to indulge my curiosity and suit up with my cotton gloves and my newly issued gear. I pulled the rope and wished for the best. It was quiet inside, so I decided to start towards the back of the secluded work area in case he was still storing freight with a fork-lift. I heard the doors open behind me and it was Dave who had just realized that one of his guys was considered missing, so he had joined in on the search.

There were only a few places and not enough room to maneuver in from the lack of space the facility provided. It was packed and dangerous with all the loose commodities and spills on the floor. You couldn't make a turn, it was so tight, that you had no choice but to hit cases. *Three*, *five* and *six* aisles were full with cases of beef, while aisle *four* had Chinese vegetarian rolls and plastic pails of concentrated juice. We split up, I walked down *seven* aisle while he checked the bin areas that carried five thousand pounds of juice in heavy plastic bags inside heavy wooden crates. I thought I heard a fainting noise from the next aisle. The humming of the freezer fans drowned out sounds, and sometimes I would just imagine myself hearing things. I heard the noise again, and I was trying to hone in on it, and then I heard scraping on the ground.

"Dave, over here!" I yelled, "Aisle six!"

Without hesitation, he climbed on the rails and unto the tops of the pallets of beef which were not shrink-wrapped properly. He told me that I shouldn't climb freight like he did, because it happened to him once before and he accidentally fell, and that's how he obtained his limp. There was no room for me to check the sides of the pallets, so I stayed in aisle five and went to the racks to find the noise again.

"Please hel–l–lp," I faintly heard and I saw Sammy laying there helpless and practically unconscious.

"Dave, four racks are on the floor!" He followed my voice and saw Sammy eight feet from where he must have fallen, with his head on its side. I saw him too but was only a foot from his head.

"Sammy, it's Coronado. You're gonna be all right. Don't move. Help is on its way." I backed out of the aisle and faced Dave who had been putting the pieces of the puzzle together in his mind.

"Dave, I'm getting help. Keep talking to him, and keep him warm."

I jumped to the rope and pulled but the doors opened just the same. I had to get some if not all of the guys to move all the freight out. We needed clearance for the Police, Firefighters, Medic Team, and whomever we needed to help him, and that was going to take a while. The first person I saw was Nelson, who had just spoken to his son from the payphone, and I told him to tell some of the guys what had happened while I found Lenny to call 911. Nelson was in charge of the USDA pickups. They were mainly surpluses from the government given to churches and schools, and every day these programs helped to feed a lot of needy people. Fortunately, he worked from a booth on the side dock, where the railcars were, and he hadn't frequented the freezer that much either, but he had a voice and James, Keith, and a few others grabbed some machines and began moving freight unto the front dock.

Nearly an hour and forty minutes had passed and the rescue squad had finally brought Sammy out of the cold freezer. He was pulling freight from the middle of the jammed aisle because he only needed five boxes. He didn't want to spend the countless time pulling out all the other pallets for such a minimal quantity. He slipped on the pallet which was nearly nine feet off the ground, and his head landed on a wooden pallet which was only five inches from the ground. Needless to say, he was in excruciating pain while he was brought out on the stretcher. That could have been any one of us, and I wouldn't stand for the pending dangers that the freezer entailed but I didn't work the freezer because I had already proven my worth and had graduated from the ice cavern.

Nelson and I decided to visit Sammy the next day at the hospital. He was admitted to University Hospital in Newark, and Nelson already knew the area so we found a parking spot, put quarters in the meter, and walked into the building.

"Good evening. We're here to see Sammy Faultas. He was admitted yesterday in ICU."

The receptionist checked her listings and could not find a "Sammy Faultas".

"He was involved in an accident from a refrigerated warehouse. I'm sure he's here." I stressed.

"We have four different names under Faultas, but no Sammy."

I pulled out my Qualcomm cell phone and proceeded to call the job. Frankie answered and I asked him.

"Yo, Frankie, I'm at the hospital visiting Sammy but he's not listed. Do you have a room number?"

"Hang on..." He had me holding for nearly two minutes while the receptionist was overlooking her records, and Nelson was impatiently pacing back and forth.

I couldn't believe what had happened next.

"Coronado? This is Barry." Barry was the company manager, and he was a stern prick. "Sammy is under the name, Ahmed Makram." He handed the phone back to Frankie, and even if Frankie knew what was going on, he wouldn't tell us. We hung up and asked for Ahmed Makram and the receptionist gave us the room number and the passes to visit him.

As hospitals go, it was a maze and we had to remember the way out but we found the room and there he was in a partial body cast half-baked from all the medication he was receiving.

"Hey, Sammy, it's us. How 'ya feelin'?"

He looked at us and hadn't said a word. Nelson came over to the right side of the bed while I stayed on his left by the doorway.

"Yo, Sam, it's your best friend, Nelson," he said as he suspected that he wasn't in full comprehension.

"Who are you guys? What the hell are you doing here?" Nelson and I just looked at each other in a confused state, and told him who we were and that everything would be all right. He did not appreciate us being there so we casually left him alone. The fall must have knocked him out. Perhaps he had amnesia, or maybe it was the over-dosage of drugs in his body. Whatever the reason, we found our way outside, and started to think about who Sammy really was.

The next day at work, the word was out about our findings, and everyone had their theories, and most even suggested that he was a company spy or a mole, but I was more concerned about his well-being and his family so I started a collection for the days he would be missing from work. Nearly all the guys chipped in and I held on to it until the next time I would see him. It was only one hundred and sixty dollars, but he would appreciate it. We never found out what his story was, nor did I ask him personally when I saw him two weeks later in the parking lot retrieving his belongings from his locker with his wife and two sons, but he hadn't understood the generosity when I handed him the envelope filled with cash. I told him to take care of himself, and that he had a strong case against the company.

"Al Salam Alaykum." I spoke as Faruq.

"Assalamu alaikum wa rahmatullahi wa barakatuhu," he responded. He drove off with his family never to be seen again. *Why had we met? Was I the one who was meant to save his life?* Then I started to think about why I was really at the warehouse in the first place wasting my talents away. What did it all mean?

Drugs were an issue amongst the lumpers. Lumpers were people who worked independently with a truck driver to help them unload their freight. Sometimes I would see them along Turnpike exits near fast-food joints, where they would propose the drivers for their services. In the morning, these six guys would be normal and work diligently and work hard for their cash. "Rabbit" was one of the "cut-throats" at the job. He would do anything for a buck, and would probably knock out your grandmother if money was involved, but even worse he would lie just to get the next job. The other lumpers knew his style so they tried to avoid him as much as possible, but if they were short a person, and "Rabbit" was the only one around, you'd better believe it they would ask for his help. It's all about the almighty dollar for these guys.

During lunch, they would catch a ride with Tyrone to Newark, and when they came back, they were different. One day I found Derek leaning on a pallet and he looked as if he was sleeping. I beeped my horn trying to wake him, but he just stayed there and I even placed my forks under the pallet and slowly moved it away. Derek was still in the leaning position, and no matter how hard he tried he wouldn't fall.

"Hey, Master Corey," he said jokingly in his sleepy state under his breath. He called me that because I was always proper and upstanding with him and the rest of his cohorts, and I never saw it be derogatory in any sense. That's what heroin did to these guys. It made them peculiar, scratch and pull their faces off, and made them hungrier for the next load so they would have money for the next bag. Of course, they each would deny any wrongdoing but it was very obvious.

"That's defamation of character," Derek said to Frankie after Frankie accused him of being doped up. After lunch, the bad lumpers would have super strength and knock out a 53ft. container, filled with frozen seafood, within the hour, while Benny, one of the good ones and a favorite of Barry's, would make a sandwich inside his container and take breaks in between. It was a give-and-take with them and since I was the dock runner, and depending on how fast I worked to remove pallets from their doors, the faster they would get paid, so in turn, the lumpers had to or pretended to, respect me.

I got my hands on some smokes that "fell off a truck" one day. I started to keep my distance when "Rabbit" told Lenny and Frankie that I was selling cigarettes for two dollars a pack. I sold nearly twenty cartons a week for two months just from the lumpers alone, and when I suspected management had found out from "Rabbit", I stopped.

Issues started to heat up and the guys wanted to start a union. We had been there for six months making a lot of money for the company with a lot of taken risks which could send us to the hospital, such as the case with Sammy. We started to organize with the first and third shifts so we could all unite. We couldn't join up with the Longshoreman Union, although we would have seriously wanted to because they were the union with whom were still in arbitration with the former crew. We went with the Teamsters and soon we held secret meetings with a delegate. Al was a leader who was going to take us to victory, and thirty of us met with him on a Saturday afternoon. We voiced our concerns and it was going to take a little bit of time, but the important thing was to remain patient.

A month had passed and I was told to report to their sister warehouse in Newark. I told them that I signed a contract to be employed with the operation in Port Newark but they, in turn, told me that it was slow at the facility and that they were obligated to ensure me forty working hours a week. I guess it made sense, but now was the opportunity to go on strike, and not be transferred. Most of the guys were weak and caved in so if I hadn't gone, I probably would have been terminated so I went.

I started at five in the morning, and Roger, Lenny's cousin, was my supervisor. He kept me out of the freezer and realized my skills as a truck loader. Even the truck drivers liked me because I was really fast, partly because we were non-union, and we didn't have more breaks in between. I remember going to a secluded part of the facility numerous times just as the sun was rising, asking and praying for direction and strength. I became more grateful for having a job, for allowing me to see the rising sun and most thankful for the opportunity. The building itself had thirteen floors, and all the windows were cemented shut. A rustic brown water tower stood at the top and was on standby in case the building went up in flames. You could see the building while driving on Route 1 to 78, on the right-hand side towards Newark next to the train rails. On the south side of the building were rail tracks where Conrail would pass by twice a day with freight, and on the other side of the fence was a state prison. It's been said that a few prisoners had escaped once and sought shelter in the warehouse, but were immediately apprehended by local authorities.

After two months of working there, nearly half of the guys I worked with at the Port, were transferred. I had bought my first mutual funds, and I would check in on its progress every morning before the bell. That's what kept me going throughout my stay there, and, again, because I felt I was just wasting my time there. I was called into the boss's office, and unexpectedly, I was offered a supervisory position after a few weeks. I told them that I would think about it, because I had plans to leave the job altogether and pursue a more lucrative career. I was good at what I did, and the better thing for me to do was to move up and become a Supervisor, but I had already known of the pending strike, and besides, I made more as a laborer. When I left the job after work, Al was outside with his strikers holding a peaceful demonstration. I pulled over and asked him how the union was working out. We spoke briefly when the boss slowly drove by the two of us and gave us an unsatisfying look.

The next day, during lunch, I was playing chess with Charlie the lumper, and Roger interrupted us to speak with me alone. Charlie left, and he told me that I had to report back to the Port on Monday. I couldn't believe the abuse I was taking, but what else could I have done? I said goodbye to all the guys, and that if I heard anything about the union, that I would get word to them. I reported the following Monday, but management was surprised to see me there. Apparently, I was to report on Sunday night to work the night shift. They wanted to see if I was loyal to the company before they promoted me to Supervisor. I explained to Barry that I was told to report on Monday and that it wasn't my fault. He told me that next week I was to start working the night shift, and I was to receive a fifty-cent differential.

When I asked Al what I should do, he told me to stick it out a little further, and that the union would surely form but it had been three months and no stronghold. I had given up on Al and with Barry, and decided to hand in my two-week letter of resignation that following Monday morning. There were no more false hopes, and no more taking advantage of me because I did for *me* and decided that if I could make it in the office there, I could do it almost anywhere. I was exposed to more politics and I was better in that, one day, I would become my own boss, and learn from my mistakes and from the mistakes of others. Like Sammy, I pretended to be someone I wasn't. When I was found out, the only choice was to leave and to find out who I would become.

CHAPTER XIV

I had already gotten used to having some freedom from my parents due to my years of perceived obedience and discipline. I had my tinted cherry-red Vette, at least that's what my car registration said, and I drove almost everywhere with that car. Periodically, it would have its problems and my mechanically-inclined uncle would guide me or work on it under its hood, but more often than not I would take care of it myself. Driving home from Mike's house one day on the freeway, I heard a popping noise and saw smoke coming from underneath the hood. Naturally, I pulled over to see what had happened and the first thing that came to my mind was that I hadn't any anti-freeze in the radiator and that the car simply over-heated so I popped the hood and didn't see anything leaking from the radiator or the hoses, but underneath I could see the anti-freeze. I then noticed that the fan belt had broken off because it was already worn, and the leak was coming from the water pump. The car just needed a breather. I was ten minutes away from home, and I only needed to wait probably another fifteen minutes for the engine to cool, then I could restart the car and drive off.

Maintenance was a factor and before long, I was an uncertified mechanic. I would drive everywhere and felt confident in knowing that if the car gave me troubles, I would know how to assess the damage but the one thing I couldn't fix would be if I were involved in a car accident and that would be an unfortunate turn of events. That Chevette would start shaking when I drove past 80mph on the highway but it would zip through city streets with no problem. One time I decided to drive on Chapel Ave, in between the cemetery lots, and speed up down the hill from Garfield Ave towards Caven Point Road where the train tracks crossed and it was elevated enough that it served as a mini ramp so as I approached it with high speed. I remember my adrenaline racing as well and when I hit that ramp, I was airborne for a quick moment but I landed a little too hard. I was excited that all the parts remained intact on the vehicle but unfortunately, it wasn't until two days later that I noticed a crack on the bottom of the passenger-side windshield. I needed a new one of those after a week's time because the crack got long enough to reach the top.

When I found my very first car, I only paid a hundred dollars for it, from a junkyard, but it was in terrible shape and it didn't even have an engine. I was thinking that this would be a cool project to get into because it was like taking vital parts from wherever I needed them and to breathe life into an already lifeless idea, but more importantly, I wanted to see what could become from this empty shell. Before long I started to collect all the original pieces of the car in different junkyards all over the state.

I kind of related to this pile of mismatched body-parts because in some ways it was not unlike myself. Perhaps it was subconsciously a car that really caught my attention from the chop shop by Ruggiero's Deli but in a month's time, I had myself a '69 Mustang Fastback with a 351 Cleveland engine, and I replaced the stick-shift option for an automatic transmission but after three months of driving my hot cherry-red muscle car, it was demolished by a debris truck which had been driving in front of me on Route 1&9 South. The truck's tarp wasn't completely fastened and pieces of bulky trash fell out in front of my driving lane. I lost control and crashed into the divider and worst of all I didn't catch a glimpse of the license plates, nor were there any witnesses. I must have pounded the top of the steering wheel with the heel of my hand a few times cursing in anger.

Like Sir Isaac Newton allegedly said: "What goes up must come down." Such was my life and I lacked balance. Maybe it wasn't meant to be and it was at this point that I started to realize that money wasn't everything. It wasn't how I defined success. My car was only of material substance and I was really fortunate that I wasn't hurt in the accident. Instead of stacks of hard currency, I started to count my blessings and further realized that I had the freedom and opportunity to start again, but ultimately, I defined success through survival, and not getting caught.

One fine afternoon at the house, the doorbell rang and it was my sister's friend, Alicia. I opened the door and asked her to come in but she didn't even look at me, but rather just hurriedly walked in and spoke to my sister. She asked Gloria if she knew any places that installed tinting for car windows and she told her that I knew a few places and that she should ask me. Well, she did and we were off to Union City in her car to get it tinted and on our way there, she took JFK Blvd which wasn't the quickest route there but it gave us a chance to listen to the 3rd Bass song – *Brooklyn Queens*, on the radio. I saw the car repair shop designated on a triangular island in front of Roosevelt Stadium, and they were open for business. It hadn't taken more than an hour for the job to be completed by two Dominicans I knew, but in the meantime, she and I just talked and got to know each other a little bit in their waiting area. That was the first time we ever had a real conversation, and I was rather sad that her car was completed and that it was time for her to go.

I started hanging out more and more, visiting more and more places with my Chevette. Often from house parties, or even driving back late from down the Shore visiting my girlfriend at the time, I was breaking all the curfew boundaries at home. I walked into the house at about six in the morning and my father must have heard me because he walked downstairs and confronted me in the kitchen. He had enough of my deviance, and let me have it. I think it was because he didn't think my current girlfriend was good enough for me because I couldn't think of any other reason he would slap me across my face. And perhaps she wasn't good enough, in whatever or any capacity at the time, it didn't mean that he should resort to violence but that was the first and only time I remember him hitting me. Things started to go further downhill from there and I hadn't seen him this furious since the time I got an earring and tried to hide it from him for a couple of days by talking to him from only my right side. I couldn't hide it from him forever, so I just showed him. He didn't talk to me for two straight weeks, and when he did finally speak to me, I noticed that he went off and got his ear pierced as well. We rarely shared emotions, but rather shared experiences.

CHAPTER XV

It became so tense on a daily basis that I didn't know what I had done wrong, in my parents' eyes, half the time. That was the year that my sister was pregnant and had told my parents, but no one told me at the time, and that's when things started to make more sense to me. I had been working mandatory thirteen-hour shifts at the Port so I hadn't been at the house much. That was when I realized that whenever I said something disapproving of her boyfriend, she became very defensive and took his side. Even after I hung up the phone on her while she was still talking to him in the kitchen, and then regrettably slapped her in the face to make her stop talking to him, she still refused to listen to me, mainly so he wouldn't be driven away from her and from his responsibilities.

"Mom, Corey punched me!"

My mother was also in the kitchen by the back door watching our rare sibling rivalry unfold but she also confirmed that I had punched her when I believed I hadn't.

"Leave your sister alone! You do not hit your sister!" I let go and disengaged immediately. I always obeyed my parents because I trusted in their wisdom and there was no reason for me to continue in this behavior. They taught me their rules and how to follow them, early on.

When my sister and I were younger we all lived in a quiet one-way street, that apartment where I got that splinter, and I heard a commotion from the front of the house. Apparently, a boy who lived across the street, who happened to be around the same age as us, hit my sister. I don't know why, but I didn't see it happen. I ran down the stairs and when I reached the street level, I noticed she was crying. The adults shouted to him to leave her alone and I think they all secretly wanted me to take care of the problem.

"He hit your sister! Are you going to let him get away with that?" I heard a neighbor incite.

The boy taunted me from across the street but I could not do anything about it. I wasn't allowed to cross the street. Those were the rules. I wasn't taught revenge or even hand-to-hand combat. As if there was an invisible barrier preventing me from taking a step unto the asphalt, my mind only computed the rule. I felt helpless and defeated for letting the surrounding others and my sister down, but knew that in the end that what I had done was right.

I never forgot that day, and I think that's why I reacted the way I did. I felt that there was something I could do to prevent a negative involvement between my sister and a boy by stepping in and telling her, as her big brother, that she shouldn't talk with him anymore, except that this time I hit someone, her, and it was inexcusable.

Her boyfriend apparently made her happy, and she didn't want me to interfere. I could easily have summoned a couple of guys to take care of him without any question and he could have been wiped off the face of this earth, but I did not take that route. It was not for me to decide who lives or dies or even gets hurt, and more importantly, he had to help take of my sister's child. Besides, I hadn't really been playing the role of brother lately, and perhaps some of this was my fault.

I was not as involved in my family's lives as I used to be. This life of petty crime, my involvement in the streets and my subtle desire to make it on my own had distracted me from what was truly important. I wasn't engaged in the daily routines of my sister, I didn't know who her true friends were and I certainly didn't know she even had a boyfriend. I strayed from the family to pursue my own interests.

Because I was two years older than my sister and we attended the best private Catholic schools in our urban city, in my opinion, it was a bit lucky and convenient for me to get along with some of her friends. I once asked her classmate Veronica, who lived about twenty minutes away in the Heights, out on a date and we went to the opening showing of *Goodfellas* in Secaucus, NJ. I remember waiting in a long line outside the theater booth surrounded by couples in suits and dresses as if we were going to a party or a family gathering. I leaned over to her and thanked her for coming out with me on a crowded venue like this. When we got our seats, we sat near the left rear corner of the theater, and when the lights dimmed out there was a strong sense of excitement because I heard the applause when the show was about to begin. As I looked at the left row floor in front of me towards the screen, I could see a couple of tall brown bags. They weren't the ones for cans of coke or beer but taller for wine. About thirty minutes into the show cigars were lit but somehow it didn't bother anyone. This was a non-smoking theater yet no one seemed disrupted or inconvenienced by the subtle puffs of smoke.

Lastly, in one of the great scenes in the film before Henry laughs at Tommy during the "How am I funny" scene, Pesci's character mentions being in the middle of the weeds while on a bank job in Secaucus. There was a thunderous roar, laugh, and appreciation that he mentioned the city in which we were currently in. I felt connected and involved in a culture that I belonged. That was the best-ever hands-down opening to a memorable film I had ever attended, and I don't think Veronica would ever forget it either.

Joanne also lived in the Heights, about two blocks north of her friend Veronica, and she was fun to be with too. We would often walk over to Leonard Gordon Park on Manhattan Ave and play tennis. That was really fun, different for me, and energetic. Afterward, at times, I enjoyed walking with her around the buffalo and bear sculptures and along the hilly and shady walking paths. We would walk back to her house and see her younger brother and sister playing on the front porch, her mom would be cooking dinner inside and we would hang outside until her father came home. He was a Sergeant of the local police force and he was really cool with me. He didn't act surprised or overly-concerned with me being around his daughter. He even offered me a beer a couple of times but I'm sure it was just a trick. We would all come in and relax on the couch in the living room and just hang out. I enjoyed and respected this family unit because they welcomed and respected me.

My sister was on the high school basketball team and I would often go to her games and check them out, but that's when I started to get interested in her friend Eva. She was probably one of the very few that had "poufy" curly hair on top of her head, as what seemed to be the style with all the girls in Jersey, during our current time in the 80s. Eva was athletic and had a nice firm body, but around this time I started to really think about my relationships with girls. I did not want my sister to think that the only reason her friends started to hang out with her was that of me. I enjoyed being with them and discovering my unique attractions to each of them but I realized that I couldn't be with all three of my sister's friends, also because they were friends with each other as well. I decided that I couldn't continue dating or even seek boyfriend/girlfriend status with either one of them because it would hurt the friendships we already had. Unfortunately, it became worse than that when I ignorantly started to ignore them and the girls stopped talking to my sister, as well.

And perhaps that is the point I wanted to make is that I have not been the best brother and have ruined relationships with my sister and her friends. Out of the five of her friends that I had dated, she is still friends with one. Twenty-percent is better than zero, but I have to admit I need to work on being a better brother and a better person to my sister. I love Gloria, and I don't tell her enough. My parents told me that if I wanted to stay out until whenever I wanted to, I should pay for the insurance and the costs to maintain the vehicle. I think all insurance companies are scams and fed on fear, or maybe it's just because Jersey had the highest insurance costs, but I refused to pay the car insurance premiums, so I decided to move out of the house. The decision could not have come at a better time since my sister would need my room for her newborn anyway, and perhaps this was a way to put my family first while allowing the space for myself to grow as an individual. Now all I had to do was to find an apartment or maybe someone that I could share one with.

I called my uncle Pedro, told him about my current situation and he let me temporarily stay with him at his apartment. He was thinking about moving out himself so I told him that it wasn't a problem, and as long as he didn't mind that, we were to become roommates. He wanted to move closer to his job in Elizabeth, NJ. His daily commute in his blue four-wheel drive Ford pickup was not suitable for him so we moved out there.

Even at the age of twenty, it wasn't easy to just pick up my things and go. I hadn't really spoken to my parents about what I was feeling and I spent most of the morning and early afternoon packing my things and moving them out. My father hadn't said anything, but my mom, I'm sure, was feeling a bit like the whole thing was her fault and it wasn't that I was leaving them, but rather that they thought they had a handle on the situation that concerned me. I turned the other cheek when I was asked not to intervene with her boyfriend, so I asked them to do the same with me. I wondered if anyone would be standing by the window staring and wondering if I would come back.

With my lifestyle and basic removal of family I wasn't really one who had time to nurture stability and love. The idea of feeling free was a natural concept I embraced and the thought that I was in control of my life brought me to a higher place. I drew my power from learned instinct and survival that fed from experience and adventure, no matter how reckless or unbecoming it was in my family and society's eyes.

I had not even told them where I would be staying, and I especially asked my uncle not to tell them. He understood, respected and accepted my wish, so now they had to face a dilemma with each of their children. My mind was made up, and my sister did what she had to do under her circumstances.

CHAPTER XVI

Driving northbound on Kennedy Blvd, less than a fifteen-minute commute from Bayonne Park, I approached the statue of the US president for whom the park was named after - Lincoln. To me, he broke up the monotony of watching tightly grouped super-dense houses along the busy boulevard and from the jay-walkers who not only crossed when the signal light is green but also from the middle of the streets where there are no clear-designated crossing lanes. Before it was Lincoln Park in the early 1900s it was known as West Side Park. *Lincoln the Mystic* greeted me on the east side of Lincoln Park while seated with his hands crossed between his knees. The original bronze sculpture had already turned green just like a penny would if you left it exposed to water or moisture for too long, and his solemn yet calming demeanor gave me a warmth of feeling relaxed every time I entered his domain.

It seemed that I always got the red light at Belmont but when it was legally time for me to turn left, as the light turned green, I drove past him and headed westbound towards West Side Ave. I pressed the Play button on my car CD where Public Enemy's *Welcome to The Terrordome* cued on. It was soon after that I gazed at the majestic water fountain that resided there. The 53-foot high fountain was restored by the county and rededicated on July 10, 1990. In the water, pool frogs spouted out water and an eagle stood on top. I stayed to my right unto Lookout Drive where I proceeded to make my way to the north corner of the park.

I noticed a couple of guys on a nearby bench I had only seen before years ago, as they were probably scouts or just residents who haven't left the neighborhood. I pulled into a parking lot next to a Tennis wall, on Duncan Ave and Route

1&9, and found a parking spot. I took my 9mm just in case and encased it in my concealment holster in my right rear pants belt-line. It was crowded because of a local cookout and community function and as balloons decorated the entrance to the North park entrance, tables of food were lined up against the background of children playing in the newly-developed playground. Girls were playing with the Double-Dutch rope while some of the boys were chasing each other in a game of Tag. Frankie Smith's *Double Dutch Bus* was playing in my head, but the young ladies were singing about Sally, Suzy or Lucy as they were twirling the rope. Walking closer, I noticed a couple of the local politicians and law enforcement big-wigs. One of the servers recognized me and said something to this big guy next to him.

"Toss him an apron!" he told him, whereby he did and I grabbed it in mid-air.

I put it on and went on his side of the table, and with a firm handshake and an inviting smile, we hugged.

"What's up, Juju? How've you been, bro?" He looked comfortably dressed in a pair of jeans and a buttoned-up shirt with his signature black Fedora but this one had a yellow feather in it. His beard grew longer over the years, had almost a cone-shape to it and it extended an inch or two from his chin but was missing a hairnet.

"What's up, Corey man?"

A father and daughter walked over to our food station. With Jerome's tongs, he placed a burger on each of their buns, and I picked up a frankfurter with my tongs asking each if they would like one.

"This one is for my mommy," the cute girl in the white and blue dress said.

"Can I get two please?" he asked me since he did have two hot dog buns opened already.

"Sure!" I responded.

"Daddy, can I have one with sour kraut?" she asked.

"Sure, sweetheart."

After the two left, Juju motioned other guys to take our place, we took off our plastic gloves and we started walking and talking with our clean aprons on.

"You remember Jaquan and my cousin Beau, right?" he asked.

"Yeah. It's been a while. What is all this?" I asked.

"You like it? Remember when the big nasty buildings were here and when all you boys would go across the street to the batting cages just to practice your swings? Not no more, bro."

"You mean no more stealing bait trucks in under a minute here? I think you guys broke all-time records for that crap." I glamorized.

"It's no way to live. Both my mom and brother died here in these Projects. It wasn't for me. After I got out and did my time, I decided to start over and try to do the right thing. I wanted more out of life and all of these people too." He explained.

"You found God in there?"

"I don't know if it was God or not. All I know is that I believed in a deity otherwise all of my prayers wouldn't count. I mean, who else could I turn to?"

"How much time did you do?" I questioned.

"Any person who knowingly has in his possession any rifle or shotgun without having first obtained a firearms purchaser identification card in accordance with the provisions of N.J.S.2C:58-3, is guilty of a crime of the third degree. Four out of twenty years." He quoted.

"And while I was away in that small cell all I could do was think about not being there, and being outside enjoying the freedom of the open air and sun. Fuck, even the moon. Thinking about wasted time, my family I abandoned and never saw again when I got caught, and all the things I wished I could do when I got out. And I'll tell you what…there was one mother fucka who helped me get back on my feet, listened to my crazy ideas while playing chess right down the park, and taught me how to use my hands to build things. That was Felix."

I listened intently.

"He was the one who suggested that I give back to the hood and the community because only then would I feel like I accomplished something bigger than myself. All of this wasted parkland across the street, he jokingly said that they should build a golf course for the rich mother fuckers and that we could sell them coke and shit."

I began to laugh.

"Or be their caddies and charge them a good amount. Thing is, they built their golf course and we didn't get anything out of it. I organize block parties for my peeps in my City. People respect you when you feed them. Chill Town! No other place like it. Big dreams, Coronado. You have to think big."

I nodded in agreement. We then stopped walking and faced each other.

"Your uncle and I made lots of money selling shit, and I want to thank you for introducing me to him. He was a good man. Sorry you left the business but when that shit went down with "Sonny" Grieco, you had no choice."

He pulled out an envelope that contained my last finders-fee payment owed me because of vouching for Mr. Feliciano. I took it. *I'm not that dumb.*

"Who shot Felix, Juju?!" I demanded.

"I know one thing, it didn't come from me, and he knew that one day he would have to pay for his sins. You might want to ask Grieco himself. He would have the resources to find out quicker than any one of us."

As we shook hands once again, I thought that it might be the last time that we would, and as I looked at the beautiful landscape of Lincoln Park, I also noticed that those huge brick buildings that made up Duncan Projects years ago were no longer there but rather replaced by the Gloria Robinson Court Houses and that the golf nets were so high along the busy road so as not to damage any vehicles from any flying golf balls.

I went back to the food line and made a burger with onions and cheese and a hot dog with sauerkraut and mustard, and grabbed a can of Welsh Grape for the road. I drove on Duncan towards West Side, making that left so that I could go down Montgomery Street towards Downtown, and finished my lunch before I made it passed the National Guard Armory and pulled over and parked before the Bus Stop that existed in front of the Medical Center Luncheonette. I got out and stood on the corner of Baldwin and Montgomery looking east and realized that I was just staring at the New York City skyline.

Life is so precious and fragile. I looked around and began to appreciate Jersey City more and more because it was diverse, complex, and filled with energy and hope. If this was to be my last day, I would feel that I had lived enough with all the things I had already experienced. If today was to be my last, from visiting Mr. Grieco, it was suitable that I visit the place where I was born: The Jersey City Medical Center, but it didn't exist anymore. Instead, it was turned into luxury apartments.

Either way, sometimes it isn't easy to distinguish whether things truly exist or not. Like my fear of meeting with possibly the man responsible for the death of my uncle, or the fact that I was even born at the Medical Center. Apparently, birth certificate and vital statistics records were switched and unorganized in 1972. When I applied for my US passport, I was told that my Birth Certificate wasn't proof of my birth but rather I had to contact Trenton, the capital of NJ, for verification on when I was born. Oh, and by the way the fee that the Office of Vital Statistics and Registry charges, the last time I checked, was $25 for the initial search and one certified copy or certification of the record or No Record Statement, and $2 for each additional copy of the same record ordered at the same time. Nothing is free in life.

"Yo, man, you got a quarter." Some stranger out of nowhere asked, and when I reached into my pocket the sound of multiple jingling coins was audible.

"Yo, lemme get some change so I can get something to eat." He insisted.

I pulled my hand out of my pocket and told him that we would go into the Luncheonette and he can order his lunch. He didn't want lunch.

"Nah, man, I'll just take the change."

"Now you get nuthin'! Get the fuck outta here. Change your location." I told him as I took a step closer to him as if to smack him. He left. *Ulterior motives.*

I sat at the fire hydrant on that corner soaking it all in, plotting my next moves and wondering what it all meant. There are certain decisions in your life which change the course of your history. The phone rang and when I answered it, I just listened, then hung up.

****

The new place was a crypt, but the rent was a mere fifty bucks a week which my uncle Pedro and I gladly split. It was only one room and we had to take a shower and use the bathroom out in the hallway. It came equipped with a small oven, a kitchen countertop with cabinets which only had room for the sink and a dish dryer dispenser, one mattress and one love seat that my parents had given him years back. We only needed the place to sleep, so we dumped all of our belongings in a corner of our hundred and fifty square foot pad, and I slept on the couch. I didn't know if things had gotten better for me, but at least I was somewhat on my own.

The money was coming in like crazy, from the cocaine business, especially on Starlight Ave. I mostly hung out all night and woke up around two in the afternoon along with my uncle who always woke up an hour before he had to go to work. I decided that I would go to Angel's place to see if he wanted to pick up some goodies for tonight's scheduled games or to just grab a bite to eat at Tutta Bene on the corner of Woods Street. Every Tuesday, Louie, the owner and cook, baked his homemade lasagna and he would even page me sometimes to remind me, and I would stop what I was doing and travel from Starlight to his restaurant for lunch. Angel's jeep was parked outside, so I proceeded to ring the doorbell a few more times. There was still no answer so I began to leave the steps and head back to my car when an old relative of mine, a blast from the past and one of my previous favorite customers, appeared in his red van.

"Maricón...what's up?" he asked as he lowered his radio from the salsa music he was listening to.

"What's up with you?"

"Hop in." He opened the door and I obliged. He had a small fan plugged into the cigarette lighter adapter to help cool him off since the only air conditioning he had were the rolled-down windows. Mr. Feliciano used to buy ounces of bunk from me long ago so he could resell them at higher costs to people in richer communities. He was partly a reason why I have made my success as an agent, and over the years I had been thinking if he had left the business and decided to pursue a more lucrative career but one out of two wasn't bad. He was also my Uncle Felix, Angel's father, and the last time I saw him was many moons ago.

He took me out to lunch to Louie's place and that was where he brought me up to date on his current ventures and future plans and had tried for a long time to get in touch with me but I had gone underground and left only a small trace of my whereabouts. He had hooked up with Buddy and Juju for all of his wholesale supply needs when I left because I introduced them to each other before I did leave the bunk business. Of course, there was the one-time thousand-dollar fee to turn him on to my contacts, and I had already known that they were still conducting business because once a month Buddy and Juju found a way to have a courier send me my cash in a disclosed envelope which equaled to the seven percent of all sales made for using my customer. In return, I vouched for Mr. Feliciano and made sure everything was on the up and up.

We both grabbed a seat at the counter and he ordered the meatloaf while I ordered the lasagna. He glanced at his pager which had been set to vibrate if any calls came in, and it didn't look as if he was going to return the call.

"This guy keeps calling me, man, but I'm out." Felix murmured.

Louie was an Italian guy, medium build, average height, and brown straight hair which he wore down to about his shoulders. He wore his white apron and behind the counter, you can see his homemade sauce in a huge stainless–steel pot with a wooden spoon inside. He was really cool and down to earth. Mr. Feliciano had known Louie through his accountant and they both admired the professional receptionist their accountant had, and always found time to swap stories about encounters with her.

"I thought that was her," said Louie.

"I was supposed to have lunch with her today, but she said she had a lot of work to do. Maybe tomorrow. Hey, why don't you invite her here for lunch, Lou?"
"Hey, Lou, great lasagna, man." I interjected.

I tried to bring them back to reality and back to business. I grabbed a small portion of the Italian bread which complimented the meal and dipped it into the sauce. As I savored the sauce and the grated cheese which I sprinkled, my lunch partner kept talking about this woman and then finally, he stopped talking and started to eat. Fantasy time was over, and his meatloaf was getting cold. He grabbed the ketchup bottle and sprinkled some on the side of his plate.

"So, Corey, where do you know this guy from?" Lou asked me as he cleaned the countertop with his rag, and kept a close eye on his sauce.

"Eh, you know, around."
We both continued to eat, and while I dipped my bread again, Louie handed him an envelope.

"Give me two again," Lou whispered as Mr. Feliciano opened the envelope and counted the cash. He closed it and took another bite of his meal. As I sipped my soda through the straw, I looked outside the big windows to see if anyone was looking at us. There were scattered clouds in the sky, and there was hardly any traffic. A mother was carrying a young boy as they walked past the storefront, and she glanced at herself with the help of the reflection of the glass. We were sitting on stools which had our backs to the windows and the five tables which made up the small restaurant, and there was Joe. He was an older Italian man in his sixties who always had the corner table seat during lunch and was always reading the newspaper. He hardly said a word, but I was sure he was a great listener. When I was satisfied that the feds weren't going to bust in the place, I continued with my meal and slowly digested it. His pager went off again.
"Este maricón," He blurted under his breath.

"Why don't you just call him and tell him that you'll meet him later. Here... use my phone." Louie brought the phone from the back room, and the cord reached the counter.

"Yo...what's cooking?" He held his conversation while Louie stirred his sauce and I just continued to finish my plate.

When we were finished, I was asked to "take a ride into the City". I haven't heard that from anyone in a long time. Somehow, I traded the beautiful outings in New York for darker reasons. It was understood what was to happen, and I would possibly get a cut of the proceeds for my risk and cooperation.

My pager had gone off and when I saw the number was from Angel's house, I figured he saw my car parked on his block, but it was a bit too late because the wheels were already in motion. I thanked Louie for the great meal and asked him what tomorrow's special was. He said it was his Lobster Ravioli with pink vodka sauce, and with that, I asked him to save me a seat. I said goodbye to Joe, and he just looked at me and continued to chew on his toothpick.

We took the Turnpike towards the Holland and made for the Westside Highway. The local Spanish radio station gave an update on the traffic and weather, then introduced the next tune: *Hojas Blancas* by El Gran Combo. We stayed in the middle of the five-lane freeway so we would blend with the other motorists and passing Forty-Second Street, at a distant red street light, we witnessed two busty blondes wearing their "skimpies" slowly walking back and forth in front of a stretch white limo in which I possibly saw what may have been their pimps in the back seat. Further on to our left was the infamous Intrepid, and soon after that, we were at a stretch towards the 125th street exit. Upon exiting, there was a mechanic's shop and a McDonald's near the underpass. We made a left after the underpass and a right into what I called "no man's land".

At the red light, a guy came out with a squeegee and a spray bottle. He started spraying the windshield before he asked Feliciano if he wanted it clean. The water wasn't even clear and it looked a bit yellowish. He moved his van ahead up a foot or two, put his wipers on and told the guy that he didn't want it cleaned. He left us alone and went to the car behind us and did the same.

We made a left onto the main street and I looked around to get familiar with any emergency escape routes in case anything went wrong and as we stopped at the red light, I could not help but notice all the hungry opportunists staring at us. Our license plates were a dead giveaway that we not from around there. We were only a city block away from our spot and as we approached it and passed the arrival point because it was a One-Way towards the main strip, we were stopped at another red light. We had to make a sharp right, when the light would turn green, because of the triangular-shaped block.

I asked him to drop me off while we were stopped so that I could walk the rest and it would give him time to find a safe parking spot. He did so as he drove ahead two blocks away so no one else would notice the red van or the plates. I was sure to keep my hands out of my pockets so I would look relaxed and less vulnerable and although I used to stop by to pick up freight here every other week, there were always new faces around so I had to look for my boys. I noticed where Mr. Feliciano parked so it was time for me to approach the front of the building and make my move.

Usually, three guys stood in front of the gray twelve-story building, but all I saw were white men with dark, bulky vests. That was strange because it didn't look like they belonged there. Alas, I saw Tomas standing on the opposite corner, and he saw me. In an inconspicuous manner, he gestured to me that I should meet him around the block towards the main street by the pay phones.

I kept walking nonchalantly facing forward, but something told me to glance at the white men again. *Oh, boy.* They were DEA, about fifteen of them, and they were obviously looking for someone and it sure as hell wouldn't be me. I reached for the receiver of one of the pay-phones while Tomas grabbed the one next to mine. We had only pretended to talk into the phones but really spoke to each other.

"Hello, old friend. Wait another hour until the Feds leave. They're looking for someone else."

"Bueno. Nos vemos aurita." *Good. We'll see you later.*
I hung up while he stayed on the phone to make it seem as if he were still talking to someone else on the other end. I had walked completely around the triangular block and carefully approached the van which was still a block away. Another vendor came up to me and asked me if I needed anything. These opportunists don't give up. He wore a

brown coat with green jeans and looked rather scary. His brown cap cast a shadow over his face so I couldn't get a better look but I didn't want a better look so I had to decide what to do.

These types of transactions only took fifteen minutes tops and any longer than another fifteen minutes grace period would be a breach of services. Mr. Feliciano had been in the van nervous by now for it was nearing past a quarter of an hour. He spotted me talking to this new fellow and I glanced over at him, I signaled that it was all right. We didn't have the time to waste hanging around this area, and we couldn't leave empty-handed, so I took a chance. He nodded his head and lifted his arm to view his watch. Julio, as I quickly called him, and I, walked around the corner out of site to a six-story residential building not far from where the van was parked.

He opened the front door with a key, so I knew he had to have occupied one of the apartments in the building because if not, he could have buzzed in with the intercom system and alerted others. He held the door for me as my mind was in overdrive. *What if this was a sting operation conducted by the local authorities?* He was too ugly to be on the payroll. *Are there more than one people involved? What was waiting for me inside?* The partial broken black and white floor tiles and the brown-peeling paint suggested the poor maintenance of this building. He led the way to our third-floor ascent, and I cautiously walked up the long marble stairs looking at each door as if someone were going to jump out and grab me.

Less than five minutes in here, and so far, so good. A door had opened when we reached the second floor. It was a mother and her daughter, and after closing the door behind them they wistfully passed me on my left walking down the stairwell. I looked at the seven or eight-year-old girl when we passed each other, and she smiled at me with the cutest grin. Hopefully, she had not been exposed to the dealings of her neighbors in the building. We finally reached our floor and I followed him to the end of the hallway and he had his keys ready to open three locks.

I allowed a few seconds to pass before I entered his apartment. Apprehensively, I entered and he asked me to sit on his couch while he went to the kitchen to get his stash. I was too uneasy to sit so I stood and caught a glimpse of our escape vehicle outside through the heavy green curtains and, by now, my partner was leaning against his vehicle waiting to see me again. Julio came back into the room with a small bag and a pesa (Spanish for a scale) and this was a triple-beam. The triple-beam scale was the most practical, used and common tool for coke dealers because it measured in grams, ounces, and pounds.

"Two, right?"

"Yeah, two ounces," I said as I pulled out a stack of singles layered with a twenty-dollar bill on the outside. If I had told him I wanted two ounces when we first met, he would have known that I had about sixteen-hundred dollars on me. I always used that line on the other guys from my regular spot. The guys whom I've done that to before know me already and it had always been our secret but the newer guys would approach me and ask what I wanted. I only told them two grams to see if they would even bother with me and if they didn't, it was their loss. Those who have bothered to accommodate me received a nice surprise because they worked off the commission. For each gram they sell, they get 'x' amount of dollars. A gram cost about twenty-eight dollars from there, and two costs fifty-six and so forth. It was fairly competitive and there were a lot of vendors. Free enterprise is great and so is competition but Julio was a bit bewildered but also surprised.

"I thought you said two grams?"

"Yeah, but you look like someone I can do a lot of business with. How much will you give it to me for?" This was a little too heavy for him. He didn't have that kind of quantity and so he took his small bag and scale back to the kitchen and reentered the living room.

"Fifteen. Wait here. I'll be right back."

From his waistband, he pulled out a small pistol. It was silver and looked like it could do some damage.

"Don't worry. It's kind of rough around here." He said.

I heard the three locks, lock one after another. My heart was racing. I have never been in this type of complicated situation before and now he certainly knew that I had enough money for two ounces, so what if he came back with others? He could have robbed me right there. *What if it took more than fifteen minutes?*

I took another peek out the window and I hadn't seen the van. I looked around the room to see if there were any clues as to what I had to do next. A Botanical candle was unlit in a glass dish on a small wooden table in the corner of the living room, and it was surrounded by small wooden idols. Inside the dish were pennies and other coins probably placed there by many of the patrons who frequented this place for protection from evil? I threw in a dollar just for good measure. It was too high for me to jump out the window, and probably too suspicious if I walked out the front door and a couple of minutes later, I heard hollering in the hallway. A loud thud crashed into the door as if someone or something was thrown unto it, followed by two popping noises.

I ran towards the kitchen, and I hid in the bathroom located next to the stove. I didn't have time to unzip my pants and urinate in the toilet although I felt like I had to. There was silence, but I couldn't stay here forever so I walked into the living room and towards the front door. I unflapped the cover to the peephole and saw a man lying there on the ground motionless. I stepped back a few feet until I was almost in the middle of the room because I panicked and didn't know what to do. The doorknob was slowly turning and I slowly crept back towards the couch but after they were satisfied that the door was locked and they couldn't get in, the knob resumed back to its normal position.

I looked over at the kitchen with a stern face and headed in search of Julio's stash. I opened a few cabinet doors above his sink when I saw, next to his scale, the very same bag he showed me earlier. I grabbed it, but not after I struck gold by noticing dollar bills slightly hanging out the insides of a coffee can. I grabbed the can to waist level, and snatched the five wads of hundred-dollar bills wrapped tightly in rubber bands, and put them down my pants. The only thing that stood in the way, was whatever waited for me outside that door. I ran to it, looked through the peephole, slowly unlocked the door and slowly peered out.

Poor Julio. He had been shot in front of his own place and continued to stay motionless. Blood trickled from his mouth, and the upper part of his shirt had been bloodied. From the inside of his jacket, tucked in his front waist, was another bag that I almost didn't immediately notice. He must have finished his deal with his agent and was ambushed by some other agents. I grabbed the bag which could easily have been five ounces and didn't hesitate to tuck it down my pants as well. I suppose it was a territorial dispute because he had not been robbed. I wiped the cold sweat from my forehead and tucked in my shirt. As I quickly walked down the tenement stairs, the mother and daughter were walking up carrying two bags of groceries in brown paper bags. The little girl stuck her tongue out at me, and I dared not do the same but held a gesturing smile within.

I walked out of that building anxiously waiting for Mr. Feliciano to come to my rescue. I was so excited to see the sun and its rays as it hit my face. The same man who was in the front of my regular spot walked toward me with his bullet-proof jacket, 9mm pistol, and about fifteen other DEA agents. What broke my attention to them was a voice calling to me.

"Yo, man, you got a quarter?" a random stranger asked.

"No. Sorry," I said as I regained my bearings.

I casually walked towards the end of the sidewalk to cross but I was stopped by a van, and the driver had opened the passenger door for me. I was terribly glad to see him again. He smiled at me knowing that I was all right. I closed the door and locked it for safe measure. The last man had entered the building and as I looked up, I noticed the little girl looking out the window, down at me waving goodbye. Mr. Feliciano made a left at the corner, and we dared not look back. *There had to be a better way than this.*

We soon looked for signs for the Westside Highway but in the meantime, we drove south towards Manhattan so that we could either escape via the Holland or Lincoln Tunnel. When we finally did see a sign, we were careful not to make the right turn at the red light, and as though it were the only exit out of the neighborhood, we kept a watchful eye of possible ambushes by the police. I had made this trip together many times before and each time there was something that disabled me from taking the same route out of the neighborhood, but inevitably the multiple possibilities of exits almost always lead us to the same exit. It was like the Children of the Corn but in the city.

He had asked me if he could use my place to sort and pack his goods so he could get it ready for distribution that afternoon. I suggested to him that he put in a little extra towards my share for all of my troubles and when he obliged, we were off to the crypt. My uncle wouldn't be home until eleven thirty, and he wouldn't know if anyone else was there. Besides, my plan was to fix up the place and to get it ready for our evening games. It was just going to be a small poker game with a few of the guys. He parked his van across the street and we approached the old building with great observation and attentiveness because we were not safe until we were tucked away in our own environment and element.

He liked the place because it was quiet and non-conspicuous, and the concept of just having a place for sleeping quarters enthralled him. I quickly cleaned off the small wooden table that was standing beside the wall, and he placed his paraphernalia and began doing his craft of chopping and weighing. I made sure the shades were closed so no one could look in, and turned on the lamp to illuminate the evil that was taking place and also, I kept busy by folding all the clothes that were still in garbage bags and neatly placing them in a corner next to the couch.

Like Frankenstein, I looked at my protégé and could not stop to think about how I created a monster out of him. I taught him everything I knew about the business and he was hooked. All the ins and outs, the tricks, secrets, but most of all the golden rule – "do not get high off your own supply." By me showing him what he found out to be enjoyable and addictive, I collected on all transactions, no matter how small, by the simple introduction and insurance of all the connections I made in my past. I still hadn't told him about the stash I found on Julio as I left his apartment. That was for me to sell to him at a later date because if he knew I had it now he would have taken credit and possibly even want it for less than it's worth. You have to always be thinking in this game, and whoever has the most without getting caught, wins.

I was almost finished with the apartment and Mr. Feliciano was on his twenty-eighth gram when I heard the street sweeper coming. I looked through the shades and realized that he was parked on the side that would be swept that day. I told him and as he looked for his keys, he asked me to resume and to separate the next ounce into eighths. He knew that I wouldn't take advantage of him, and so did I because he was the only one I trusted in this realm of trading, and I never told him that even though I'm sure he felt the same way.

I finished wrapping two bags when he returned, and when he resumed, I went to wash my hands so they wouldn't get numb. It was "fish scale" and was called so because of its shiny layers every time a chunk was taken off just like a fish's scale. It was potent stuff, and I taught him that he should never waste his time cutting or mixing his product with any other ingredient. If anything, he should cut down on the quantity and sell it as such, as opposed to messing around with the quality of the product.

"I'm done, Mariconsito. Toma...here's your cut, and since I made my first $100,000 last month, thanks to you, here's a little extra. I'll see you tomorrow for lunch at Louie's?"

"You got it. Your treat, right?" I asked.

"No. Your treat, maricón."

Why did I teach him how to be a wise-guy? He asked to leave his scale and other paraphernalia at the apartment for future uses, and so I cleaned it extra carefully and hid his things in the closet. He had a small portable black digital scale which if he got caught with it would have meant instant jail-time and sandwich bags which he would put his stash in. I put my cash, the initial sixteen hundred plus the two hundred he had given me for the ride plus Julio's cash stash from his coffee cans, along with my private stash, Julio's stash, in my safe, and when he returned, I asked him to drop me off right at a liquor store close to where he found me. Before parting, we exchanged information, so we could contact each other in the future, as immediate as tomorrow, and before long he received another page from his beeper, and dropped me in front of the local liquor mart.

CHAPTER XVII

Before I went inside the liquor store, I decided to call Angel from the payphone that was located next to a solicitor. I wondered what he was going to do with all the spare change he periodically collected from passersby. He looked like any other person, but he wore a baseball cap and kept looking at me as I walked away from the van towards the phone which didn't have too much graffiti on it. He thought I was going into the store, and that would have been his cue to ask me for change, but since I only went in to make a phone call, he hadn't asked yet. Calls were only a quarter, and I dropped it into the empty phone box and dialed the seven digits.

The change dispenser was missing its chrome molding.

"Yo. What's up? I'm right around the corner. Uh-huh...all right. I'll be inside." I conversed.

I hung up and he told me he was going to meet me at the liquor store and that's where we were supposed to go earlier but he wasn't home, or rather, there was no answer at his door. I quickly entered the store before anyone could even breathe a word to me and even though I hated drinking beer from a can, that was the way to go so we wouldn't have to pick up the possible broken glass. Besides, I didn't want anyone to hit anyone else on the head with the bottle if they became too rowdy or out of hand.

I grabbed a bottle of vodka for my personal stash, and we decided that five cases of beer were good enough. He came in through the automatic glass doors and found me down the aisle right away. Angel was laid back and looked comfortable with his denim shorts, a white T-shirt, and sandals.

"Yo, bro, what's up?" he asked me.

"Dude, I came by before. You must have been sleepin'."

"Nah... I was in the studio downstairs mixing some beats. Yo, I'm gonna produce my own label and shit."

"That's great, man. I'd like to stop by some time and check it out." We were walking around and looking for the cases of beer, and when we saw the price for the cases of cans, we grabbed the five cases.

"You set for tonight?" I tried to confirm.

"I've been practicing from the card chute and it's running smoothly."

"All right. Let's get this stuff to the apartment so I can clean the place up some more. Peter's comin', right?"

"Yeah, he knows about it and so does Frank. We'll be there earlier to help you set up."

Angel went in half with the bill and paid for his pack of Newport cigarettes separately, while I separately paid for my fifth of Smirnoff. We walked outside to load the booze into his jeep when the guy asked us for change. We just walked off as if we hadn't heard him.

After he helped me with the beers and left the apartment, I locked the door and put the chain on it too. I looked around to see where I would pick on the cleaning aspect, and I hadn't known where to put all the junk. I opened a bottle of iced tea from the fridge and took a swig. I decided that, before anything, I would take care of my own business first and see for myself just how much Julio's life was worth dying for. Under one of my boxes of stored clothes in the closet, I had my safe with all types of goodies in it.

With a couple of spins of the dial, the safe was opened and I started to bring out the sandwich bags, the scale, and the most important part, the stash. I turned the digital scale on and placed an empty bag on it, so I could reset it at zero because the bag itself weighed about ten grams. When I took off the empty bag the scale naturally read negative ten, and now I was ready to tally the total weight of the bag and its contents. I was impressed, and just sat there trying to come to a realization. I took it off and put it back on again because it totaled four hundred and forty-eight grams which were the equivalent of four ounces. The street value for a gram was fifty dollars, and if I had the time to sell it all in grams, I would make over twenty-two thousand dollars, but if anyone, like Mr. Feliciano, wanted it in a one-shot deal I would probably have sold it for about fourteen thousand easy.

I thought about Starlight Ave. If I sold it there the guys wouldn't have to go up the Hill for a long while and risk either getting ripped off or arrested. The quality was superb and they would be getting the finest product available. I would only be about a twenty-minute drive away via Route 1&9 or I could meet them at the train station which was only a five-minute walk from the crypt. Either way, there was a supply and demand and opportunity.

I put it all away, wiped it clean again and decided to leave it in one bag and wait for the huge sale. It took me about two hours to make the room presentable and get it ready. All I needed was the blackjack table from Angel's house and his eight decks of cards with the card chute. My game was Craps and I knew every odd, bet, crap and scam about the game. The dice were more favorable for me and I enjoyed being the pit boss and overseeing the numerous bets made behind the "pass line". The "pass line" was where a player put his minimum bet of five dollars and let the dealer know that the player was in the game and unlike blackjack, where the players bet against the dealer, craps involved playing against the dice, therefore why would anyone be angry with me?

Eleven o'clock was game time and Brougham showed up around ten-thirty. Peter came over with the blackjack table and was ready to help start the craps table. All the beer that could fit into the refrigerator had been cold already, and the ones that didn't make it remained hidden under a dark blanket in the back corner of the room behind me and the craps table.

"Where's Angel?" I asked Peter.

"He said he was comin'. I think he's hanging out with his girl, Frankie, and his girl."

"Well, no one was to know about the operation. How is it that their girls know?" I further wondered.

I never gave up my shirt and tie clothing regime from going to Catholic school and wearing uniforms throughout my teens, including Prep school. I never got into the urban outfitting of proposed style and relax-fitted apparel. Because I didn't look like everyone else, I never really looked like I fitted in with the others except that I knew these particular guys and they didn't care.

The doorbell rang again and five more guys showed up. I had put some very low music on in the background and had asked everyone to relax until Angel and Frank showed up. It was eleven-thirty and Peter and I decided to "get the show on the road."

"Guys, anyone want a beer? It's 'happy hour' until midnight and then they're a dollar."

They each grabbed one just to calm down, relax and take advantage of the free booze. The doorbell rang again and a couple of more guys came. Abner, Angel's brother, had come over just to watch and he didn't want to partake in the games because he was studying to become a State Trooper, and he didn't want to be involved in any illegal activities. He knew that by just being there, he was a co-conspirator, but I think I might have peer-pressured him into staying. I offered him an iced tea because I knew he wouldn't accept a beer, and he pulled out a Macanudo from his shirt pocket and lit it. The side window was opened slightly, but that type of smoky environment was expected and ultimately favored.

"Anyone else for a cigar? Five bucks a piece."

I had a box of Optimo cigars on top of the kitchen countertop, and several ashtrays were already scattered around the room.

"Yeah, I'll take one. Here you go."

I asked Brougham, and the others, to please not smoke on the tables and to be careful with the ashes. Some of these guys just needed to be reminded, so I took out my Zippo from my pocket and lit his cigar, as a compliment for purchasing it for five bucks, plus I wanted everyone to feel comfortable so they wouldn't feel bad when they lost all of their money.

Peter and I finally started to get the games rolling without the other two because I hadn't even known if they would even come at this point.

"Shooter...shooter...lookin' for a shooter. Five-dollar minimum. Lookin' for a seven or an eleven on the opening roll. Lookin' for a shooter."

It was an oval table which accommodated eight players and I stood behind one of the oblong sides while Peter sat across from me on the other oblong side. My job was to pay out the winners and to get the game moving. I held the stick which brought the dice back to the shooter after it hit the wall and bounced the combination. Each die had a different number, in dots, from one to six on each of its six sides. *Seven* or *eleven* on the open roll was good, and if a *two* or a *twelve* was rolled, it was a loser or "craps". Brougham's friend, Eric, stepped up to try his luck at the dice.

"Shooter, hit the wall. All bets down."
Out of the ten dice I pushed over to him with my wooden stick, he had to pick two and only use one hand when he rolled. He rolled a five.

"Five...five...five's the point."

"Twenty-two on the inside, but move my five on the nine," Brougham said.

"Five on the field," a guy said as he placed his chip on the field numbers. "Five" was the point number, and now the object of the game was to throw a "five" before a "seven" was thrown. A "seven" thrown now had a "craps" status, and Eric didn't want that.
"C'mon...five."
He threw the dice, and then I noticed my uncle walking in from his hard day at work.

"All the guys who had their money on the pass line won their pass line amount, and whoever had bet "five", won. For every five dollars placed on the winning "five", the winner received seven dollars, and their five-dollar chip was left there until a seven was rolled or until they wanted it moved somewhere else. There were so many possibilities for winning which was another reason why I favored it, but the odds were in the table's favor. My uncle had no idea what would be going on tonight, but he handled it quite well.

"Bro..." he said as he opened the fridge and saw all that beer.

"Take one. Take two."

"Winner. Shooting for a new point. Let's go, shooter."

I paid the winners out accordingly and Peter also made sure there was no foul play. The doorbell rang and Pedro answered it. It was Angel and Frank with their girlfriends, and they were upset that we had started the games without them. They also came in hearing that Eric hit the point, and some of the guys were winning. The girls sat on the couch while Frank ran the poker table and Angel started to run the blackjack table. A few more guys showed up including Angel's friend Joey.

Joey was a shorter guy, probably a few years younger than me, and looked like he was there to have a good time. He wore a black biker cap, carried a smile and asked for a beer.

"Sure. The first one's on me."

He sat at the blackjack table towards the far left, as the anchor, as soon as Angel was finished shuffling. Three other guys sat at the table and were casually calm as they enjoyed the environment and mood in which they could gamble as much as they wanted and not worry about anything else but losing at the cards.

The object of the game was to reach a total of "twenty-one" and not go over or to beat the total that the dealer had. Two cards were given and the play was against the dealer. The dealer had to "hit" on sixteen but had to stay on seventeen. If no cards were desired it was considered a "stay". It was a rather impersonal game in which hand movements determined whether a card was wanted or not. Pointing or tapping the cards signified wanting another card, and waving passed or over the cards meant that no more cards were needed.

Marcos cut the deck and the game was about to start.

"Place your bets. Two-dollar minimum." When Angel saw that all bets were placed, he gave a quick wave above the table to iterate that there were no more bets to be placed. Joey took another drink from his beer, perhaps, to slowly dull the pain of losing. The cards were being dealt one by one clockwise starting with the Marcos, who was to the left of the dealer, face up. The dealer dealt his first card face down. One more time around but this time Angel dealt his second card face up with a seven showing. The table lamp brightened the green felt and accented the whites of the card borders.

"Dealer has a seven showing...possible seventeen."

Noise was coming from my craps table as the players anticipated Abner hitting the point. Abner was somewhat in the spirits and decided to try a round or two.

"Five-dollar hard tens, two-dollar "acey-deucey", and a two-dollar "yo," Abner exclaimed. A "yo" bet was a combination totaling eleven and, in this game, it was always a six and five combination.

"Five-dollar 'yo'," I yelled.

"Five-dollar 'yo'," Frankie responded from his poker table.

"Five-dollar 'yo'," Angel patronized.

"Yo" Abner yelled as he threw the dice and rolled a "yo eleven."

The table went wild, and the guys were feeling his excitement. Brougham raised his cigar and gestured to Abner that it was a great roll, while I carefully paid him out his winnings. The other guys were feeling the mood and quickly threw cash on the table so I could convert it into chips. Abner threw the house a five-dollar tip which would be divided at the end of the night amongst the four of us. I grabbed the chip, tapped the table three times with it and placed it in a glass box that was designed as the tip box.

Meanwhile, at the blackjack table, Joey was deciding whether he wanted to hit on his fifteen, a king and five combo, because of the possible seventeen for the dealer. He tapped his cards. Angel dealt the next card which was a four.

"Nineteen. Dealer has..." He flipped his first card over and it was a four. "A four. Eleven."

"Dealer hits and gets...a 'one-eyed jack'... twenty-one." He collected the losing chips from each player clockwise, first, then discarded their cards. They hadn't stopped there. As we had hoped, they doubled their bets to cover their previous loss. We wanted the players to come into the games betting high and enjoying the possibility that they just might beat the house, but the odds were always in the house's favor. The girls had seen enough and decided to leave and they did look out of place, and I hadn't expected to see them in an environment like this with all these other guys. They each told their man that they were leaving, and said goodbye.

The poker table was running a little slow so Frank did the right thing by shutting it down temporarily and joining us at my table. We were not allowed to drink until the end of the games when everyone left, but it didn't apply to Peter who was on his fourth can and probably smoked half of his pack of Newports.

"Yo, man, I want to play too."

He brought his ashtray which stood about three feet from the ground on his wooden table and he threw twenty bucks on the table. Peter's job was to tally everyone's bet in an inconspicuous manner. He especially made note of the "sleeper" players we had such as Abner and Peter. Their major function was to entice or entrap, other players, to join in on the games. They acted as the relatives who wanted to win a couple of dollars and weren't entirely negative about the whole operation. They would each receive whatever monies they invested back at the end of the night when we divided the earnings, plus their cut of the operation.

A few hours had passed and we decided to announce a "last call" when four o'clock came around. We had been quiet enough as to not disturb the others in the building, and luckily no one got out of hand. Joey had been winning on the blackjack table and was up about three hundred bucks and while his winnings came from Marcos who lost nearly five fifty, Brougham decided to leave after only losing a hundred bucks and having a great time doing so. The craps table was done for the evening and I was busy putting the chips and dice away, while Pedro had gone to use the bathroom in the hallway. The crowd started to file out thanking us for the hangout. Joey, however, felt lucky and decided he wanted to stay and try his luck at the poker table.

Joey sat at the table with Angel and Frank at a small round table, while I paid out Abner and Peter for their help in the evening. I asked Abner if he wanted to stay a bit longer, but he said he had to get up early that morning to work out at the gym, and after that, he was to go and see his girlfriend, Kimberly. Peter left with him and I heard the two of them say goodnight to my uncle as he was reentering the room from his trip from the bathroom.

"They're still playing? I'm tired from work."

"They'll be done soon. How was work?"

"Man, I can't believe it. Fourteen hours overtime this week. I love it." I asked the guys if they wanted anything to drink. Frank said that he did, and winked.

"What are you having, Frank?" Angel asked.

"The same thing I always have after these games. Corey knows."

I poured a glass of orange juice with some of my vodka on top. It wasn't even a teaspoon, but it was set there to give it an odor in case there were any nonbelievers. I walked over to the table and asked Angel if he wanted any. I winked at him.

"Sure, why the hell not. I'm overworked here anyway."

"Comin' right up."

Joey became a little curious, but he was still undecided whether he wanted to join in on the poker game and hang with the big boys. When I turned my back to get another drink, Angel was asking him if he wanted one and that they were drinking Screwdrivers – a mixture of orange juice and vodka.

"Make that two more," he said.

"Two more comin' right up."

Angel started to shuffle the cards, and since Frank was sitting to his left, he cut the cards. It was "dealer's delight" which meant that whoever was dealing the cards would be deciding what the game was. In this case, it was "Seven-Card Draw" with sixes being wild. I came over and placed Angel's juice with a smidgen of vodka, next to him, and placed Joey's glass of vodka with just enough juice that he wouldn't be able to recognize the lighter color of yellow in his glass from the others, next to him.

I walked over to Pedro who had turned the radio a little higher and lit a cigarette and told him that the game would definitely be over within the hour. I slipped him his cut for playing the craps table, and he just told me to get some cleaning stuff for the apartment with it but took twenty bucks of it to play the NJ lottery later. He kept himself busy by looking through some store circulars which periodically came to the apartment, and he took note of all the specials and sales occurring in each store.

I made myself some orange juice, which I had a strong distaste for ever since my grandmother would serve me Tang with every one of my meals when I was younger, but it was very important to keep the appearance that we would all be drinking. I grabbed a folding chair, turned it around and sat on it waiting for an auspicious time to get into the game so I could "ante up", or bet the minimum. After watching a couple of hands go by, I saw my opportunity to play my part.

"I'm in."

"All right, Core, it's your deal. What's the game?"
I grabbed the deck and shuffled it, with a few passes, and shuffled some more. I sat between Joey and Frank and when I was finished shuffling, I placed the deck on the table and allowed Joey to cut the cards. He tapped the top of them which signified that he was satisfied with the cut.

"Seven-card 'no peek' and 'Suicide Kings' are wild. Beat a nine," I said as I cut the deck nearly halfway showing a nine of diamonds and put the pile back in place. I dealt the cards and whoever had the highest had the option of "checking" or "betting." There were only twelve dollars in the pile when Angel decided he was out of the game because he hadn't thought he could beat Joey's pair of fours. He, on the other hand, felt that his fours were powerful enough to win him the round so he bet two bucks. Will and I each put in our two bucks.

"Two fours showing...I have a possible flush...and Frank has..." I dealt his card, "two Queens. Frank, check or bet?"

"I check."

"I bet another two bucks," Joey said confidently.

"I'm out," I blurted.

"All right. It's just youse two."

This went on for quite a while with Joey winning more and more. That was part of the game within itself. A few rounds of drinks later, we started to act as if we were drunk enough to lose silly hands and gave Joey the confidence and upper hand in winning. He had been up a few hundred, but not enough to clear a thousand. It was Frank's deal and he switched the game to "Guts". That game was a bit simpler and took a bit of courage, hence the name. Two cards were dealt to each player and the one with the highest card won. If the player lost, he would have to match what was in the pile, while the winner would win the pile. If two players lost the hand, each would have to match the pile, and so forth. If the player had a two of a kind, the loser would have to pay double the amount in the pile. Finally, if the winner had two aces and the other player lost, the payout was triple the pile. The player only lost if he decided to stay in the game, and lost with the lower card.

After a couple oh hands, I started talking to my uncle who was keeping himself out of the game and concentrating more on his sales on Sears tools.

"Anything good?"

"You don't understand. There's a beautiful sale starting tomorrow." I could hear the riffling of cards as the others were casually talking about the card game to be held the following day. I finished concocting our potions and made sure Joey got his potent mixture.

"What's the pile at now?" I asked.

"One forty-four," Joey stated as he was intent on winning all of it.

"I just tried to bluff since there was a lot of cash. I thought you might have been scared to stay in, but I guess I was wrong," I blurted in a buzzed state. "All right, Frank, wheel 'em and deal 'em."

"Dude, cut 'em." I did and we were off to another hand of "guts".

"Angel...a four...Joe opens with a deuce...Corey shows a ten...and I have...a Jack. Down and dirty." He dealt our second cards and we held them up pretty sternly above the new jackpot.

"One...Two...Three."

Since Frank had a Jack showing it was only fair to say that he had the highest, but when we each held on to our cards, we felt that someone had a pair, or just brave enough to think that their card could beat Frank's Jack.

"Oh, man," I said in disgust. The others had the same look on their face except for Joey who immediately turned his cards over revealing a pair of deuces. He seemed pretty excited to think he had won but I just happened to pull off a pair myself. I grabbed my winnings, and they each put in two hundred and eighty-eight leaving the total in the pile to be eight hundred and sixty-four.

"This is crazy, man. There's eight hundred in the pile."

"Eight hundred sixty-four to be exact," Joey exclaimed.

"Well each of us won, and now maybe it's your turn, Joe," Angel consolingly told him.

We figured we had the bite on him so we wanted to lure him in and finish him off. He was hungry for that money. He had been winning, or under the illusion that he had been winning, for the whole evening and it would have been nice to break the bank and beat the house, so before the next round was dealt, I grabbed the bottle and two shot glasses, because I only had two, and two regular glasses and poured some vodka in each.

"Bottoms up."

"Cheers, big ears," I said as I looked at Frank and Angel while I took my shot. While Joey was busy trying to shake off the gradual buzz from the alcohol, he had been fed during the course of the table action, and while he was drinking his shot, Frank placed the necessary cards he needed on the bottom of the deck. I looked Joey in the eyes and even tapped his shot glass after he drank it to further distract and misdirect him from Frank. With a couple of false passes and sleight–of–hand, I was ready to cut the cards. He placed them in front of me and I just tapped them signifying that I was satisfied with the deal.

"All right. This time both cards are down. Down and dirty."

He dealt our two cards each, and Angel said that he liked his hand. Joey was deliberately dealt two Kings, and he was definitely tempted.

I interrupted and told them that I was confident with my hand, so I licked the back of my Ten and let it adhere to my forehead.

"Well, shit. If you're gonna show your Ten..." Frank did the same with his Jack and stuck it on his forehead. Frank and I taunted each other on who had the higher card and that I had better have something higher than his Jack to beat him. As we were bickering, Angel asked us if we were still in and that it was our last chance to give up. He got bold.

"I'll even throw in this ring to show how confident I am." He placed the ring, he had found by the woman who lost her finger on that freeway, on top of the table and it was gleaming with tempting treasure.

"My Ace beats your Ten and Jack, so you better have an Ace to at least beat me." He hadn't shown an Ace or either of his cards which left him out to become a potential bluffer.

"All I have is my red Vette outside, and I think you're bluffing so here are my keys. I don't think you can beat my

Ten. I call your bluff." I threw my car keys on the table and left them thinking.

"Joe?"

He looked around and stood quietly, thinking about his options and how maybe this could be his break. He was feeling a bit happy and from the booze we were consuming, he had to have thought we were totally out of our minds too, but he had a solid pair of Kings. Perhaps he thought I had a pair of Tens and Will had a pair of Jacks, and that was why I called Angel's bluff when he had an Ace showing, but Joey had his pair.

"Frank?"

"I'm not saying anything until Joe decides. It's his turn to check or bet." My card was still stuck to my forehead and Frank's wasn't going anywhere, and Joey must have thought we were clowns.

"How much is that diamond worth?"

"I would say about a couple of thousand."

"And your Vette?"

"I paid a little over a thousand for it. I have all the receipts."

He took a swig from the remainder of his screwdriver and professed.

"I'm in."

He threw the keys of his '86 Buick Riviera on the table. I got up to the window to take a look at it as it was parked across the street. I sat back down and asked him if he wanted to sell it to me, but he refused because he had already placed it as a bet and because he was that confident that he would not and could not lose that hand.

"I'm out," Frank said. I've got nothing." He threw his cards on the table but dealt the hand.
"Ready? One...Two...Three."

It was silly to think that either one of us would be out after we placed our high stakes. I peeled the card from my skin and flipped my other card revealing my two Tens. There were *oohs* and *aahs* from the others, and even though it wasn't Joey's turn he showed his pairs of Kings and we shouted out loud that I was beaten, and that I lost my car. Amidst Joey's glory, Angel turned his cards over and revealed two Aces, which mysteriously appeared thanks to Frank's wizardry. Joey couldn't believe it but we immediately made it seem that it was a night of chance and distracted his thoughts of misery with beliefs of the "easy come, easy go" cliché. Along with our car keys, Angel grabbed the cash that came with it and placed it in his pocket.

I took out my cash, fastened to my money clip, from my left pocket and started to count out two-thousand five hundred and ninety-two bucks that I had just lost from the Aces which paid out triple, while Joey held his head straight and flushed with the idea that he had lost everything he had come in with. Frank had no problem paying his two-thousand plus wager, and after Joey tried to make sense of it all, reached into his pocket and just about covered his loss, although he probably wouldn't mentally recover.

Joey embarrassingly decided to go, but we tried to tell him that there was over seven thousand in the pile and he still had a chance to win it all back. Ultimately, he was out the next round with and Four and a Six and officially lost. I made a small stink on how I should have stopped while I was ahead, but that was the curse of the gambler – not knowing when to quit. As a consolation, Angel offered to take him home, but he decided he would rather walk the two miles back to his home. When he left, the three of us split all the money that we had been keeping in our right pockets, I took my car keys back and the only lingering factor was what to do with the Riviera.

No one wanted it, but I made an offer and bought it from my share and now I was the owner of the car and it only cost me three hundred for each of them totaling six hundred and they were more than happy to accept. Problem solved.

"Were there any problems tonight?"

"Nah, Nicky was in for three hundred and he said he'd square up with me tomorrow."

"All right, but that's a hundred towards me and gas money for my new ride."

"I got this."

The following day Angel went over to Joey's to get the title, and that same day I straightened everything out with the Department of Motor Vehicles to make me the new proud owner. After the proper documents were filed accordingly, I went to Tutta Bene to celebrate with a nice meal.

CHAPTER XVIII

"Hey, Louie. Hey, Joe."

"Corey, what's up? Here, try some of my Lobster Ravioli."

"Sounds good." I plopped on the stool at the counter and looked around, but no one was there because I just made it before the lunch crowd. We made small talk as the smell of his tasty concoctions filled the place, and left me with a wonderment of hunger. The door had opened and a slender professional woman in her late twenties entered and filled the room with her aura. She had long blonde hair and long legs, and it was when she sat two stool lengths away from me, did I smell her enticing perfume.

"Hi, Louie."

His back had been turned but when he heard her voice, he stopped stirring his sauce and automatically walked up towards her from behind the counter.

"Hi, Veronica. How're things? You look good today."

"Well, thanks. I'm here to meet Feliciano. Have you seen him today?"

"Yeah, he was here earlier. Let me page him."

As Louie used his phone to summon him, she glanced over at me with a smile and looked back away towards Joe who sat at the corner table, as usual, reading the paper.

"Hey, Joe, what are you reading?"

"Stock picks, my love. How else is anyone going to afford to take you all over the world and to buy lovely jewelry for such a pretty girl?"

"Oh, Joe, pick us a winner."

I hadn't said a word. She was in the spotlight and I wanted to learn more about what she was about. I took note of her persona and of what Joe said, and I temporarily thought about taking my money and investing it in the market but was distracted by Mr. Feliciano's presence into the restaurant. She played it cool and remained on the stool, and he instinctively walked over to her and sat to her left.

"Hey, sexy. Have you been here long?" Felix asked.

"I just paged ya'. What's up?" Louie greeted him.

I walked over to the refrigerator which had the vast selection of soft drinks and decided to leave the others alone. As I grabbed a bottle and made my way out the door, I motioned to Louie that I would be in the front.

Once outside, I took in a deep breath and hailed another glorious day in which I was free to do anything I wanted. I had walked away from most of my troubles and quarrels and it was just me and the world. I twisted the bottle open and only took a sip of my water, and why not – I had all the time in the world to finish it, whenever I wanted to. Angel had turned the corner and approached me.

"What's up?" he asked.

"Where are you coming from?"

"Nicky's house. I saw him this morning and he told me that he didn't have the money, so I told him he had until today."

I heard a loud thunderous sound coming from a block away.

"What the hell was that?" I asked.

"It's probably the M–80 I stuck on his windshield."

I looked at him in confusion.

"I took a cigarette and cut it in half, stuck the M–80 fuse towards the filter and lit the cigarette. Oh yeah, and I taped the cigarette to his windshield which the whole thing gave me enough time to walk over here and here I am."

"You're nuts," I told him.

He walked off, and I started to go back inside when Veronica opened the door and smiled at me as she walked into her black Mercedes which was parked out front. The guys saw me but mainly kept their eyes focused on her through the large windows. They snapped out of hypnosis and Mr. Feliciano greeted me.

"Interested in selling your car? I got a buyer who just needs it to get back and forth to work."

"My Vette? Six hundred and nothing less."

"Sold. Let me call him. I told him seven. You don't mind that I made a hundred off of it, do you?"

"Nah. Besides, you can start driving me around now."

"Maricón."

I owned the Riviera now and it was great timing and ideal for me. The money I would make would be given to my father since he bought the car for me as a high-school Graduation gift for exactly the same amount. Retribution was at hand and was a small token for all the things my father had given me. He got off his phone and told me that it was a deal.

My uncle Pedro wanted to leave our crypt because it was too small for both of us, plus he missed his friends from his previous apartment. He outweighed his options and decided that he would sacrifice the commute to his job after all. I didn't mind because I got a chance to see Mr. Feliciano, gain some extra cash and own a new car. Another start to a new beginning was forming and it couldn't get any worse. I took everything that happened into perspective and tried to learn from it.

That night, I decided to hang out at Angel's basement studio to unwind and get into some music and after a few hours the doorbell rang, and not a moment too soon when we stopped listening to some new import records that were sort of monotonous.

"Is your brother home?" I asked him, to see who would open the front door.

"Nah. Can you get that?" he insisted.

I went upstairs and opened the door only to see two apparent hoodlums staring at me.

"Wassup. Is Angel here?" the one with the North Carolina Tar Heels cap asked. "Yeah. He's downstairs. Come on in." They both followed me down to the basement and Angel was seemingly delighted to know they were there, but I wasn't impressed by the mood of a surprise. I hate surprises. Things started to become dull, and I just wanted to mellow out and perhaps just even watch television in the living room upstairs.

"Yo, man, you wanna just go for a ride? Kev and John live in Union. It's only down the road, and we'll grab something to eat on the way back."

"Let's hit the diner, Angel." John proposed.

"'Bump that', I don't have money for the diner. We're dropping your asses off first."

"Let's go," I demanded. I didn't want to make a project out of the whole thing, and I certainly wasn't pleased about being associated with two guys who pretended to live in the ghetto.

"Nice watch." John blurted about my silver Tissot wrist watch. I wasn't sure if he was being sincere about his compliment or it was just good enough for him to try to steal from me later. Typically, while growing up in the urban city, a couple of bandits who have made mention of my watch were intending to rob me of it.

John was maybe fifteen with a burgundy pro-basketball cap, which he crookedly wore, a navy-blue windbreaker, with matching pants, and white sneakers. He hadn't a hint of facial hair, and without his present gear, he appeared to be an average clean-cut kid. Kevin had the Tar Heels uniform except that it looked like it belonged to an actual basketball player judging on the length of the pants, because they drooped down from his waist, and he wasn't that tall.

I drove my new car, Angel sat 'shotgun', while Kevin sat behind me and John next to him.

"Yo, slow down, Yo."

"That's the car that was rockin' by the schoolyard yesterday. It's got two eighteen-inch Pro-Pyles in the back. They're not mounted, and a Bose Gooseneck. See it hiding under the seat? And a Kenwood Benzi. Jackpot." I slowly crept away because I didn't want to be involved in any funny business.

"Yo, we gotta come back later tonight," John said as if *we* meant a part of me. I drove off and made it to the main street and thought to myself that I should relax, and not let these two jerks bother me.

I kept looking in my rear-view mirror, and they noticed that I was on full alert. I would make the best getaway driver. I always noticed everything, and tried never let anything get past me. I guess they tried to diffuse my concentration, or to try to lighten me up, so John tried to change the mood.

"Why don't you have a Puerto Rican flag hanging from your mirror?"

"I was born in America, and I'm proud to be an American as well as being a Puerto Rican, so why don't I have an American flag? As a matter of fact, I rarely see any American flags hanging from any part of a car. Either no one is American or they're not proud to be one. I think they're all waiting for a major disaster to happen so they can all unite and say, 'Hey, we're American.' What kind of flag do you have on your car?"

"I don't have a car."

"Well shut the fuck up then..."

I was being followed by a couple of marked police vehicles, and I let the rest of the carload know.

"If he turns on his lights, I'm hauling ass. I ain't gonna stop."

There was silence in the car, finally, as if they were all shocked that I spoke about being deviant.

"Just turn at the next corner and we'll be out of Hillsdale."

Just then the blue and red lights were turned on and my passengers were wondering whether I would actually yield to the authorities or not. Like the lawful wuss, I pulled over immediately and reached into my back pocket and retrieved my license and registration from my wallet. I rolled down the window and anticipated the officer's walk to my side. A bright light shined from the rear window, but it didn't deter the two guys from moving around so frantically. I continued to look straight, and from my peripheral, I noticed another officer approaching the vehicle from the passenger side with a drawn pistol facing the ground.

"Remember when the cops pulled us over in Stanhope? Of course, you don't...you were passed out. Try to stay awake for this one." I reminded Angel.

"License and registration please," the officer demanded.

I handed him the already prepared documents. His flashlight focused on the vital information, and when he realized my papers were in order, he asked me for my insurance card. Another flashlight was pointed towards Angel from the passenger side and when I reached over and opened the glove compartment, the spotlight was focused on its inside contents. The radio scanner which I purchased from Eddie at the Feast for forty dollars, was in the process of falling out but Angel reflexively stopped it from hitting his knees.

"Gun!" the officer's partner yelled seeing a dark object on Angel's possession.

He had quickly placed it towards the back of the compartment while I tried to search for the necessary paperwork.

Before I could sit up straight in my seat, the officer had pulled out his firearm, pointed it at my head, and ordered me to get out of the car. His partner started screaming at Angel to keep his hands up. Angel froze and did what he was told.

I hadn't even looked towards the back seat. I didn't have permission to.

"Slowly open the door with your right hand," the partner yelled.

He did so, and I was dragged out of my vehicle and told to put my hands on the trunk. There were so many lights. I thought it was only the one patrol car, but as I looked around there were two detective vehicles because they were unmarked, two marked cars and each of the officers had their guns drawn. Angel was escorted back to one of the other patrol cars and questioned. The officer who pulled me over told the two guys in the back not to move, while he obtained the insurance card from the glove compartment and also helped himself to the scanner. Another cop approached him and investigated the scanner. He looked at it, or should I say, admired it. When he turned it on, it didn't take long for it to pick up a frequency.

"This looks better than ours," he said to his partner.

"Where did you get this?" he asked me.

"From Radio Shack...it's tuned into the City frequencies, not anywhere local."

He turned back to his partner, while my hands were still frozen on the trunk of my car.

"These frequencies are programmed, and they're pretty long."

"Yeah, I don't think he could have changed the frequencies and reprogrammed them in this short of time."

"How can we compete with this equipment? Our radios are shit." A cop said.

"Listen, buddy. All the other guys are minors and you're the only one of age...so turn around. We have to arrest you. Luckily, your passenger has a license. Does he have your permission to take the vehicle out of here?"

I told him that it was fine. I was in shock, so I went along with the whole thing not even questioning why I had been arrested. My Miranda Rights were read to me, and I agreed to remain silent. I kept thinking that this was all a joke and this whole thing was just to scare me to the very end, but I was handcuffed and placed in the back seat of a patrol car, and it wasn't funny. Angel looked over at me and told me that he would have me bailed out, and then all I heard was the dispatcher from the policeman's car radio.

"You go to school?" the arresting officer asked.
I told him the name of the University where I was currently being educated as a Freshman in '90. The officer looked at his partner as if he felt guilty for arresting me.

"I pulled you over for a broken headlight. You're being charged with possession of an illegal scanner in your vehicle. What appeared to be a firearm falling out of your glove box gave us probable cause to search your vehicle."

"I bought that scanner from Radio Shack. We launched into space using Radio Shack parts," I objected.

"Having a legal scanner, in a legal vehicle, in transport, makes it illegal."
"Do you have money to post bail?" another officer asked.
"No. I don't have cash on me and I don't have that much in the bank."
I could have told him that I had purchased the scanner that day and that I was bringing it home, but I didn't have a receipt for it. Not having a receipt is not entirely illegal, and possession is nine-tenths according to the law. The theory was that the authorities were worried that while some criminals were in the process of committing a crime,

or stealing cars which was what they thought we were up to, the former would tune into the police frequencies to monitor if an alert had been sent out. The fact that my frequencies were tuned to the City made it less likely that I was up to no good locally. I don't write the laws, but I just try to obey them.

They escorted me to my new rest–stop. It was my own holding cell equipped with bunk beds and on the way there, I overheard two officers talking amongst themselves about me.

"Union is the number one town for car thefts, then Newark, then Hillsdale."

"Where was he?"

"Hillsdale, but his car was spotted in Union looking into a vehicle."

"Any broken glass?"

"Negative. Everyone was clean and nothing was vandalized, but since we were all at the scene, we had to charge him for something."

I couldn't sleep. I did some push-ups, general calisthenics, but most importantly I wanted to be aware and prepared for my bail-out. The fluorescent lights in the holding cell were too bright anyway. I asked myself how I got into this situation. *What was the precipitating event that led me here?* After several scenarios and angles running through my head, it became obvious that there was something or someone that I needed to avoid. *Angel.* My decision to roll with his careless mentality, his association with two derelicts and whichever absent-minded hoodlums, and his disrespect for order and rules, had led me astray from the organized, clean and reputable businesses I was regularly and associated with. Karma will get them, I thought to myself, and I do not want to see them ever again. Embarrassingly, I made a bad choice of friends and character and didn't recognize it until it was too late. I got into trouble every time I hung out with this dude. *If I don't cut him out of my life, I will get into worse situations.*

It was like the time I asked him to do a run for me in the City. I gave him $2,500.00 to buy me a pound of weed. He had been with me to the spot a couple of times enough for him to be recognized and vouched by me, and he would get compensated for going. When he didn't contact me until hours later, I became concerned. Finally, after receiving a page that he arrived at the bottom of my street block, I got dressed and met him there. He proceeded to tell me the story of how he was "jumped and robbed by armed men". He hadn't gone alone because he brought those two knuckleheads with him, and one of them decided that it was safer to hold all that marijuana on their person instead of leaving it in the car while they shopped for their own drugs, and when I saw him in the backseat I ran up to the car and opened the door to fuck him up, but Angel insisted that it wasn't their fault and that I should chill and he would personally pay me back. Ultimately, he still hasn't compensated me for my investment. No money, interest or weed. *Trouble*.

How did it get to be this way? Our mothers were sisters and that made us first cousins, so it may be safe to say that we shared some similar behaviors and values taught to us through one side of the family's experiences. We only lived about a twenty-minute drive from each other, he lived in Elizabeth, and I, in Jersey City. He attended a public school and probably had the same number of friends as I did. I was afforded the luxuries of attending private schooling and my parents did so to prevent any negative influences that the Streets may offer from not having an educational background. With every decision we each made in life, no matter how minute, it drew us closer to our own and unique fates. Of course, there were those instances that were beyond our choice or control.

While my dad spent most of his time working at a company full-time and pursuing his degree part-time, he found time to be a part of our family during the day. Angel's father left the house way before most of the neighborhood was even awake, in the morning. Most of the time he would work late well into the evening helping customers with their plumbing issues, electrical or mechanical concerns. He hadn't spent much time at home with his two sons, nurturing nor creating many fruitful experiences with them and was busy providing the family with his money instead which he believed to be more important. Angel called him dad while I knew him as my uncle Felix.

They had taken away my personal belongings, like my watch, so I had no idea what time it was, but when an officer came to my cell with a bologna and American cheese on white bread and a black coffee, I thought it was probably lunch-time the next afternoon.

"Sir, do you have anything else other than bologna? Maybe a ham and cheese, or a bagel with cream cheese?" I politely asked the officer.

He wasn't rude about it as I wasn't being a wise-ass and I think he knew that.

"No." Then he left the cell room.

What must my parents be thinking if Angel told them? I was hoping to be freed before they would wake up. Bail was only set for $90.00, but I didn't have access to the funds.

"You're freed on bail." A clerk told me.

The officer unlocked the cell and I followed him to the possession room. He gave me back my belongings and I wanted to know who bailed me out and as I tried to decipher the voice, I could not comprehend that it was Mr. Feliciano's brother.

"Thank you very much. If you need any paint supplies, or anything from the store just let me know." I exclaimed to him in utter joy.

"Just give me the ninety-dollars back." And then I thought about how he bailed me out in the same style that

I bailed Malik out with his gambling debt. Goodbye, Elizabeth.

CHAPTER XIX

My uncle Felix always wore a coverall jumpsuit, either a gray or dark blue one to protect his clothes from getting dirty from grease, oil, dirty sewerage water or even bird poop for that matter. His hands were often so dirty that he rarely touched his face even if he had an itch on it. He was the guy who would blow the snot out of his nose while blocking his other nostril with a finger knuckle, then wipe it on his jumpsuit by the leg area and wipe it off.

He was great with his hands and it was what made his money, other than his immense hands-on knowledge of being a contractor. They were rugged and his fingernails were short and some were crooked from everyday use of hard to get areas, and probably from banging them with a tool on occasion by mistake. He was a hard worker and took on any job that he could handle. He was one of those mechanics that would not only fix your car but would do it in a timely manner, not charge you a whole lot and explain to you how and when the next maintenance check-up should be. He was reliable, an earner and a keeper but most of all he was fair, so if he felt that he was being taken advantage of he would let you know it.

I would often sit in his van as he drove from job to job. I admired the freedom of being your own boss without having to clock in at a specific time plus he will never know how stuck he would feel in an office cubicle for eight hours a day. The best part about hanging out with him was not only learning how to do plumbing and electrical work but going out for breakfast early in the morning at a local diner. I usually craved Taylor Ham. It was developed in 1856 by a John Taylor of Hamilton Square, NJ. In North Jersey, residents continue to use the term, Taylor Ham, while South Jersey residents generally use the term, Pork Roll. Central Jersey has the best of both worlds, I guess. Jersey is full of diners and I enjoyed a nice Taylor ham, egg, and cheese on a soft roll with salt, pepper, and ketchup accompanied with a cup of coffee.

Uncle Felix could start a conversation with anyone since he was a people-person and I guess you really have to be if you're dealing with the public all the time. In Sales, you have to sell a product and he would not only sell himself as a certified contractor but also as an ambassador of just being friendly to combat his loneliness. Although he had a wife and two sons, he felt the need to work as much as he could to get all the things he and his family needed so he sacrificed most of himself to achieve that but the problem was that there wasn't much long-term socializing on the road. He would fix someone's problem and then go on to the next solution and perhaps this was partly a reason for the attraction of having daily customers mixed in with his regular clientele. He might fix a boiler once a year for a customer, but to see Ralphie every other week so he could get his party fix was another.

Ralphie met up with us at a diner in Linden. Across the street were a gas station and a Truck-Stop where his truck was parked and he would regularly meet him for breakfast during his short stay in Jersey.

"Mornin'," I said to him as I raised my cup of coffee in a kind gesture.

"What's up, gentlemen? How's it hanging?" he said with a smile. His blue plaid shirt was unbuttoned and the black t-shirt underneath revealed that he might have enjoyed listening to AC/DC but sometimes shirts are just shirts. He wore blue jeans with a big belt buckle and a pair of black boots. Ralph Sorenson drove an Over the Road (OTR) truck who somehow manages to visit the East Coast twice a month from southern Texas. His load frequently changes but mainly they're clothes from the cotton that's manufactured and produced in Texas. As he sat down, he received a warm greeting from Felix.

"What's up, maricón?"

I chuckled as I excused myself and got up to use the restroom. I didn't like being around or even near the deal anymore. I was more concerned with not getting caught or being an accessory, and besides it was none of my business.

By the time I was finished, I would head back in the dining area and Ralph would be on his way out the door with what appeared to be a take-out bag but was really two ounces of coke wrapped in two Ziploc bags and a brown paper bag. It was really 225 grams because he would throw in an extra gram for Ralphie on the road to stay awake. Whatever he did with the drugs was on him and he was solely responsible, and I wasn't a part of it.

Mr. Feliciano worked hard for the things he got. Nobody gave it to him because he was an earner and so he didn't want to lose those things he accumulated over the years. To prevent seizure of his house or personal assets he staged his stash in a one-bedroom apartment, really a safe-house, for himself, on the top floor of an old building in a Puerto Rican section of Downtown Jersey City. He knew the old man who owned it and periodically he would also do maintenance on the water heaters and boilers for the building. He also took care of the pigeon coops on the roof by feeding them, all in exchange for free use of the small apartment.

No one else knew about that place. He never did any deals anywhere near that sanctuary. It was his secret hideout. He did most of his transactions in parking lots, sometimes in front of a convenience store one, or even one at a fast-food joint. He did it wherever it was convenient for him on his route or on his next contracting job.

That, mixed in with random pages and calls, led to the magic of having his own mobile business and freedom to meet anyone at any time. His biggest client was a lawyer friend of his who helped him out on previous jams and tickets. I used him when I was involved in a car accident in Hoboken the previous year. I was making an ounce delivery of blow to a guy who was partying in Weehawken, off Palisade Ave while I was in Downtown, JC. I cut through

Hoboken to take Paterson Plank Road but then the train was coming so the arms came down to block that route. I then decided to cut through the city streets so I took Jackson Street until I could make a right. It was an undeveloped area, more industrial than residential and so when I got on 7th Street to head towards Clinton Street, I kept going because there was no Stop sign.

The problem was that the corner of 7th and Madison didn't have a Stop sign either so at the intersection, I was struck by the other vehicle at my rear quarter panel of my Buick Riviera. The lawyer took care of my case and I was awarded my due monies from the Insurance companies.

The car was totaled and I was taken to the hospital for treatment. I called Mark when it happened and he had a guy take all of my belongings from the car before they took it to a towing contractor's custody. He managed to retrieve the ounce and had it delivered for me, two boxes of vintage Playboy and Penthouse magazines that I hid from Alicia so she wouldn't get offended, and my Triple-Beam scale I used to weigh product. Man, I missed that Riviera but it was fun while it lasted.

CHAPTER XX

I drove my '86 Buick Riviera headed on 1&9 North towards the Pulaski Skyway because I didn't want to drive amongst trucks, passed Newark Airport and the Port of Newark, all the while listening to *Who's the Man* by House of Pain. I always enjoyed driving on the Skyway over the Passaic River and looking at the New York skyline from up there, while looking below I could see industry and commerce and busyness. The Skyway was dedicated by the State of New Jersey to the memory of the American Revolutionary Hero General Casimir Pulaski. I got off on the Broadway Exit going down the ramp and passing the landmark of the Wilson Carpet guy on the left. After passing the Duncan Projects, Lincoln Park and finally reaching route 440 and Communipaw Ave, I decided to take West Side Ave. to Starlight instead.

In just a few minutes I would be approaching Miss America Diner on West Side Ave., instead of the Colonette Diner on the busy freeway, because its presence looked and felt more historical to me. I finally made it to Starlight, somewhat near passing Grieco's, but parked near the corner, as I more than often found myself parking at. I saw Jay's dog and his leash was tied to a grey pipe outside and attached to the pizza parlor. Jay was inside pacing and talking with Salami. Before I decided to walk in, I knelt down on one knee and pet Binzo who reciprocated his affection towards me by licking my face.

I heard a voice speak to me as I was vulnerably at pet level. "Red Beard's been asking about you. Keep an eye out." One of Grieco's men said to me as he casually walked by. I didn't know what he meant or who this Red Beard was but I became a little more vigilant on my surroundings, especially on how he walked up on me without me noticing. I nodded to him that I heard, acknowledged and understood.

Jay came out and I quickly stood up.
I extended my hand to shake his and palmed a small bag of "yayo", "What's up, dude? Here's a little something for you. It's a new product and I want to know what you think." We finished shaking hands and he was extremely excited because most of the time he feels like he gets shorted or ripped off.

"Thanks, dude!"
"Let me know." I told him.

I walked inside and saw Salami. "What's up, dude?"
He and I talked about Gotti, The Godfather I & II, and just regular casual Italian mob stuff for a while, at least until Jay sprung in the pizzeria and wanted my attention.

"Dude, you gotta come with me. There's someone I'd like for you to see.
C'mon." He walked towards the door expecting me to follow.

"Be right back, Josh."
I got up, looked out through the store-front windows and followed him outside. We only walked in between the liquor

store and the laundromat to a local fruit stand, where a guy in his mid-fifties was sorting out the different colored peppers from the neighboring plum tomatoes that fell in its basket.

"Bean, this is Corey. He's the guy who gave me the stuff."

Ben "the Bean" Becker was originally from Massachusetts and moved to Jersey when he was in his teens. His father opened up a fruit and vegetable stand for the local community and throughout the years expanded to sell candy and some school supplies to the nearby public-school kids. Ben was overweight and he wore layers of shirts to conceal his obesity, but no one really cared about that except himself. They called him "the Bean" because he was from Boston "Bean Town" but he was convinced that it was because he was far from looking as thin as a string bean. He wore a grey gumbalini to conceal his baldness.

"Hey, so you're Corey. That's some pretty good stuff. Got any more?" he chuckled.

"Bean and I have been doing this for years and it is far better than the crap up the Hill!" Jay exclaimed.

I looked at Jay because I knew him longer and served as my go-to guy, just because I wasn't completely certain about Ben, and at the same time thinking about how this would be my beginning into cocaine. The product was validated, safer to use than going up the Hill and I would only deal with the guys I knew. "Tell you what. I got grams for forty and eighths for a buck twenty-five." The Bean didn't hesitate and stated that if it were the same quality as what he just tried, he would want an "eight-ball", so rather than allowing them to know that I had it on my person I told them that I needed to go get it and be right back within fifteen minutes.

I went back to Steve's Pizza and ordered a slice. Josh was reading the Daily News and I sat across from him.

"Washup with Jay?"

"Oh, nothing. He wanted me to meet Ben from the fruit market."

"The Bean? Dude, that guy isch the only one I know that could do an eight-ball in two linesch."

"Really?" I asked.

"And the only one I know who could do scho musch blow and schtill not losche weight."

"That's funny," as I started to laugh.

"Slice is up!"

I got up to grab my slice and sprinkled parmesan cheese, garlic powder, oregano and crushed red pepper on it, and placed it on the table to cool off.

"Be right back."

Josh went back to his newspaper as I felt in my left pants pocket an eighth that I had already packaged in a plastic bag for distribution. The grams were in my right-side pocket, in smaller plastic bags.

When I reached the market, I noticed there were no customers, and there were some herb plants on a nearby shelf so I reached for a basil plant and dropped the product in its place so there wasn't direct contact with the guys. Without looking at Jay I told him that it was on the shelf. Both their eyes went up as they hadn't even noticed the transaction. Unfortunately, Jay handed me the $125.00 and I immediately took it so it wouldn't be in plain sight for too long. I put the plant back on the shelf in front of the bag to conceal it temporarily until they were ready to grab it for themselves. I went back across the street, folded my slice and ate it.

Within a couple of days, Donny and Joe found out through Jay about my stuff. They had already partied with them and tried it for themselves. Donny walked up to me while Joe stood behind, "Got anything?"

"Yeah. Grams for forty." "Got anything smaller?" "Nah. That's it.

"All right then. I'll take one."

He took two twenties out of his pocket and palmed it while I palmed my bag, and we shook hands exchanging and transacting. He was one of the best at making it look natural. I was glad we were on the same page with that because most of our deals were out in the open so as not to get any of the local vendors involved or in trouble by conducting business in their stores.

I had involved myself in this new market. I no longer dealt weed, didn't run any numbers and tried working a real job with benefits, but the cocaine business was beginning to look very lucrative. I had already gone through the initial risk of having the product and I just needed to maintain discretion until I finished selling all of it, but because I was busy before I jumped on this scene, I hadn't noticed that there was another dealer, a small-time hustler, peddling blow. His name was Alfred, Al for short, and he was a skinny Puerto Rican guy about my same height but had the attitude and persona as if he was from the Bronx or one of the guys selling the product in the City. He would periodically stroll unto Starlight with his pregnant girlfriend, Anna, so they could go to the market and buy groceries.

Since Big Dave knew him, he told him about me. While Anna was in the store, Al pulled out a Newport cigarette from its case and then approached me.

"Hey, you got a light?"

Although I didn't smoke, the Scouts taught me to always be prepared, so I happened to be carrying a Zippo lighter. It was the same one that Eddie gave me years ago for being in his wedding party.

"Yeah. Sure." I lit his smoke.

"Me and my girl got an apartment up the block and she's due soon." He took a long drag and leaned against the brick wall putting his right leg up on it.

"Oh yeah?" I engaged myself.

"I told her to take it easy so I'm out hustling to save for when the baby comes.

Nothing big but enough to pay the bills, you know?"

Malik walked towards us. "Wassup, Alfie? Where's your prego wife?"

"Getting some milk, bread and hopefully cigarettes."
He laughed as he walked on by and into the grocery store, holding the door open for Anna as she was walking out.
"Gotta go, bro. Thanks for the light."
"Later."

Alfred was from the neighborhood, trying to survive and make it. There were no threats, advances or reasons for uncivility. There was plenty to go around and we didn't interfere with each other's business. Besides, because he didn't have enough startup capital to invest in the product, he only sold dimes whereas I didn't accept anything lower than $40.00 per gram. That was until things started to take a different turn.

A couple of weeks had passed and business was steady. Guys were selling weed on two different corners, people hung out at the pizza place, kids would walk by eating from bags of chips, and the music was always playing from somewhere. Donny always paid me in full even if he had to co-op and split the funds with someone else, but I guess he ran out of cash until next payday. "Hey, dude, did you hear about Ron?" he asked me.
"No. What?" I was curious, as he lit up a Marlboro.
"He was on that junk and took a bad batch. They found him over-dosed behind Paradise East, by the tracks."
"Nah, man. That's fucked up." I started to let it sink in.
"Yeah. He's been to rehab a couple of times to clean up, and even signed up for the Navy, but when he got out, he went back into it. Rode that dark horse bad. I hate to ask

but can you give me a bag until Friday, when I get paid? I promise." This was the first time he had asked, and with the money I made off of him already, it would be near break-even if he didn't pay. I looked at him and hesitated.

"C'mon, man. I promise. I've taken care of you all the other times. I'm good for it."

"This one time, Don. No arms and no shorts. You know the rules." as I held out my hand and shook his.

"Thanks, man. I promise.

You'll get it on Friday." A few moments later I was approached by Ben.

"Got anything?"

"Yeah."

"The usual. Come by the store." He said.

I followed him and sold him an eighth. He also had a part-time gig working at the Meadowlands Racetrack as a security guard and he enjoyed watching the Giants, Jets and all concerts at the neighboring stadium, so he needed these boosts to help him stay awake.

"Hey, this is between you and me, all right?"

"Yeah. Of course. I don't know what you're talking about."

Jay and Binzo came from around the corner and they saw me chatting with Ben.

"What's up? He asked us.

"Wassup, dude?"

"Hey, Bean, did you get anything?"

"No. I gotta go to work."

"Hey, Core, can I talk to you for a minute?" Jay asked.

"Later, Bean" I expressed to Ben as I walked away with Jay and his dog.

"Hey, can I get a ball?"

"Yeah. One left."

"I'll pay you on Friday. I ain't got the money until payday."

"You're the second one to ask me today."

"Yeah? Who else?"

I couldn't tell him because then he would hound them for a freeze or line.

"Some dude who comes around sometimes. I told him no arms and no shorts."

"I can let you hold on to something, as collateral. They're my favorite shit."

"Yeah. I don't know. I'm not a pawn shop."

Joshua walked by us and I asked him where he was going.

"Gonna get a shcratch-off. I feel lucky today." He walked into the liquor store to buy lottery tickets that were called "Scratch-Offs" or "Rub-Offs" but I called them "Rip-Offs" because I never won from them, and then I got back to business.

"Dude, I'll have it for you on Friday. Wait here...I'll bring it." He left while I walked back towards the laundromat. It must have been a full moon or this is just how it is. Donny came back and his pupils were wide and dilated, his eyes were glossy and he kept grinding his jaw. He was "beaming". He could hardly talk but as he tried, it was slow and intermittent. He wanted another bag but I told him that I couldn't because I ran out.

"C'mon, dude. Just one more."

Then Jay walked upon us and handed me four black boxes.

"What the fuck is this?"

"My KISS dolls. They're original and they got all their shit and everything. They're worth at least a couple hundred dollars."

"What am I gonna do with these? Where'd you get these?" These dolls were like the ones from my old classmate, Jack Roberts, and he especially self-painted and designed guitars out of paper and specialized them. He brought it to school once as a show-and-tell. I know they were Jack's at one time but now they were mine, for now.

Donny seeing us bartering decided to take advantage of the situation and slowly offered me the title of his car. It was a piece of crap with a shoddy paint job but it took him from point A to point B, and especially to the manufacturing job he had.

"Guys, what the fuck? All right. Tell you what. Don, get the title. Jay, I'll hold on to these." I gave Jay the eighth when Don turned his back and hurried to get the document, which didn't make too much sense since he didn't need the title to drive his car because he could always get a new title made. When Jay left, I waited for Don and when he returned, we did the exchange, then I walked towards the grocery store.

What I didn't know was that Salvatore Grieco had walked out of his restaurant with two of his guys and started coming my way. One of his guys had a red kerchief in his coat pocket, while Salvatore's was white. I stood up straight, took my hands out of my pockets and wondered what he wanted. The sidewalk was lined with used cigarette butts and crushed soda and beer cans along the street curb whereby this was no literal red-carpet event. Perhaps, Sonny crossing over to our block had nothing to do with me, it's just that I had never seen him leave the close proximities of his place of business and here he was approaching our place of business. I looked around at the buildings to see if we were being watched or surveilled because I was more concerned for his safety than my own. There were no police cars, marked or unmarked, parked on any corner ready to drive and swarm into arresting action. It was just Salvatore and his crew coming towards me.

As they got closer, he reached into his pocket and pulled out a metal case wallet that held his cigarettes, and opened it so that he could tap twice on the filter side to pack it, before lighting it with a Zippo. Regular crowds were going about their own business but I saw three guys just appearing unto Starlight from Woodgrove Ave. and looked like they were dressed like Run DMC with their Kango hats and matching black jackets, coming at a forty-five-degree angle to where we would all eventually meet up. As they stepped off the sidewalk from across the street, behind a parked white delivery van, they quickened their pace and were already coming towards our side of the block. It took me a short while to figure that they weren't the Feds as the middle guy pulled out a shank and was about to lunge it into the Grieco crew.

I stutter-stepped forward towards Sal as he made it to the front door of JC's Deli and Liquor and quickly pointed at the men.

"Sonny, look out!" I yelled.

As the hoodlum got closer, Joshua ran out of the lottery store with a Rip-Off in his hand about to tell me that he won on the ticket but that never happened. The blade swiftly entered his body as he mistakenly walked in front of Sonny and took the knife for him. I ran and tackled the guy, wrapping my arms around his body and dropping him on the floor and slightly knocking the wind out of him. The guy with the red kerchief fought off one of the guys knocking off his hat in the struggle, while the third hoodlum shot off a round and hit one of Sonny's men in the leg.

"Stand him up! Get him up!" Sonny shouted to me after he kicked him in the head.

When I got the guy up, I took off his hat to reveal that it was Alfie, the newbie with the pregnant wife. His ambitions and desperation got the best of him. There are no short-cuts in life. You have to earn. The other two were continuously getting punched and beat up until they lay there motionless on the ground. This was when I released my grip from Alfie to tend to Joshua who was on the ground covered in his own blood.

"Dude, you're gonna be alright," I affirmed.

"Is that Schonny?"

"Yeah. You saved his life. Gotti style. Classic." I sensationalized to him.

Big Dave came out of the laundromat from calling an ambulance.

"Help is on their way!" he shouted.

"You hear that? Help is on their way." I said in my best comforting demeanor.

"Tell my sister that I love her," Josh whispered.

"I'm sure she already knows, but I will, Josh."

Joshua "Salami" Russo died in my arms. That never happened to one of us, and I never thought that it ever was a possibility since we weren't a weapon-toting crew. For us, it was just business and something to pass the time with. It was what we did, and perhaps it was just what happens when you get too close to this lifestyle, like Julio in Spanish Harlem except that Joshua died a hero and not just a victim of circumstance. He was my friend.

I heard at least three gunshots followed by another two or three. I didn't look up or over. If I were to be involved in the mix it would happen now. No barrels were pointed at the back of my head that day. I slowly rose up and walked away. That was the last time I ever stepped foot on Starlight, and the last time I wanted to involve myself in the racketeering and drug business.

I got back in my Buick Riviera, the car automatically leveled, and I made it back to Route 440 towards the 1&9 where for the first five minutes I drove silently through Chill Town managing and focusing on my escape. An Ambulance sped past me, most likely on its way to Starlight, but for me, it was "lights out".

When I was at the apex of the Hackensack River Bridge I looked over at the PSE&G plant and stared at the billowing smoke coming out of the stacks. I hit my steering wheel with the palm of my hand and screamed out "Fuck!" until I exhausted my last breath. It was over and now it was just a matter of my survival. This was real life, and death. There were serious consequences for my actions and it didn't hit me, I mean really hit me, until now. There was no other choice but for me to stop what I was doing. I felt that there was enough time to turn my life around and do something more productive and positive. *But what?* What else do I know what to do? I needed a vacation. I just needed to get away.

CHAPTER XXI

It didn't take long before my uncle Pedro and I found an apartment through one of his friends. Joe was a Realtor in our city, and within a week of apartment hunting and evaluating, we gathered all of our belongings and moved into a brand-new affordable condominium with a great location in Jersey City.

Rent was reasonable considering we would be splitting it, and any fees, in half. The condo came equipped with two bedrooms, a living room, a kitchen which had all appliances available, and hard wood floors and between the both of us, we had so much junk that I had to throw half of mine away. The train station was nearly a stone's throw away, and his local hangouts were even closer. Within a couple of days, the neighborhood knew that we were in town.

We frequented a Spanish bar called *Gilbert's*, on Marin Blvd. and 1st Street, where two Latin barmaids would take care of us every time. I stuck with bottles of cold *Zima*, while he had the same but mainly preferred Budweiser. On the weekends, loud salsa and meringue music would be playing from an attached room in the back with a large dance floor, and it wasn't as smoky as it was from the continuous cigarette-smoking in the front bar area. We mainly stayed at the bar, enjoying the crowds watching a muted television program or just hanging out by the jukebox. Two bouncers patrolled the front door and made sure no minors were allowed in while I was content with having my corner seat, and periodically my uncle would introduce me to his people.

Lucy came to me and asked me if I wanted another beer. She was about five-foot seven, twenty-four years old, with a pair of hips that you knew could move when she danced. I told her that it was a good idea and my uncle would have another too, and it was bottoms up with our old bottles. I favored Lucy over Trixie because she was more my age, although most of the guys tended to favor Trixie because she was older. She was a little shorter, with a blondish hair color tied in a ponytail. They both had golden skin, and both were certainly an attraction to the bar but instead of focusing on the ladies at the bar I decided to give Alicia a phone call. She only lived a few blocks away and I hadn't spoken to her in a long time. When she answered the phone we briefly talked and I was reminded on how she was too young to legally consume alcohol and so she wouldn't be able to join me for drinks, and besides her mother would not allow her to be out so late. We had a nice conversation and it was the precipitating event that led us to continue a healthier relationship.

There was a couple dancing in the center of the dance floor. She wore a nice party dress while he looked slick in a dark suit. At times he would just stop and pose, or even slick his hair, while she would turn or dance around him. I was staring and trying to figure them out when one of

Pedro's friends came over to him and told him that he and his girlfriend would be going to another bar a few blocks away and that if we wanted to join them, they would be there for another hour or so. I didn't have a problem with it, since the place was becoming a little too noisy for me, and I wanted to mellow out in a quieter environment. He told Don that we would meet him and Jackie in about fifteen minutes at Vera's.

We arrived there at about twelve-thirty, and since it was only a Thursday, the pool table and the jukebox were the means of entertainment besides the cable television broadcasts. I bought the first round of cold beer and he inserted his fifty cents into the pool table so we could play a game of "last pocket" eight-ball. My uncle lit a cigarette and picked a cue stick so he could "break" while I racked. I came back with the beers, placed them on a nearby table because at that point he was selecting three songs from the jukebox and after I racked, he came over to the table and I handed him his beer.

"What did you pick?" I asked.

"Some good songs, Sobrino. You don't understand."
The music kicked in and after the second round, so did the alcohol, but we were not drunk from the booze, but rather from the vibe. He put on some good jams from Tito Rojas, Mark Anthony, and Jerry Rivera and when his songs were over, I put in my dollar and waited for my songs to play. Don and Jackie sat at the bar drinking their Remy Martin and Rum and cokes. Tommy, who worked for a warehouse

facility that only sold Kosher products, sat a few stool lengths away and was always there on Thursdays. He kept babbling about all the products that had a special symbol on them, especially on the soda can he was drinking out of.

He hadn't known what else to talk about.

"What did you put on?" Pedro asked me.

"Marvin Santiago's *Vasos de Calores*, Eddie Palmieri's *Vamanos Pal Monte*, and then I finished it off with Hector Lavoe.

"What are you crazy? You trying to wake these people up?"

Just then the bass and the trumpets sounded off from my medley of tunes I requested. My pager went off, it was about one o'clock, and I had no idea who it could have been. I looked down and I told my uncle that I would be back and that I had to use the payphone. I walked over and passed by the small crowd towards the front of the bar, and reached for the payphone that was behind the entrance door next to the last stool at the end of the bar. When I dialed the number, I was surely surprised to hear my sister crying at the end of the receiver.

"What's the matter?"

She tried to talk but she could not control her sobbing.

"Where are you?"

I only understood her to mention that she was by the mall right down by the water Downtown. We were only minutes away so I told her that I was on the way. I slammed the phone and walked back towards the back where a serious rhythmic orchestra was playing from the jukebox.

"I have to go. That was Gloria. She's crying." I decided that was all he really needed to know, plus that was pretty much all I knew about what was transpiring.

"I'm coming with you. Nothing better have happened to her, man. She's my niece."

He finished the last of his beer and left the pool cue on top of the table. He lit another cigarette before he put his camouflage jacket on and then we were off to see my sister.

It had only taken a few minutes before I saw her at the mall by herself weeping and drying her eyes with the sleeves of her jacket. I pulled up next to her and she wanted to jump in the back seat. I hadn't said a word for the first three minutes, or until she regained her composure, and only then did I ask her if she was all right. I glanced in the rearview mirror and noticed that she wasn't mainly wiping her eye from the tears, but rather concealing the puffiness and swelling it was forming. I pulled over and put the gear in park.

"What the fuck happened? I'm gonna get that mutha fucka. Where da fuck does he live? Where is he?"

She started to get emotional again. "I" she couldn't form words again, "don't know."

"What kind of car does he drive?"

"A green station wagon."

I thought about how Angel took care of Nicky's green station wagon back in Elizabeth. My uncle listened but didn't get involved just yet. I put the gear in drive and proceeded to take her home. I had the window down slightly so we could all breathe in some fresh air.

"I'm taking you back home. It's almost two in the morning. Mom let you out this late? Forgettit. You're staying home where it's safe, and I want you to take care of that swelling and get some sleep. You hear me?"

I took the back roads because I didn't think he would want to be seen in the obvious main roads especially if he were speeding off to what he thought was a safe place. It was a quiet ride back uptown, and I was surprised that my uncle refrained from smoking another cigarette. We hadn't forgotten that she was a couple of months pregnant, and we did not want anything wrong to happen to her or her child. When we got to the house she quickly got out of the car and started to walk away.

"La bendición."

"Dios te bendiga." Our uncle responded.

No matter how distant my sister and I had become over the years, she was still my sister and deserved all great things because she was loved, but more importantly, because I loved her. We were family. I left so my parents wouldn't hear a motor running for a long time in front of their house, and I didn't want to wake them up and alarm them. I made a right unto Starlight and pulled right over at the corner, in front of the deli, and used the payphone to call

Angel. He picked up and was on his way from Elizabeth with a couple of guys. He was to meet us at the Polynesian restaurant's parking lot in a half an hour, but in the meantime, since I knew where this guy, Gustavo, lived, I decided to pay a visit and see if he was home.

I've never been inside his place, nor have I had any excuse to pass by before, but we when I did reach the street, I started to look for a green station wagon. We hadn't seen one and so I parked right in the front of his basement apartment anyway. We got out of the car, and my uncle wasn't hesitant at all, and we were about to bust the side door down when we realized that the door was already slightly opened. I went in first and climbed down two steps into a dark foyer which smelled damp and old. A dim light appeared from another door a few feet from our left and it looked like the light source was coming from a television set, but I hardly heard the volume and so I quickly decided on the plan of attack. My uncle had found a baseball bat leaning against a wall of the dark basement, and grabbed it for fear of the unknown.

I kicked the door open, although it was already, to stun and surprise the occupants so we would have the upper hand. A guy in his early twenties was relaxing on a bed watching the television, and quickly sat up when the opening door hit the wall with a loud bang.

"Where's Gus?"

He looked at me and then at the bat my uncle was carrying. He stood quietly and as we walked closer, I stood near the foot of the bed staring at him. His hands were on the bed covers, and he didn't have anything in his hand, nor had he attempted to defend himself, but he was startled and stunned.

"Do you know who I am?" He nodded his head. "I want Gus. Where is he?" As if we were playing good cop/bad cop, my uncle stepped in.

"If you got any shit in here, you better get rid of it. The cops are on their way."

"He fucked up. Where is he?" I demanded.

I believed he genuinely had no clue where Gustavo was and I also believed that he had not returned to this place. Apparently, this guy was staying with him as a roommate and probably thought twice about staying there any longer because my uncle swung the bat and busted the television set. We left and we hadn't heard a noise coming from the apartment as we walked up the two steps back out the side door and to the car. We went to the parking lot to meet up with Angel.

He was there with three guys in his jeep and another car with two more guys. I walked over to him while Pedro lit a cigarette and stood by my car.

"What's up? We're looking for a green station wagon. Let's check Country Village first."

Upon looking at the vehicles and recognizing some of the faces, I realized that each one of them had a weapon on their laps. I hadn't seen so many weapons since we went to some mountains late at night off Route 22, and we were being chased by what seemed to look like members of the Ku Klux Klan in their full robed gear. I am not sure how I made it that evening but I drove down the Watchung Mountains without my headlights on to evade the chase from them, after stumbling upon them as Angel and I were walking in a field one late night. Considerable time had passed and I lost that rage which filled me when I first realized that he must have punched her in the eye, but he crossed a line and he had to pay – an eye for an eye.

We crept through the Village and there wasn't a vehicle in sight. After ten minutes, my heart started to race as I saw a green station wagon with four occupants and I was glad to have the nine of us to take care of their four. Angel was in the lead car and when he realized that the wagon was about to make a left unto Forrest Court, a narrow and quiet residential street, he accelerated and cut him off to get in front of the car. Halfway down the street, he stopped, and four guys from his jeep stepped out with pipes, a wooden bat, and a screwdriver. The wagon that was in front of me stopped and in fear, decided to reverse but he had nowhere to go. The three guys behind my car had already parked behind me and walked towards the battle scene with their own weapons.

I opened my door with no weapon but my hands, and even they weren't in the shape of fists and walked right up to the window. I stared right at the driver's eyes. Unfortunately for all of us, this green station wagon was occupied by a Philippine family, and they looked terrified.

Neighbors had put their porch lights on and a woman stepped onto her porch to warn us that the police were on their way. There was nothing that we could have done that night because these people in the Village were involved in a neighborhood watch and I wasn't about to call their bluff so we drove to the outskirts of the city and parted from there. It seemed that it was forbidden for me to take care of this guy as if the gods needed him for some other silly use in his life. I left it for time to tell.

My uncle and I decided to head back towards the condo, but before then we went back to Vera's to see if Don and Jackie were still there in the chance that they would want to come over and hang out. Thomas was still there talking about his job and some type of Kosher crackers when Don, Jackie, and Annette were sitting at the bar enjoying their drinks. It was nearing "last call" so Pedro purchased two six-packs to go, and asked them if they wanted to stop by. I was tired, had been through some day, but didn't mind the company because they would ultimately just distract me from what was creating tension in my life – family drama.

CHAPTER XXII

Living arrangements were a definite improvement and it marked yet another beginning for me. I was back in Jersey City but now attached to the Downtown area scene. I could feel the bustle of the faster pace and the energy of the suited professional every morning, as I took my early morning walk to get the local paper and a coffee. Car horns, fumes from passing buses and the occasional rolling up of the storefront gates added to the daily noises and feel that I enjoyed. The tall buildings, bodegas, subway entrances and the pure logistics where I lived added to the liveliness and desire to live on Columbus Drive. It was what "Downtown" should feel like and I discovered and landed in its new territory. That was the "day" aspect versus the nightlife that Pedro initiated.

Being here also brought me closer to Alicia's house. Our streets intersected at some point down the road and thought perhaps we would meet again someday. Instead, I fell short of walking the entire distance to the Paulus Hook area and went to visit and see one of my favorite women in the entire world. There was a shortcut to the park that not too many people knew about unless they came from the other end first. Off Jersey Avenue and Grand, by the Boys & Girls Club of America, there was a trail to the State Park where I strolled through nature past the marina and embarked unto the backyard of one of the most sacred grounds in my life. That is when I saw her.

Although the feud between her original home-town has bickered for many years, she will always have a space in my heart – one that would supersede and transcend all boundaries of admiration and unconditional respect. She belonged to me. She belonged to Jersey City, and if anyone said otherwise, I just didn't want to hear it. In fact, if anyone tells you that she belongs to anyone else other than New Jersey, tell them that you don't want to hear it! It filled me with purpose and being and so I needed to find that proper channel of expression. I actually walked the narrow spiral staircase that led to her crown years ago and it was magnificent. I decided to walk back to the condo and relax. Until next time, Lady Liberty. *Au revoir*.

The only luminescence in the darkroom was coming from the tiny bulb located in the fifty-gallon fish tank that was located on the strong and sturdy dark walnut three-drawer chest that separated my bed from the wall. I laid there quietly staring at the fish as they swam care-free, gracefully maneuvering and chasing each other through winding caverns.

I sat back on my queen-sized bed and propped my head on top of two pillows and stood there motionless as I folded my hands and rested them on my stomach. I was at a new start in life and direction because I was my own boss who didn't have to answer to anyone, and solely responsible for my own decisions. I could not hide behind the rules and regulations, the policies and procedures already put in place by corporations and established businesses. Even though I was back in my home turf, the others would probably still think I had still moved away but it wasn't a big deal because I wasn't hiding from anyone.

I looked around and saw a stash in my closet on the shelf next to my record albums, with a note on it from my uncle simply saying "try me". I grabbed the pack of rolling papers, along with an album, and started to break up the healthy buds, started sifting and separating the seeds using the inside album crease, and started to get into the spirit of things. When I was about to roll a heavy bone, I walked over to the stereo because I couldn't find the remote control and decided to listen to some tunes.

In the corner of the closet was his small bong and so I decided to put the second sheet that I took out, and folded it into my wallet. I did remember to take the very first sheet of the new pack, crumble it and place it in my mouth. I superstitiously believed that using the first one was bad luck, so I swallowed this one. I was often told that if I ever ran out of sheets, I could have used that very first one. Even I had my own techniques and rituals, but one thing was for sure, "three lights to a cigarette" was bad luck. It was thought "taboo" to light three cigarettes using the same match or lighter. The theory was that during battle, by the time the third cigarette was lit, an officer was shot. Maybe it's where we get "Three sheets to the wind"? *Who knows? Where did I hear these things from?*

I took out my Zippo from my pants pocket and placed it next to me on the bed, but it clanked when it hit something. It was the remote control and so I placed it in my back pocket. I pinched a couple of buds and started to pack it into the bowl when I saw that it didn't have a screen but that was just a minor setback. I set the bong back down and stopped any songs from playing until I was fully ready to engulf myself in melody and mood.

I opened the door and proceeded into the kitchen to fix myself some iced tea. I reached above the sink and reached for a glass, walked over to the freezer and filled it with two cubes, then poured the tea until it reached the top. A fluorescent light hung under the cabinet directly above the sink, and the white countertop allowed me to notice a couple of water spots on it. I grabbed a coaster from the counter and placed my drink on it. I cracked my knuckles and twisted off the small chrome connecting at the end of the sink spout and when it was disconnected, I removed the small screen located inside and screwed back the piece.

I grabbed my glass and dragged a comb across my head. I was set to experience a state of nirvana, while I clutched the screen and was about to enter the sanctum that I called my room. I pressed play on the remote and the wheels were in motion. *Within You Without You* was the first random selection and it sent shivers down my spine and the hairs on my arms stood up as the zither introduced the Beatles tune.

I was back in business. I inserted the screen into the bowl of the bong, packed it with a nice size bud, and ignited it with much determination with the lighter. The fiery pit glowed as I took only a few "pulls" before I decided to take off my shoes and get undressed. I fiddled around with a little organizing in the room and decided to feed a little food to the little fish. I was feeling a bit jovial but always maintained that I was never buzzed yet. My little pals swam to the top little by little, each time taking a nibble from what they were given. I sat at the edge of the bed just staring at their movements.

The James Gang came on from the "Rides Again" track, and when it did, I took another pull and laid back down on the bed. I cast my fate to the wind and after a few minutes, my mind drew a blank and I drifted off into a new dimension in which I was care-free like the fish in my tank. The jam of the *Closet Queen/The Bomber* kept me conscious until I disappeared further and further into a realm of beauty and love. The last thing I heard before I blacked out was the sound of a snare drum rappin' and tappin' evermore, and in an existentialistic state, I suddenly appeared inside the bong's tube riding down the straight slide landing in a body of water.

I noticed two bodies staring down at me from what seemed to be a pool. I could not swim to the top but came very close, and before I tired myself and almost reaching the surface, I realized that the two people looking down at me were my sister and father and it was very reminiscent of the day I dove off the deep end from the diving board while we frequented Lake George, and remembered neither of them helping me. That was the day I learned to swim, by survival, without help as if I were a fledgling baby bird thrown from a nest to test my flying skills. I almost drowned that day, but with perseverance and drive I learned to truly swim that day. I was liberated. That was the year when a lot of people were walking around with jerseys on that displayed the number 84. I remember sitting on a street stool, sitting quietly posing for a portrait that artist Ron Peer was drawing, and my father asking me why people were wearing the number 84. I told him that I wasn't familiar with any famous football players and that I wasn't really sure why or who they were celebrating. He reminded me that it was 1984, the year and not a player that was in fashion. I was only twelve but knew who Orson Wells was already. In my vision, I surfaced into a white room and everything was clean.

I could hear cymbals crashing, and I walked over to a two by three-foot blank canvas picking up a brush and intrinsically splashing blue oil paint on my empty slate simultaneously with the rhythm of the crashing sounds. I looked up and saw an aircraft, with two propellers, hurling above me. It was a fighter-bomber, and to avoid being its victim, I jumped into the landscape portrait I had just painted of an ocean with friendly sea creatures. *Some imagination.*

The waters were calm and I wasn't afraid of what was below. I heard Ravel's *Ondine*. I closed my eyes and embraced the serenity of me and my canoe that wasn't made of wood but of a plaster material. I was on a good-sized joint that was canoeing but not sinking and I didn't have to worry about being randomly drug-tested because I was my own boss again. I was clean, refreshed, baptized.

CHAPTER XXIII

A few months living in the Condo and being closer to my girlfriend, Alicia, I was spending more and more time with her and it unfortunately periodically intervened with my uncle's work schedule as part of the agreement of living away from his job was that I would drive him to and from work, in Elizabeth. He was in the process of purchasing another vehicle after he was involved in a car accident, months before, and the insurance company was taking their time on paying out his settlement. Eventually, he decided to move back which led me to find a place of my own. Alicia said that the second floor of her grandmother's house was vacant and that I could possibly move there, and upon asking her mother, the condition was that I needed to move in with her male cousin because he was about to take full-time courses at the local University.

I first met Christopher at his parent's house on Christmas day. Alicia and I had gone to Lakewood, NJ, the night before to celebrate Christmas Eve with my family. It was a nice trip, about an hour's drive, into Vernon and as we passed city roads and headed north, I could not help but anticipate meeting her godfather and his family and partake in a different cultural, festive holiday. Through winding roads and hills, I started to notice the beautiful land and serenity of Hidden Valley.

"It's about five minutes from here," Alicia said as we passed an amusement park on our left. Driving by, she suggested that we first see the family ice-cream store – Dairy Whirl. It appeared to look like a very successful investment, not isolated from the main road, and several other establishments were only a couple of minutes away. It had a huge parking lot, which is key for any business, and sported an emblem of a blonde girl in a ponytail slightly bending over to give her cone to a younger boy. We had not gone inside for we were expected to arrive any minute at the family's residence. She was right about how close we were to our rendezvous and it wasn't long before we drove up another hill, in her four-door burgundy Corolla, and parked in the street in front of their house. The driveway was taken by some of her other relative's cars. Several trees surrounded the landscape, and we didn't walk on the grass. Instead, we trod on the paved driveway where I saw a canary-yellow Corvette parked outside the side garage.

"That's my cousin's car and his girlfriend, Julia, and down that short hill you can see my Uncle Steve's house."

Julia was standing outside smoking her cigarette when she noticed us. Alicia had met her before at *Trap's* in Hoboken. We rang the doorbell, but there was no response so we walked inside because the door had already been open and once inside, I was a bit nervous to meet everyone. They had not heard the doorbell because of the auspicious music playing and random Polish dialogue from downstairs, and that's where everyone was. To the right were five steps leading to the basement, while five steps in front of us lead to the first floor. While we took off our jackets and proceeded to hang them in the hallway closet, her godfather had come from downstairs and greeted us.

"Hey, Apple, how are you?" Apple was the nickname given to her when she was a child by her uncle.

"Uncle Roman, this is Coronado."

We shook hands while we greeted each other and her cousin came up to check on Julia. She was fine outside, so he saw us standing on the top of the stairs and then I saw my future roommate. He was a bit taller than me and had long blonde hair in a ponytail which was tied with a rubber band. He had a jovial look on his face, and I could tell he was an easy-going person. He came up and introduced himself.

"Hey, man, I'm Christopher, Alicia's cousin."

"Corey...nice to meet you."

"Chris, why don't you go downstairs and have your mother come up to check on dinner. How's everything, Apple?"

He turned to me and offered me a drink. I asked for a juice or a soda.

"Everything is good," she said as he went to the kitchen and fixed me a glass of Vodka and cranberry juice. Just then the family had come upstairs to prepare the table and to serve the dinner which had been magnificently been prepared by her aunt and grandmother.

"Hi, Chocha. Hi, Teta. Hi, Babcie." Alicia had given her two aunts and her grandmother a kiss, and I had just assumed that Babcie meant grandmother. I followed by doing the same. "This is Coronado." I was a bit embarrassed because of what she had called her aunts. Those two words translated into Spanish were fresh and naughty words, and I stepped aside as the women were getting busy setting out the china, silverware, and glasses. There was nothing I could do but to grab my drink and take a gulp. Christopher had fixed himself one too and we sat in the living room by the Christmas tree.

We talked about our living arrangements together and how we were going to proceed with moving furniture and such. It was no problem to me as I saw this as a good thing because I would be living above Alicia and her parents, and the only way that could have happened is if her cousin lived with me there too. He was briefly telling me about his ambitions when we were called into the dining room. There were tons of delicious food but I didn't know where to sit, and I was still too shy to make an assertive move so she sat me next to her while the others started to pass the roast beef and the mushrooms around.

She grabbed my plate and started with kapusta and golabki which were cabbage and a form of sauerkraut. Her uncle Steve asked her to give me some homemade white horseradish, so she piled it up and everything looked and smelled delicious. The roast beef came to me and I smelled the garlic. It was a great compliment with the mashed potatoes and the kielbasa with sauerkraut. It wasn't long until everyone started to eat, as I waited for Alicia to serve herself. Her uncle had put on some Christmas music from a CD player in the basement while we feasted, and when I finished my first serving, I was very content.

I looked around and got familiar with her mom's side of the family. I sat to her right because she was a lefty, and we held hands under the table as much as we could. Just when I thought dinner was over, ham and perogies were brought out from the kitchen. Her aunt would not forget to refresh the rye bread and butter which had already been set in the center of the table. I was in the festive spirit and joined in the usual conversations had over dinner. They asked me if I wanted any more, but I couldn't. I was stuffed.

When we finished our meal, the guys suggested that we take a walk into the bright starry-night and slip away from the women. The six of us strolled down the street in pairs of three, with me and one uncle on each side. Uncle Roman had led us to his neighbor's house down the road towards the Dead End. The two-story house looked rather plain on the outside. The residents had been gone on a business trip for nearly two weeks now and he had promised to watch over their home for another two. Walking towards the right side of the house, he pulled out a set of keys from his comfortable slacks and proceeded to open the door.

It was a hidden treasure for me and while Christopher and the rest of the cousins decided to get started on a game of billiards in the basement, I wandered around and received a full tour of what appeared to me to be an esoteric setting. The small kitchen was to the right, as you climbed five small steps unto the main floor, and was separated by the very large parlor by a countertop with a few vases setting on top. The parlor had a very high ceiling with two walls completely engulfed with books. It was an open room with two couches and a couple of soft plush chairs that served as borders from the remaining rooms. A dimly-lit lamp hung over the glass table which was strategically placed at the center of an imported Persian rug.

As I looked around, the others had already walked up to the second floor and were walking along the balconied extension. Uncle Steve looked down at me as he stood in front of an oil painting, and asked me to come upstairs to further on with the tour. I found the stairwell towards the right corner of the dimly-lit hallway, but before I ventured on, I noticed something in the reflection of the glass in the front foyer of the house. The complete abode had hardwood floors which were so clear and shiny and I thought it had recently been refinished. I walked towards the front door and slowly turned around. I stood about fifteen feet away from a wall, and as I took three steps forward, I stopped and found myself frozen in time. I had been engulfed staring at a 5'x 4' oil reproduction of Rembrandt's *Polish Rider*.

"We'll be in the basement."
I hesitated a bit and made my way back to sounds of billiards crashing each other.

"Hey, you know how to play?"

"Yeah, a little bit." Uncle Roman opened a bottle of Dewar's and poured me some in a scotch glass. As he poured one for Uncle Steve and then himself, the former took the bottle from the latter and handled it for safe keeping. He was a short, a bit stocky young father of three girls, and a husband to a beautiful wife and mother. His light brown hair was slicked back with a comb and his trim olive-green two-piece suit complimented his mustache. "Do you know where we're from? Do you know who we are?"
I looked at him as if he were asking a trick question.

"Carpathian Russian, right?"
He turned to me in surprise, and without any expectations from me, he grabbed me and gave me a kiss on my cheek.

"Look at this guy...Puerto Rican Prince...he knows us. I love this guy," he said with an exuberant smile. He grabbed the bottle of Scotch and refilled both of our glasses. Uncle Roman came over and offered me a Dunhill which I accepted, and I took a drag after he lit it with his silver Zippo.

CHAPTER XXIV

Chris and I were about to throw our first Halloween party at the apartment. Wearing a costume was not mandatory for what was to be a ghoulish night indeed. Alicia and I went to the party store and chose decorations from an assortment of goodies while Chris was attending classes and afterward, he worked as a waiter in a Hoboken seafood restaurant.

Finishing touches were being made as we taped plastic spiders on the walls, hung miniature mock-skeletons, draped our ten-foot long wooden dining table and twirled black and orange streamers from opposite corners of the kitchen. I bought a keg of Coors Light and ten bags of ice, and let it chill in the bathtub in the kitchen. I almost forgot the tap for the keg with all the cases of Bud and Heineken that were being piled in the car. Preparations were set and all we needed for our ten o'clock gala to start were guests who had been notified weeks prior.

Alicia would be waitressing at the local northern-Italian restaurant, Zesty's, around the corner and she would not get off from work until about ten. I stopped there around then to see how everything was going, and to know if any of her co-workers were joining in on the festivities. Keith and Brian were reluctant to go at first but when they found out Tina was going to be there, they rapidly changed their minds. Tina was a slender Italian girl with long dark brown hair with a naive personality. It wasn't that she was slow, but rather, not experienced in some fields and it probably attributed to the fact that we hadn't talked much, except for the casual hello and goodbye, and I never heard her express any of her views on anything, but what I really liked about her was her smile.

They all finished bussing and waiting tables that night and all that was left to do was to clean up the place in preparation for the lunch crowd the next afternoon. The restaurant did not have a liquor license, so patrons were more than welcome to bring their own liqueur of choice. Patrons mostly carried in a bottle or two of their choice wines to complement their pasta dishes, but since they could not drive home with an open container, if it were unfinished, the workers usually kept them for themselves. Needless to say, we raised our glasses filled with red Merlot and toasted the evening together.

I had left them early so they could finish cleaning, and to get a head start on what was to come. Angel had been ringing the bell when I turned the corner and noticed him outside of the front steps along with his younger brother, Abner. They were a bit early, but I liked that. The others came fashionably late and I suppose they did not expect to see different colored light bulbs in each room. The kitchen had a red bulb that was illuminated by a small lamp on the mantle. The computer room sported a yellow bulb, while Chris's room was green. His room had been painted this lime green color which he had purchased from Stanley's and my room, on the other hand, was a soft blue to match my blue and white striped fold-out couch. The doorbell rang and I went to see who it was while I was putting on some tunes, but Angel was kind enough to get the door, one flight downstairs, for me before I could even make a selection.

The door opened and as I glanced over, I noticed it was Sergei and a buddy of his. My roommate met Sergei at school during Economics class and although I met him before, to my knowledge this was the first time he had ever been to the apartment. Under his arm, he held a small keg and one I've never seen before.

"Privyet. Hello. What's that you're holding?" I asked him.

"Russian beer."

"Fantastic. Let me put that on ice for you."

I turned to his friend and extended my right hand while I tightly held the keg under my other arm.

"Hello. My name is Coronado."

As they entered the apartment, I heard the front door downstairs open. It was Alicia and her friends from work. I gestured for Sergei and Ivan to enter and to make themselves at home while I was trying to be the best host and waited to greet the next wave. Keith and Brian brought bottles of wine from the corner liquor store and I took them and tried to find room in the already packed refrigerator. Tina and Alicia each bought a four-pack of wine coolers for themselves to substitute any consummation of beer.

Jack and Chan, best buds and in the inner circle of closing down Hoboken bars on the weekends, were looking for the bottle opener which hadn't been visible next to the chips and dips on the table. With limited lighting, I felt to create the aura of Halloween and to give off a relaxing mood. I met them both through Alicia's sister. They were originally her friends and often we went down the shore and played drinking games all night long. There were ten of them that night I drove an hour and a half to see Alicia, who had been with her sister's crew at a rented motel down the Shore. She didn't believe me when I told her I was coming and when I rang the bell, she was surprised I made the trip.

We played the traditional game of "quarters" in which the object was to bounce a quarter into a glass and if you missed, you had to drink and if you made it in, someone else had to drink. I instituted the game of "Oh Captain, My Captain" where one person, the appointed captain, clasps their hands together and points to someone while the persons to the left and right of the captain had to row until the new captain was appointed and their left and right had to row. Sound confusing? While intoxicated, games like these were amusing.

Jack was a great drinking partner. At six feet, two hundred and something pounds of Irish blood, this guy could drink with this fish anytime and still come for more. Chan was from Trinidad, and he was a whiz on the computer. He had helped me many times on installing software and installing new hardware upgrades on my new computer. I opened a new AOL account and helped me optimize the speed in which I could access this concept of the World Wide Web. He was also a conservative party animal who never went overboard, but always hung with the best of them. I grabbed the bottle/can opener, took their beers and opened it for them. I saw to it that their hands and drinks were never empty.

It was a well-diverse, mingling crowd until the door opened and Christopher walked in from work around midnight with his girlfriend, sister, and her boyfriend. It was as though the noise had stopped and all you could hear were my beer gulps. We had been invaded. The alien Elvis Presley walked into the scene while his partner wore a resembling costume. Chris's girlfriend had on a nice disguise while he wore his waiter uniform. Although it wasn't required to bring a costume, it did add to the theme of our celebration. Unfortunately, though, they felt overdressed and embarrassed, and for most of the time stayed in my roommate's room. I didn't wear a costume or mask because I had been so many people and carried on so many roles that I already felt as if I was living in other people's shoes already. I was just content with being the ultimate host, catering to the needs of others.

A curtain, because we couldn't have a door due to fire code regulations, was hung on each of the doorways to a room, and also trapped their respectable colored lights within. Chris dug the layout and he hadn't expected it. He said hello to everyone and mingled with everyone and was delighted to see Sergei there, and they chatted and were hanging out. That's the way he was and I liked him for that and because he was a good host that tried to please everyone and everyone else. After a while, he entertained himself by picking up his acoustic guitar and strumming out some melodies.

I told everyone that if they wanted to smoke, they should do so in my room because it had a window in it and that if anyone got caught drinking with their left hand from then on, they had to drink again. That was my "Bull Moose" clause – another one of my drinking games. I had already laid out several ashtrays, and I periodically cleaned them out but it didn't take long before the cigarette smell could not over-power the smell of bunk being lit from the room. Angel was sitting at the head of the table near the fridge and I sat to his right. I sat down to take a breather and to watch everyone have a good time. Chan had given up the bottled beer and was pumping out of the keg from the tub into a tall red plastic cup we purchased earlier.

"Are they smoking marijuana?" Brian asked as he looked uneasy.

"Yeah. I guess," I responded as though it wasn't a big deal, and turned to Angel to ask him if he remembered that night in Stanhope.

"That was a trip. I don't remember much..."
He stopped midway through his sentence and looked at the far end of the table.

"Yo, cuz, your boy looks like he's gonna pass out. He's pale."

I looked over and it was John just swaying mildly with his red cup in hand.

"Nah, he's fine..."

Angel jumped out of his chair and having an initial reaction from his sudden movement, I got up. He ran towards Jack and said that he was about to fall. It was perfect timing because Angel grabbed him by his sweater, I grabbed the drink from his hand, and the three of us fell gently to the ground. Jack's head hit the floor with a soft thud, and he was turning white.

"Oh, shit. He's gonna die right here."

"Jack...Jack...wake up."

I started to tap his face while Angel felt for a pulse.

"Where's Alicia's sister? I'm getting some water to splash on his face."

The others must have been in shock because they hadn't realized what had happened amidst the large crash to the floor. Chris walked from behind his curtain.

"You throw a bitchin' party, dude."

Her sister came from the computer room and tried talking to our patient. I looked at Angel and asked him how we couldn't save him from falling.

"Deadweight, man. Gravity and inertia."

I looked at him as if he knew what he was talking about, or perhaps he did. I opened the windows to get fresh air in. The recycled air-conditioned air was no match for the type of heat generated with all these bodies. After a few long minutes his face gained back its color and he opened his eyes.

"Jack, are you all right? You're back from the dead. Happy Halloween," I said as I was relieved to see him recovering. We stood him up and with me on one side and Angel on the other we walked him over to the couch in my room where he sat in front of the open window. I offered him another beer, but he just wanted water.

"Whatever you want, Jack. Stay here as long as you like." I walked back into the kitchen and saw Sergei and Ivan drinking from their keg.

They both raised their cups at me.

"Za Vashye Zdarov'ye."

"Cheers, big ears," I replied.

Chris picked up his black Fender guitar and played a "Cougar" Mellencamp song I hadn't heard in a while. Of course, he changed a word or two but it was cool.

"*A little ditty 'bout Jack & Chan. Two American kids growing up in the heartland.*"

Sergei pulled out a small cigar and handed me one. I gracefully accepted it and tried to pull out my lighter from my pocket when I noticed he was struggling to find his light. When I did so, I had also pulled out a small red-clothed bag that had pull strings attached to it. His eyes opened and he was a bit intrigued with its possible contents. He reached into his pocket and pulled out a small black-clothed bag.

"Let's see your stash," I said for him to show me his contents first.

I was stunned when he opened his bag and revealed about ten loose-cut diamonds. I thought it was pretty funny because when I opened mine, it was a magnifying glass to specifically inspect diamonds and jewelry. He was equally amazed at my apparatus, and it complimented each other. I noticed Ivan keeping a close watch on the surroundings, while Sergei allowed me to inspect his treasure.

"Where did you get these?" I asked him.

"From a guy I know. We fly to Kyiv tomorrow."

"In Russia?" I was interested in logistics.

"Close. Ukraine, outside of Russia."

"Why don't you sell them here? I know a diamond dealer...a good friend of mine." I asked.

"They pay better over there. The currency is different and the market is more open. Loochshiy." *Better.*

Tina had noticed us by the tub, and I suspected she saw the shiny, glittery contents of his bag. To avoid further exposure, he quickly put his stash away, and I followed by putting my magnifier away and in my pocket. Angel walked over to me to confirm that Jack was fine.

"Sergei, you met Angel earlier." That was the last time I remember seeing either of them that night. *Good night.*

CHAPTER XXV

Christopher decided that he wasn't going home to see his parents for the weekend, but rather he felt the necessity to stay here and search for a new line of work. He usually left on Friday nights, but since I saw his bags still in the kitchen, I thought he would probably leave early Saturday morning. I grabbed a clean towel from my drawer and brought it with me, as I opened the Formica bi-fold countertop which concealed our basin tub, in the corner next to the kitchen sink. I adjusted the water temperature to a warmer setting and I closed the top so the running water would not wake him. Quickly checking the cupboards and the inside contents of the refrigerator, I took note of the bacon and eggs that would content our waking appetites and the iced tea container that was a couple of inches full that would only fill one mug.

After making the iced tea, I stepped into the hallway to use the facilities, but not before I checked the water level of my bath. It was quite dark in the apartment and the blinds of our six-foot windows were still closed except for the one in my room because the sunlight acted as the light source in the hallway through the translucent glass on my painted-shut door. The door did not have a lock on it nor had it been opened in years. The light in the hallway was on a timer and was routinely scheduled to go on at five-twenty-eight according to my watch. It would shut off around four-thirty in the morning, and if I needed to use the bathroom after then, I would need to put my bedroom light on so I wouldn't fall down the twelve long steps of the elaborate and ornate Brownstone building.

When I was finished, I went to the faucets and turned them off. I undressed of my boxers and T-shirt and hopped up and in, starting with my left foot which acted as my temperature gauge. It was just the way I enjoyed it. I entered in so fast and smooth that I made the "plopping" noise unprofessional swimmers make when they are drowning. I dunked my head and when I slowly submerged until the water was leveled at my nostrils and my ears were still covered, I heard murmuring. I looked up and Chris was there, half-smiling at me.

"What's up, brotha?" he asked as he munched on a piece of wheat bread.

"To what do I owe this surprise?" I asked jokingly as he scratched his ass and opened the refrigerator door.

He took out the already-made iced tea and drew one of the blinds to get more sunlight in. The blinds of the window next to me were still shut so no one would see my naked self when I stepped down from the tub. I unplugged the stopper and waited for him to go to his room or to look away just long enough for me to stand up and dry myself off. He threw on some shorts, a shirt, and his sandals and said that he was headed to the corner store for some orange juice. I wrapped the towel around my waist and changed into fresher clothes in my room.

"Dude, want anything from George's?"

"No, man. After this, I'm making us a fat breakfast. Do we have any milk for coffee?"

"No. I'll be back in a few." He said.

When I finished buttoning my shirt and tucked it into my blue jeans, I went back to the tub and diligently washed it clean, closed the top, and put the white dish rack back on top to conceal the tub's whereabouts. After washing my hands, I grabbed the eggs, bacon, and sausage links which were in the freezer. I did not waste time and in an instant, he returned.

He threw the Jersey Journal on the table as if he were on the front page.

"I can't believe it is 1993 already," he stated.

"Yeah and I'm already twenty-one."

He left the half-gallon carton of milk out and began putting Bustelo coffee into the strainer for its next brew. I cooked breakfast over an old *Prizer* stove which also served as our heater during the winter and while he sat and poured himself a glass of juice, I finally opened the last set of blinds and then the room was filled with immense sunlight.

"There you go, man. Now you can see the paper."

The food was just about ready, and he got up to pour us each a cup of coffee. When we finally settled, he casually explained that although the tips he made at the restaurant and bar were great, he needed to make a career move. I took the newspaper and looked through the classifieds.

"Accountant...cab driver...hairdresser, yeah right. Wait a minute. Dude, call this one... it's all you. You're perfect for it plus it is right down the street." I encouraged him.

I turned the paper around so it was facing him and then I pointed at it with a strip of bacon. I took a big sip of some of the good, rich coffee and waited to hear his reaction. He read it in its entirety and asked me where it was located. I told him it was literally a ten-minute walk from here.

"Great, man, I'm gonna call them right now."

He took a sip of his coffee and decided to eat his eggs and his entire breakfast before it became even colder.

The position called for an advertising representative for a Hemp company. He was a true believer that marijuana should be legalized, and to gain further knowledge of the industry he decided that hemp products would be a great way to start promoting his ideas and beliefs. He was really excited and into it so much, that he called and was very content with the way his prospects were looking. When he hung up, he had a big smile on his face.

Since the house phone was now unoccupied, I used it to dial Alicia who was probably downstairs with her parents. She answered the phone.

"Hello."

"Good morning, Alicia. Did I wake you?"

"No. I was up. What are you doing?"

"Chris is here. He's not going home for the weekend. You wanna go out later and catch a movie or something?"

"Sure. I'll be up there in a bit."

"All right. I'll see you later."

I wanted to do something completely different since I sensed that change was in the air. I was inspired to attempt something bigger than myself so I looked into my closet and pulled out a paint set that my father had given me. I wanted to paint something for Alicia and to give it to her as a surprise gift so I went to the cabinet underneath the sink to fill a jar with warm water to clean the brushes. I wound up staring at the canvas board for nearly an hour before I gave up. I needed more inspiration.

I learned how to draw, shade and paint from my father, and never received any real formal training in a school or class. He taught me the Color Wheel, light and darkness and complimentary colors and after so many years of just watching him create something out of nothing I really understood composition, still-life, and portraits. Some of his original works were always displayed in my parents' house.

She and I hung out for most of the day but when I returned, Chris and I bunked it and went for a ride towards the waterfront and listened to some tunes. Before returning back to the apartment, we had decided to patron a fast-food joint that was only five minutes away from home. He sped through the street as if it were his last meal, he was so hungry. I was feeling nostalgic from sitting in the passenger side of the orange Volkswagen Beetle he purchased from my dad, since it had just been parked in my parents' driveway all these years anyway. When he reached the parking lot that shared neighboring establishments but were all closed due to the late hour of midnight, he calmly let go of the accelerator and whipped a turn into the drive-thru. I had frequented this food chain for nearly my whole life and the menu had seldom changed, however, Chris felt that he should peruse through the menu to make his selection. The voice prompted a greeting and the question of what was to be ordered.

"Give me a minute," he said to the intercom while his head continued to search for his hunger relief. He was ready to order.

"What are you going to have?" he asked me.

"I'll take a number one, and hold the onions, with a Coke."

"Hello? I'm ready." He spoke into the intercom.
The voice responded and was ready to take the order.

"I'll have a number nine with cheese and an Orange soda."

"It already comes with cheese, sir."

"Wait. Make that a number four with extra pickles and an Orange soda."

"Anything else?"
He turned to me and asked me to repeat my order because he had apparently forgotten. I repeated myself.

"And a number one, hold the onions, with a Coke."

"Anything else, Sir?"

"Is that it, man?"

"Yeah, that's it." I confirmed.

"That's all," he commanded to the voice.

He shifted his car into gear and proceeded towards the first window to pay for the food. I gave him my share, he paid the attendant, and while we waited for our change one of the employees was taking the trash out to the dumpster. Chris turned to me and wanted me to roll down my window, and so I did.

"Hey, man, you throwing that garbage out?"

The young employee looked our way and nodded yes.

"Throw those two bags in the trunk. We'll take 'em."

He didn't know what to make of it. He should have just thrown the trash out like a good worker, but for some reason, he hesitated to do so. Chris popped the trunk open and helped the guy put the two smelly bags into it.

"Dude, what's up? I can't believe you just did that."

He pulled up to the second window to pick up the food, and I had been wondering if they made it without adding their own ingredients since he had been so indecisive in ordering.

"You never piss off the people who make your food," I told him.

Apparently, the fast-food joint held a contest and whoever collected all the pieces to their puzzle had chances to win all sorts of prizes and it wasn't until I held my Coke, that had a contest entry on it, that I realized that he wanted to sift through the bags of their garbage in case anyone had thrown their pieces away. He was sick, but he had his own get-rich-quick scheme.

When we got to the apartment, I helped him carry one of the garbage bags to the second floor. He closed and locked the apartment door behind us, and started to pry open one of the bags.

"Whoa, dude. Let me eat first, at least."

I had work gloves at the house and face masks in case the stench over-powered us. I checked the bags to make sure we got everything, and everything was there. I wanted to make sure that I ate before I would start sifting, but I was also cautious not to vomit it all out if the project smelled too bad. We didn't win a thing but got a lot of pieces of the game and some extras.

"Better luck tomorrow!" I said.

The following day Christopher got called in for an interview and asked me to come to check out this new place with him down on one of these old buildings on Washington and Bay Street. The area looked quite desolate as we walked by what seemed to be old and neglected brick buildings and empty lots of broken glass and debris. As we drew nearer, a tinted Cadillac pulled over and the passenger side window rolled down. I looked at the driver then I looked over at Chris and nodded him good-bye and told him that I would catch up with him later. This visit didn't concern him.

As he walked away enough of a distance the back door opened and out came Mark. I already recognized Lexy behind the driver's wheel.

"Oh! Marón! Look at you. How've you been?" Mark asked me.

"What's up, dude? I'm doing alright."

"You still in Elizabeth? Waddya doin' here? It's good to see you."

"Yeah. You too. Nah, I live down by Paulus Hook over there. Just goin' for a walk with a buddy."

"Where we're standing will be gold someday. Nothing but buildings, skyscrapers, businesses, shops, people walking their dogs...gold!" he expressed.

"I'll be lucky if I find a penny on the ground with all this glass and crap. Waddya doin' down here?" I curiously continued.

"I'm going to visit my grandmother. She lives in one of those high rises by the Mall, by the water."

"How's she doin'?"

"Good. Hey, so you straight? Need anything?"

"Nah. I'm good."

"Yeah?"

"Yeah."

"Let me know if you need anything, huh?" he gestured as he turned to get in his car.

"Stay outta trouble." He jokingly told me.

"Yeah, yeah," I said as I closed the door for him. He rolled down his window to tell me one last thing.

"Thanks for everything and take care."
I nodded to him as they continued north on Washington while I walked away and picked up a rock from the ground. I threw it as far as I could almost, hitting a piece of left-over block of concrete that had been long forgotten. Incidentally, the noise caught the attention of a rat who quickly scurried along.

What a fantastic skyline! The view of New York City from across the Hudson River was spectacular, and such an amazing country where anything is possible. *What did I want to do with my life? What is my destiny? If I could do anything with my talents, what would it be? What are my talents?* So many questions and there aren't enough hours in the day to accomplish all the things I want to do in this life. Maybe I'll start a hobby? I kicked some more rocks around as I walked on the debris of an uncared parcel of property. Perhaps I'll give back to the community in some way, invest in some property or even invest in myself. Anything is possible and I wanted to explore all of those options, legally, because it would be an extreme challenge to exercise my freedom in a prison cell.

CHAPTER XXVI

If there is one thing that Angel excelled in it's that in Billiards. He had certainly mastered the art of the game. I think it helped that he had a pool hall around the corner from where he lived, along with an arcade to entertain the youth in the neighborhood. He invested in his own *Balabushka* pool cue stick and was skilled in just about every game from eight to nine. Billiards occupied most of his time, as a hobby, and we would hang out and even participate in local tournaments sometimes.

One evening, it was his turn to rack the balls because I lost the last two rounds, but it was ok because it was fun and the music was cool.

"Eight Ball Last Pocket" he announced as the name of the game. Tom Petty's *Last Dance* started to play and with a loud crash, he broke the fifteen balls apart and the three-ball dropped in the corner pocket. He had lows.

Oh yeah, another thing he was good at was hooking up with the chicks. I am not entirely sure what his secret was other than being the bad boy because they seemed to like it when he treats them like trash. Whether it was in the form of whistling, a cat call or just flat out saying "hell–lo", to me it came off a bit rude but somehow it worked for him. Angel once told me that girls get treated nicely by their boyfriends and everyone else all the time, so sometimes they look for the not-so-nice guys, the bad boys, to hang out with.

Mutual friends of ours, Michele and Liz, walked in and saw us so they decided to quickly stop by and say hello. Michele reminded me of Charlize Theron while Liz had a pixie look to her.

It was a nice evening of music, social interaction, I learned a couple of cool pool trick-shots and it was still early. The four of us decided to go out and grab some dinner so we closed out our tab and went out the back door to where my car was parked, but something went wrong in the parking lot. He and I noticed it at the same time. His father's van was parked there and the rear doors were opened, when Angel saw his father and friend talking in the back of the van.

"Yo, Pop! What's going on? What up, Phil?" he addressed them both. But Phil was too slow in hiding the ounce of weed from Angel's sight. The two girls and I stood back while their interaction was taking place. Feliciano was caught, but luckily not by the police.

"Gotta go. Later." Phil said as he walked away to his car.

"What's up, Papi?" he asked his son.

"Don't Papi me. Is this why you never come home? We don't ever see you, you forgot my birthday, we don't ever do shit together? You're out here dealing drugs? And to my boys? In our neighborhood? That's fucked up." Angel snapped.

"Don't worry about what I do!" Feliciano responded. "Worry about getting a job and not getting up at two in the afternoon and coming in at three in the morning. Get a job like everybody else and stop living off of me and your mother. I'm doing this for you and your brother."

"You ain't doin' shit for me except for making mom lonely." He said in an angry tone.

"You want a hug?" His father opened his arms and walked towards him but he backed off.

"No, I don't want a hug. Don't fucking touch me."

I was talking to the girls about some of the pool shots they made that were impossible to make except for sheer luck, trying to divert the energy and attention of what was really going on. We walked over to my car and after the three of us got in I put on a mixed Club/House tape. The two of them were still at it, letting out their indifference to each other and clearing the air, and after a few minutes Angel came around to the passenger-side door and opened it.

"I fuckin' hate you. The next time I see you doin' that shit, I'll fuckin' kill you!" he slammed the door shut. I hate that. I really dislike when people disrespect me by trying to justify things while trying to resolve their own issues. That door did nothing to him. The van left.

"Where to?" I asked the group.

When we decided, we went over to the next town to a local steakhouse that served good drinks too. Angel decided to light a bone and the other two joined him. I cautiously drove the car as I was designated driver again.

Angel had no idea that Mr. Feliciano and I were involved in a little franchise together. I wouldn't want him to blame me for my involvement or taking part in his father's decisions to not be more involved in his family's lives. That was not my fault, was out of my control and frankly none of my business.

CHAPTER XXVII

The temp agency had decided that I lacked the credentials and experience to be qualified for any of the positions they had available. Certainly, there was something they could do. The telephone rang after a few weeks of looking through the classifieds and whole-hardly avoiding any warehouse offers.

"Coronado, I think we may have something for you. Can you please come down to my office so I could prepare you for your interview this afternoon?"
I did not want to waste my time, nor hers, by accepting a corporate position that I was not ready for, but it was better than buying the local newspaper and reading it while I watched the Market updates on television.

"I'll be there within the hour," I said while I was quickly trying to decide what to wear. I hung up the phone and immediately went through my closet to find the white shirt I was about to iron. A quick polish of the shoes, a fastening of my necktie and a "wish me luck" towards the sky, was proceeded by an exit and locking of the front door. I wondered what the job entailed and if this would be the legal career move.

It was Friday, and as I walked through the Financial District and towards the agency's headquarters, I noticed that everyone was dressed casually. Either they thought I was an executive or probably sensed that I was going to the agency which was located at the far end of the corridor of the building. I made it inside the offices and had summoned my agent through the brunette in her early twenties who sat behind her desk. I had already taken the typing and software programmed prerequisites and passed, so I needed not waste my time with any more tests. Pam met me and escorted me to her supervisor's office.

"I didn't find the position for you. I tried but there was nothing out there so I told my boss, the president of the company, and she saw to it that you would be placed somewhere."

I was optimistic. Perhaps she knew someone and called in a favor but whatever it was, I was about to enter the president's office with a smile.

"Susan, I'd like for you to meet Coronado. Coronado, this is Susan."

Pam left the office and closed the door behind her. I've had plenty of meet-and-greets and interview experience, so I expected it when she shook my hand with a firm grip and asked me to have a seat. She was a handsome and smartly dressed woman in her early forties. I kept eye contact at all times, had a very neat appearance and listened tentatively. She had explained to me that with my warehouse experience, office experience and the fact that I was bilingual, I was a sure-win to be a Maintenance Manager at a prestigious real estate company.

The girl whom I would be replacing was on vacation but had mentioned that she was looking for another line of work. She had not been let go yet, so the objective would be to learn from her as much as possible before she would be fired. I have always secretly wanted to be in real estate, so it did not surprise me to find this new niche to be appealing. I was eager to learn the business and, well, the girl was leaving anyway. Susan also expressed that there was a lot of room for advancement within the company and that she had dealt with this corporation many times in the past. I had a two o'clock appointment with Mr. Jacques Frisco, and she gave me the address. It was a few blocks away from my apartment and that also reinforced that I would be reliable and ready to take on this new challenge.

I arrived at the offices of the complex, but not before checking out the grounds and many, if not all of the tenants, lived there and commuted across the Hudson to their New York lives. It was less expensive to live in Jersey so it was a matter of great convenience and expense to travel the fifteen minutes via the subway. It would be a great responsibility to uphold the grounds and to ensure that every tenant was content with their living arrangements. I approached the receptionist at the window and we were separated by a large window with a small hole that I had to bend down to just to talk, and a small slot at the base of the glass if anyone needed to exchange any paperwork. I told her who I was and that I had an appointment with Mr. Frisco. She asked me to have a seat, but I walked towards a chair and started to read an article about the owners of the property which had been displayed in a glass frame on the wall. With my back turned, the door opened and the office manager escorted me in to see him.

"Hi, I'm Wendy. Mr. Frisco will see you now." Wendy did not look like an office manager and I sensed she lacked leadership skills right away. She had terrible posture and wore this tacky green dress which she could hardly fit into. Her long blonde hair looked like she was stuck in the seventies, and I guess that all wouldn't matter because she would be my supervisor if I accepted the position. The quick tour of the office looked as if it needed maintenance itself and whoever chose to have flat pink colored walls did not realize the fingerprints and smudge marks would make the office's appearance more horrific. The desks that were being used looked like the ones my elementary school teachers had while there were boxes, files, and papers all over the place. *Who in the hell would want to work in this dump?*

I entered his office and he had been on the phone with someone. He gestured me to have a seat that sat directly in front of his wretched gray desk and leaned against the wall. Talk about space, or lack of, for he barely had room for himself with all the papers he had piling up on this desk. I looked around as I sat there semi-motionless and saw, to my left, his CD collection on his cabinet shelf. Most of them were of classical music so maybe we had something in common. Pictures of his wife and two daughters were displayed on his desk and behind him on the wall was a black and white photograph of himself conducting an orchestra. He hung up the phone and apologized while he stood and extended a handshake and I simultaneously stood and reciprocated and we sat back down. He basically told me the same things Susan did and also stated that he liked my background experience. I was a sure candidate and he wanted me to start the next morning. The interview is a very important process in which you may or not be able to negotiate the terms of the agreement. Knowing this game so well, I told him that I had to think about it because the salary was below my expectations.

"Although the salary has been set by the main office, there is a great deal of growth potential and the benefits are great."

"I'm sure they are. I'll still have to think about it and I'll be corresponding with Susan to give her my decision. Thank you very much, Mr. Frisco, for meeting with me. Have a great day."

"Thank you. You do the same and I'm sure to hear from you soon."

We shook hands again as gentlemen and I looked around the offices as I walked myself to the front door and exited, but not before I thanked Wendy and the receptionist for their help.

When I went back to the apartment, I decided to start a new painting since I was inspired by the location of the real estate job, and not the job itself. I grabbed a 20x24 stretched canvas and stared at it for about fifteen minutes and since I would be located alongside the Hudson River, I wanted to do something aquatic. I thought about it some more while I gathered my favorite brushes together and prepared my mixing solvents. The blank slate remained that way until ideas started forming.

I squeezed Cerulean blue from the tube and placed it on my plexiglass palette. I enjoyed using this type of palette rather than the wooden ones because I could easily clean it better. I painted the sky, light blue with an assortment of clouds, and then started mixing my blue with some yellow to form my landscaped horizon. *It was pretty neat.* I even added a faint mountain on the right side, but the bottom half of the painting was empty and after about an hour, I decided to take a break so I cleaned my brushes and walked to the park and breathed in the fresher air. Things were starting to look up and I was feeling a little better about the way things were going. I walked over to an empty bench and sat there staring at Ellis Island as I was thinking about my options and decisions.

I started to think about what Alicia had said to me about her ambitions in getting into real estate as she had been weighing her options about her career choices and ultimately enjoyed working in the outdoors as opposed to an office position or just being cooped up indoors. She had the "Holly Golightly" attitude about being caged, and would rather buy homes, renovate them and buy more, all on her own terms and pace. I shared the same beliefs and attitude of that real estate realm, but I saw it best for me to pursue the corporate route to gain some business ethics. I pondered and sat as pigeons were slowly making their route towards me as if I had some bread for them. It was food for thought for me.

I went back to the studio and found myself inspired to create a beautiful landscape of the serene outdoors and the woods which were the homes of furry little creatures and nature's wildlife. Certainly, it would also represent my self-expression of freedom and the outdoors as well, but it mainly served as an illusion of a life outside the boundaries of my cityscape and the booming industrialism that was forming along the waterfront. It was my plan to escape the life in which I subconsciously dreaded regarding being another cog in the wheel and feeling the effects of not being able to appreciate the wonders of the world presented to me on my own terms.

I had received the call from Susan the following morning, and after a few compromises and understandings, it was agreed that I would start the following day. The gears were in motion and my opportunity to shine was for me to be responsible for an entire complex. I hadn't realized how complex it would be until I returned that morning, and was faced with my first challenge within the first hour I arrived because on that day a Hurricane came, and it struck for hours.

My primary concern was for the safety of the tenants first, and to worry about the assessment of the damage at the nearest convenient time. The rest of the office personnel were alerted to stay home, except for Wendy who lived in the building that the office served as the first floor for. She called Mr. Frisco on the telephone and told him that I was there already, and I had no intentions of leaving on my first day, especially with the vicious winds brewing outside the windows. I overcame that day and others like it for nearly a year now.

I knew our tenants by first names and would greet them as they walked throughout the premises. I would often take walks to visit the concierges of each building to pick up on possible tenant concerns that they may encounter during their day. When I returned to my office one Friday morning the receptionist told me that there was a man waiting for me inside. When I asked her if she knew who he was she said that she didn't but that he was extremely nice and didn't have any issues at all and when I walked into the room and switched the light on, there was Mark standing up from patiently waiting in the corner chair. We gave each other a quick hug and I closed the door behind me before we sat across from each other.

"How long has it been? Since last year right down the block there?" I pointed south toward my apartment. "You look good."

"Thanks. You don't look too bad yourself." He said.

"So, what brings you around?"

"I was in the neighborhood and wanted to personally thank you for taking care of my grandmother while she's here. It means a lot to me."

"Your grandmother? Yeah. Of course. She's awesome. I make sure everything's taken care of in her place. I had two of her windows replaced because the condensation that built up over the years. She has a better view of the City now and the guys in the lobby make sure that they open the door for her whenever she goes for her walks."

He stood up and I followed. "I'm having a little get-together tomorrow and I also wanted to personally invite you to come." Mark pulled a pen out of his suit jacket and wrote on a pad I had next to my work phone.

"Here's the address. I'll see you tomorrow."

"Yeah, thanks! I'll be there."

"Oh, and another thing...I put a little *something* in your car for helping me out."

"My car?" I asked.

He opened the door and kept it open.

"Yeah don't worry about it."

Respect. Not only is it my job to ensure all the tenants are comfortable in their living environment but giving a little of one's self, goes a long way with humanity. It was good to see Mark again since we've based our relationship around trust and integrity and we were from the same neighborhood, and I wasn't even phased that he knew where I worked or where my car was. *My car.* I wouldn't be able to get to it until about lunchtime because of the workload and assignments that I had to take care of. I tore the paper off the top of the pad, folded it a couple of times so it would fit in my shirt pocket.

Right before lunchtime, I went out the back door to the parking facility to check out my car. The lot itself had five floors and a decent view from on top and often we would find empty beer bottles and some fast food trash, not far from where the garbage can is placed, presumably from party-goers during the evening hours. I usually park on the second floor so I could go in and out of my space more easily without having to be bottle-necked or congested from patrons entering or exiting the facility, on the first floor.

I took a flight of stairs up and unto the second floor and walked towards where I thought I parked. I didn't see my Lincoln Continental so I stopped in my tracks. I looked back towards the stairwell and saw the number "2" on the wall just to verify that I had gotten off the correct floor. I took another look by panning left then to the right again. I double-backed and went up to the third floor because, sometimes due to congestion, I have parked on other floors. Verifying the "3" securely fastened on the next floor I looked to where I thought I parked but there were fewer cars there and I didn't see it. I pulled out my car alarm which was attached to my key and pointed it to the lot while pressing the button numerous times. *Nothing.* I went back to the second floor and did the same thing except that while I was wildly pointing my alarm-clicker everywhere I did hear my alarm. I stopped, did an about-face and went downstairs to the ground floor.

I walked to the back door of the office cut through by the receptionist's desk and asked her if I had any calls or messages while I was gone. She told me that it has only been less than twenty minutes since I had been gone it was unlikely that she could have missed such a call. I pressed the button again as I neared the front office entrance. The front parking area was small and primarily accommodated our quick delivery vans, parking for the handicapped and visitors interested in leasing one of our apartments. Although my car was legally parked out front in a safe area, I know that it was originally parked in the lot out in the back of the building and as I looked at it more closely it appeared a little odd. It was trunk-heavy.

I remained calm. There was nothing for me to fear. I didn't do anything wrong other than having my car parked in front of my workplace which was shunned against and my boss would probably have a fit from all the politically-driven nonsense talk that goes on in most office environments. I had to move it before the chatty-patty receptionist said anything to anybody who would listen. I started the car. The "Car is Leveling" light came on and my vehicle adjusted itself accordingly. I drove to the supermarket on Marin & 18th and parked it there, away from other cars, as I shut off the engine and walked to the back of the car which was noticeably lower than usual.

What was in the trunk? My Qualcomm phone rang. It was Leonard Beauregard.

CHAPTER XXVIII

I met Leonard at the Property Complex a few months ago. His company was building a hotel in between some of the high-rises, and as the General Manager, he was tasked with overseeing the completion of the construction. He and a small staff of four shared office space at our Leasing Office, and our cubicles at the time were only about ten feet from each other. Professionally, he was known as Leonard and after a while, I graduated into calling him Leo for short but there comes a point in time where even a nickname is perhaps too formal. I referred to him as "LB" for short at times or sometimes I would just call him "Pound", and when he was with the hotel staff, I referred to them as the "dawg pound".

Our interactions and close proximity to each other allowed for the opportunity to know someone a bit closer, and so at times, I joined the staff of their popular hotel chain for dinner and even drinks. I mentioned to Alicia how cool of a guy Leo was and the conversation pivoted on whether he was single or married. She convinced me that it would be nice for the four of us to go out for dinner some evening. The fourth person is a friend of hers, so I mentioned it to him and he was open to it after some initial reluctance.

It was "blind date" night and I was sitting there, staring really, for an unaccountable amount of time, at a young boy playing with his red Matchbox car on the top of the dining table, while his parents were just engaging in conversation with each other. When he looked up at me, I looked into his dark, brown eyes, and envied his innocent youth. I had then realized that I had been day-dreaming, thinking about how things used to be, beginning with my father, and becoming aware of life and how I had lived it. The boy began to smile and, from his pocket, he pulled out another miniature car, and held it up towards me, signaling that he wanted me to play with him. I only smiled back at him, and disengaged eye contact and started to join in with my dinner companions.

The four of us sat at a Japanese restaurant looking through the selective menu and deciding whether or not we were going to eat sushi with Saki. My stomach could not take Chinese food from local restaurants. Besides, I've never seen any of the workers eating four wings with pork fried rice. Alicia and I started carrying the conversation so Leo or Andra could jump right in whenever they felt a bit more comfortable or social. It was their first time meeting each other and we felt that they had a lot in common, so we insisted that they meet and try to get to know one another.

"So how long have you known Alicia?" he asked his blind date as he picked up his hot tea and began to slowly sip it, and waited to hear a response and her voice. Alicia had known Andra for about four years, but they never really spent personal time together because it was mostly work-related. She was a tall, young woman with a slim figure and her straight blonde hair stopped just below her neck. I met her one day when I was visiting Alicia at the office and I was speaking to Cheryl in the kitchen. She had just walked in, saw that Cheryl and I were speaking, and I guess walked back out so as not to disturb us, but Cheryl called her back in and introduced us. I hardly spoke to her after that as she was a quiet, diligent person who always looked busy when I visited.

"I've known Alicia for about four years." She turned to her seeking affirmation and perhaps trying to get her to say something or join in on the conversation.

"So... how did you two meet?" Leo asked us. I knew she probably would not have immediately answered so I obliged his question.

"My sister briefly introduced us, but she was a little distant towards me. When she had left my parent's house, I called my sister to the kitchen and told her that she was the one I was going to marry. It was love at first sight. Well on my end anyway." They chuckled.

I looked over at her, and underneath the table, we had already been holding hands. We had a great meal full of casual dining and talk, and more importantly for me, some reminiscence.

"Well, the night's young. Why don't we all come to my place and unwind? I've got a nice bottle of Sauvignon that's just begging to be opened." Leo suggested.

I thought it sounded like a great idea. I was with people with whom I had felt comfortable and so we proceeded to leave the restaurant and we drove to LB's with two cars – Alicia and I in hers, and Leo and Andra in his. He lived only a few minutes away, so I thought that conversation would be a minimum for them until we got to his place.

Although his favorite period of art was the Renaissance, an original Kandinsky hung on his den wall. It fit the genre of his abode because, like the painting, everything was thrown around in an organized mess. A Matisse and a Picasso complimented his antique silver-gray walls and the more I looked around, the more I realized that he enjoyed the Bohemian motif. It was a modern place that overlooked the busy Holland Tunnel from the south. Constant construction and rebuilding of the area made it difficult for anyone to get a great night's sleep. Luckily for him, the new residential building being built would eliminate the noise levels substantially coming from the tunnel but not entirely blocking its view.

I was staring at an oil painting of Napoleon he had in his parlor, while he gave the ladies a quick tour of the place and it was pretty cool for a corporate manager of a prestigious hotel, but that's what was cool about him, was that he was down to earth and we could hold normal conversations without judging the other. LB was a clean-cut guy who parted his hair to one side and grew modest-length sideburns. He wore thin black-framed glasses and sharply tailored suits that complimented his polished black shoes but was never stuffy or overbearing with power. He appreciated and enjoyed the finer things.

The phone rang and LB excused himself from the room while he took it in the kitchen. Chances were that it was the wrong number, or if it wasn't, it was a call that he was obligated to forward to his neighbor. The phone company had some trouble in the area a few days before and his number was crossed with another's in the building. His neighbor received several calls from Leo's job and he was kind enough to understand the situation and take messages for him. This reminded me of when I ran that Numbers operation years back near Third Street. Since then, Louie has been reciprocating the favor. Funny thing is, they never revealed the other's phone number to anyone else.

We continued chatting about how content to be where we were. The ambiance surely was of a calming nature, and the Miles Davis record playing in the distance gave me a relaxed feeling as I took the last gulp of my fine red wine. He came back into the room alarmed and told us that he had to step out to the Hotel for a moment.

"Can I get anyone anything before I return?"

"No. We're fine. Be careful."

I wasn't sure how long he would ultimately take but we made ourselves comfortable. I found myself staring at another one of his Picasso pieces appreciating the style and modern techniques it possessed. Andra walked over, quietly stood next to me while holding her drink, and began talking about art and art history. What I didn't know about her was that she was a curator for an art gallery in

Soho, NY. We innocently flirted with each other in tasteful dialogue and after some friendly back and forth jabbing and compliments, we clinked glasses and stared back at an oil reproduction of Picasso's *Le Rêve*, or "The Dream" in French, originally painted in 1932.

After several rings, and a couple of quick glimpses around the parking lot, I answered Leonard's phone call and was surprised at what he had to say as we went back and forth on pleasantries.

"I'm taking Andra to Denver this weekend...Yeah, we're good...Nice. Hey! Every time she comes over, she stares at the Picasso in the Living Room. She truly likes it." He said.

I thought back to how she and I had a cool moment the last time we saw each other at his place and I felt very satisfied that they were still together in that I felt like I was part of something organic.

"I told her that I commissioned you to paint it for me and she was stunned. She had no idea! She kept going on and on about how you were into Realism and that Rembrandt was your favorite artist and Modernism didn't impress you. I told her that you had a big collection of works, and showed her a couple of pictures you gave me, and now she wants to know if you would consider showing them to her for a possible opportunity to display them at a gallery in Soho."

"Get outta here, dude!" I exclaimed.

"No. I'm serious."

"That sounds great! I'll get my portfolio together and show them when youse get back from Colorado...Yeah...Have a safe trip...Have fun!"

I put my car key back into the trunk lock and turned it and when it opened, I received a blast from smells I hadn't encountered in a long time. There were rolls of wrapped meats of different kinds and sizes: Salami, Pepperoni, Chorizo, Genoa Salami and a rump of Capicola. He must have known or lucky for me that there wasn't any Mortadella, but still, there was a lot of meat in my trunk that needed to be refrigerated, and soon. I pulled the address out of my shirt pocket. He lives in Hoboken – the birthplace of Baseball and Frank Sinatra.

CHAPTER XXIX

I always enjoyed driving to Hoboken, Jersey City's neighbor in the north, because of the old factories and brick buildings I had to pass through. If I wasn't taking exit 14C on the Turnpike and driving down the ramp towards the Holland Tunnel, I was taking Jersey Avenue and crossing 16th Street into the historical landmark city that housed the set of "On the Waterfront" which featured Marlon Brando as Terry Malloy in 1954. Often, in order to access the other side of Hoboken, I would take Paterson Plank Road to 14th Street, especially if I needed to meet anyone at the Malibu Diner. My least favorite route was taking Tonnelle Ave because of the incident in '94 when a bowling ball fell unto a car's windshield, from above, killing an eight-month-old.

I hadn't been to Mark's before but it wasn't any surprise to me that he dwelled close to many of the old gambling spots and that parking spots were few and far between, especially on Jefferson St. A sun-shower came and went and I was pleased to know that the raindrops would not wet my clothes or hair. After I finally parallel-parked, almost too close to a fire hydrant, I looked at the city signs for any special parking times and permits. It was Saturday and I was clear to have a good time because after all, I deserved it from all those long hours I put in at my job. I walked around the corner towards Jefferson and followed the house addresses. I had to cross the street to get to his and when I reached the bottom of the stairs, I looked up and two guys were at the door.

As I began my climb I looked around at the neighboring Brownstones and an old lady who was also climbing her steps looked at me and looked down again to avoid further eye contact. It was quiet except for some music that got louder as I got closer to the front door, and then one of the guys opened it for me. To me, it was like the scene in *The Wizard of Oz* when Dorothy opened the front door after her house crashed in Munchkin Land. From black and white to color in the film, except that when the door opened there was no entrance to the inside of a house.

I walked through the front wall of what appeared to be the outside of all the other houses on the block but I was immediately led into a front Courtyard with a well-manicured landscape and a few other armed men. The actual front entrance of the house was on Adams St. and this lot was the rear entrance to that house. Because of the weather clearing up from the recent rain sprinkle, guests were coming back outside to enjoy the gardens and music from the live five-member band in black and tuxes who were also setting up and getting ready to perform again. It was like I was just in time for whatever occasion the party was intended for.

A robust young woman in a red dress and a pearl necklace came over to me with a smile.

"Hey, handsome. You look like you could use a drink." She said to me with innocence and without it sounding like a pick-up line.

I looked into her eyes, since her heels brought us to that level, and revealed that I would like a glass of red wine so she called one of the drink servers over.

"One red and one white please." She softly asked in a respectful manner and with a smile.

"You must be Coronado. I am Marie. My brother told me how well you take care of our grandma."

"Very nice to meet you, Marie. I didn't know Mark had a sister, and now I can see the resemblance." I continued.

"I hope I'm the prettier one." She flirted.

"You most certainly are." I gestured with a smile.

The two glasses of wine came and we raised them to make a toast. I asked her what we should toast to.

"To us and our wedding." She seriously stated while I was just playing along.

The band began to play and then Mark walked out with his grandmother in his arm and they both greeted me.

"I see you've met my granddaughter. Isn't she beautiful?" She pimped.

"A real nice lady." I countered and she was really attractive with her long dark brown hair, strong manicured hands and she wasn't afraid to smile. Mark disengaged and was about to continue to graciously host his party.

"Excuse us, there are a few people I'd like Coronado to meet," Mark said as we left the two of them.

Terracotta pots were lined up against one section of the courtyard, hosting several fruit trees and one cactus plant. I really enjoyed the mini ornate three-tiered bird bath sculpture, or perhaps it was just a water fountain that invited feathered friends, but what really stood out to me was the manicured topiary.

I recognized a Judge who presided over a case when I served as a juror in Jersey City. He wore an unmistakable full, luxuriant and bushy mustache but had a bald head with a small noticeable mole on his left side of his scalp. Jury duty was another right as a tax-paying American where I can serve in our judicial system. The case involved someone being attacked by a pipe and I remembered filling out a juror questionnaire to see if I were fit to serve as a juror in this case. The judge addressed me.

"Juror eleven, it says here that you were involved in a similar incident. Please explain to the Court." He stated.

"Well, your Honor, I was involved in a similar case because I had to use a baseball bat to defend myself from being jumped by fifteen guys from Bayonne."

"How did you know they were from Bayonne?"

"Because I was in Bayonne." I quickly responded.

The courtroom was in an uproar of laughter.

"Juror eleven, you are dismissed from this case."

Another server came and he grabbed two glasses of white wine, Pinot Grigio I later confirmed, and he began to introduce me to some of the other guests. I met some Union representatives, one from the Waste Water Plant another from a construction company, and if I remember right one from the Waterfront park system. They were an exciting group of people who understood business and teamwork. The Mayor stopped by for about twenty minutes but he had to go swiftly to attend one of his own family functions. After about an hour, maybe two, I decided that I didn't want to overstay my welcome so I decided to leave.

I started to stroll closer to the front door when I noticed a group of three guys conversing, wearing blue jeans and boots while drinking imported beer. One of them looked extremely familiar with a distinct red beard but looked rugged and serious, yet approachable like a cool uncle. *Red Beard*. They were probably some bikers Mark knew but at least they wore suit jackets and carried themselves well in conversation amongst themselves. *No. Wait.* He was no vagrant and his hands and fingernails weren't nearly as soiled as Chooch's hands.

"And then we were on a Code 5 watching these punks..." he continued to say. *These guys are cops. JC's finest undercover squad. How long was Starlight being watched? I need to warn Grieco.* When I caught another glimpse of him from afar, he looked right at me and gave me a puckered kiss. *Maybe I've just been warned?*

The DooWop group singing in the background were performing live to a song I hadn't heard in a long while, *Take Me as I Am* by The Duprees, and that's probably why they were known as "Oldies but Goodies". The Duprees had a series of hit records and founded in the early 1960s, in

Jersey City, by students from William L. Dickinson High School. Dickinson is that huge school that looks like a fort and sits on top of Newark Ave and Palisade Ave.

"Mark, nice party!" I was thankful and grateful for the invite. "What's the occasion?" I asked as if there needed to be one. Marie must have seen that I was preparing to leave, and Mark was aware of that. He put his arms around the both of us, while she held a two-foot-long baby boa constrictor.

"Your engagement party with my sister." I looked at him in confusion. He released his arm from Marie and we kept walking.

"Just kiddin'. I'm glad you came and had a good time. We have big plans for you and it involves most of those people you met in there. We are one big happy family and family comes first."

"Yeah. Nothing more important than family." I affirmed.

"How's the art thing? I want you to do my portrait. Waddya think, huh?" He teased.

"Let me know when. I think it'll look great on a wall." I confirmed.

Mark walked off while Marie came over with her snake. "You guys sure like reptiles," I mentioned because of Izzy the iguana.

"This is 'Sneaker'. He's harmless." She downplayed the fear of being strangled, mauled or bitten by a snake by making it a cute thing. Wanna hold him?"

"No, thanks, but I do have to go. Maybe next time?"

"Ok, Coronado, but next time don't be so shy with me. I won't bite, but maybe Sneaker will." She joked, I think.

CHAPTER XXX

Inspired by the view I had from living in the Paulus Hook area, I often painted scenes of the Hudson River, The Statue of Liberty and Ellis Island, and of the New York Skyline. Periodically I would capture images of Water Towers and various other towers. My Abuela's brother helped construct them back in the day and he still roams around this city in his guayabera and gumbalini. Tio Tony must know a lot of history of this place, and I should visit him some time to hear about his childhood.

Being around Mark's family felt good and inspiring. I had been working on a piece of artwork for a while and I wanted to wrap it up. I finished a still-life painting I made of a red toolbox, a tape measure, a red pipe wrench and a bottle of Malta Goya. It was an oil on canvas and completely dry so I wrapped it up and decided to bring it over to its new owner and his new stash house.

He was taking a long shower to wash away all the dirt and grime from a sewer job, and that was why I decided to watch a video on his television to pass the time. It was labeled "La Promesa", and when I pressed *play*, it was a group of five jíbaros, which refers to "la gente de la montaña" or "mountain people", in their guayaberas or a traditional button-down shirt with at least four pockets in the front, playing a combination of Spanish musical instruments including Quattros, a guido, and maracas. The lead singer sang soulfully of upcoming promises and I felt my spirit agreeing with him.

CHAPTER XXXI

I drove over to the Marion Section, an area where Arturo Gatti lived in his teenage years, but perhaps, more importantly, was laid out in the 1870s and planned as a blue-collar residential community to work at Lorillard Tobacco Company, American Can Company, or nearby railroad yards. On the corner of Broadway Ave, and Wallis Ave was one of my favorite Italian restaurants and so it was a delight to hear that I was asked to meet there at 7 pm. I parked in front of Rita & Joe's lot and walked in.

The usual guy with the white shirt, black pants, and skinny black tie was behind the bar cleaning glasses and only a few tables were already occupied. I looked around and didn't see anyone I recognized but the men's room door on the right opened and it was one of Sonny's guys, wearing a red kerchief again, drying his hands with a paper towel.

"How you doin'? You ready?" he immediately asked me as if he were in a hurry to get somewhere. He led the way into the dining area and then opened the kitchen door, whereby I looked around at the eating patrons and entered into a room I thought never to have seen up close and at first hand. There was one of the owners making desserts that I oh so loved ordering at the end of every meal there, especially the cookies. Past the preparers and wait staff, I was led outside the back door where past the cigarette butts and trash can I was suddenly in another parking lot that joined with a delivery company. He asked me to get into a golf cart that was parked there.

There must not have been a Governor switch on the cart because we were going really fast passing about ten truck docks, on my right, in seconds and weaving around a car that was backing out of its spot. A rail line was on our left, possibly the Path Train rail that goes to and from Newark Penn Station and suddenly we were on Fayette Ave. I didn't know where we were until he made a right, after a couple of blocks, unto a street that I hadn't been on in a long time and one of my other favorite Italian restaurants was on that corner of West Side Ave. and Broadway: Puccini's Restaurant and Catering.

That was the place where I was introduced to the term "a la carte". I had taken Alicia on a date here, at one time, and when our waiter came over, he also brought over an actual cart that displayed each of the entrée items and also a separate cart for dessert items. I thought that the meals were already heated and prepared enough that all we had to do was select that particular plate. There was no waiting, fast-food service, but I hadn't realized that it was just a visual representation of the actual food selection. Instead of looking at the menu I just pointed at the Lasagna and Tiramisu options. *What did I know?*

The valet guy took the golf cart from there in exchange for a black Cadillac Brougham. As a precaution, in the event I was being followed or tailed, Grieco's crew switched vehicles and caused a misdirection of my whereabouts but now I was in the passenger seat headed to "who knows where".

"Seatbelt," he dictated. He didn't say much but when he did, I somehow didn't question it and listened. We took a scenic route leading up Broadway to Journal Square, then taking Sip Ave to Summit to the Junction. Along the way, I took a closer look at the people of this city, how every single decision affects the next, and how it has made me stronger and more resilient.

"Now this could only happen to a guy like me, and only happen in a town like this." I crooned.

"Oh, we got a Sinatra fan." He pressed play in a CD that was already cued for the next Frank Sinatra tune and played it moderately low, not too loud or distracting, yet still very appealing and audible to the ears.

We were at a red traffic light and I glimpsed over. On Summit Ave, before it hits Communipaw, across from the Sunoco gas station, stands four remaining brownstone buildings where my godfather, Uncle Frank, currently resides in one of them. He is one of my father's oldest friends while growing up in Jersey City, and was there when I was baptized in the eyes of the Catholic Church. To me, being a godfather was a sacred trust between a child and its caretakers, and I am glad my father has a friend like him.

I still wasn't sure where we were headed as the light turned green and we proceeded on Garfield Ave towards Greenville. To the left was a wasteland of old factories and it didn't really help the neighborhood from its inability to provide real value to the community. A couple of lights later he put his left directional to get on the Turnpike on Bayview Ave and from there I can wind up anywhere.

As I looked out the car window, I noticed my reflection and then pondered on the moment of who I was really looking at. Where was I going, not only now but in the future and who am I? *How did I get here?* Many questions scurried to my mind as to whether or not I made the right decisions and choices in life. There were no "take-backs", no "do-overs" and could not think of many regrets if any.

I thought about my love for this city and how I would go to Liberty State Park to paint landscapes of the New York Skyline with maybe a bench, bird or rail in the foreground from our side of the river. The trees and bushes have already grown since the last time I was there and so you wouldn't really recognize the same image as in my paintings, or any of my works for that matter because of the time I lived in it. *Change is inevitable.* "All things must pass", as George Harrison once or twice said.

Continuing on Bayview we kept going on Morris Pesin Drive towards Liberty State Park. I rolled the automatic window down a little to hear the clanking of ropes of all the flags as they hit the aluminum poles they were on. Majestically, flags of every US state hung and lead to the South-East side of the Park.

"Sonny thanks you for stopping those guys from fully attacking us. There are a lot of misguided people out there who think they can just take what's not theirs, but he knows you're an earner."

Making a left on Freedom Way gave me a scenic route and tour as we headed towards the marina and the Central Railroad of New Jersey Terminal. I thoroughly enjoyed seeing and hearing the sounds of the car as we rode on the cobblestone pathway towards the water.

It was about a twenty–minute drive before the driver pulled over as close to the Terminal as he could. He unlocked the car doors and signaled for me to get out, with the nod of his head.

"Thanks," I said as I got out. As soon as my feet were planted on the ground, I looked around at the nearby parked rail cars, towards the huge red building and then towards the water where I saw Mr. Salvatore "Sonny" Grieco, and a couple of others guys not so far away from him, sitting on a bench facing the Twin Towers. I walked over to him and before I approached him, I was searched for any weapons by one of his suited guys.

"Yup." He said and let me continue.

"Sit down." Sonny directed. "Here's the thing..." he continued. "Things are sometimes not what they appear to be. Life is full of mysteries. Wouldn't you agree?"

I'm not dead I thought to myself. I loosened up some of the tension that had built up within the past couple of hours.

"Change is good. We need to embrace change." I responded.

"Take Downtown Jersey City, for example. It used to be full of Italians and Puerto Ricans with a small pocket of Polish and Russians but it was good. Colgate factory workers had jobs in Paulus Hook, bars were full and things were done, but now the prices of houses and apartments are going up because people from New York are coming over here to live. They got good-paying jobs over there but the rents are too damn expensive, for the small amount of square footage, so they live here and commute back and forth. And because of that we can't afford the rents and are forced to live somewhere else. It's called gentrification. Fuckin' believe that? Gentrification."

The horn from the Circle Line boat was loud as it was approaching and preparing to dock nearby to pick up and drop off passengers who wished to visit Ellis Island and/or Liberty Island.

"Thing is...my son has confirmed everything I have known about you. The Numbers, working at the Ports and warehousing, involved in real estate, great education...and the stuff in between you can't learn in schools. *You* did this. Now, I'm just a guy who owns a couple of restaurants and maybe I don't know a thing or two, but it'll be good to have a guy like you in my corner."

"Who's your son?" I asked.

"C'mon...we don't do names but I'm very proud of my son, Mark. You've been in the business for a long time and have adapted to the changes that life has thrown at you. And my mother-in-law, my wife's mother...thanks you for looking out for her. Sorry I couldn't come to your engagement party in Hoboken." He joked.

I smiled but was still confused as to what was being asked of me.

"Mr. Grieco...it seems that family is important to you as it is to me but do you know who took out my uncle Felix?" I insisted.

"I know you'll do the right thing by working for me. There are a few key political influences I would like for you to meet." He persisted.

"Sonny?" I questioned again.

"Carmine will take you back, but first you have questions. The answers you seek are in that building." He motioned for me to stand up and go while a couple of the guys slowly approached to escort me.

"Ciao, Coronado. Change is good and inevitable. You have a bright future ahead of you."

"Thank you," I responded but mainly for not taking my life. I didn't know what was awaiting me inside the Train Terminal. It's been there far longer than I have and will probably remain there after I'm gone. The time on the clock was 2:03, my birthday.

CHAPTER XXXII

I had always enjoyed not only being at Liberty State Park but also attending multiple events at the Central Railroad of New Jersey Terminal. It offers shelter from the elements while waiting for the next ferry to arrive or when there is a big event or concert occurring at the park. I would spend most of my Fourth of July celebrations here, however, this location is extremely enriched with a history dating back to at least early 1600 when the Native American people used it as a big landing place at the side of the river, or Lenape.

As I walked in, I could remember the same smell as when I attended Scout events and evening photo opportunities of the old wood and the connected abandoned rail yard. The place has many times been restored, painted and preserved as a Historical landmark. Standing by Track 14, which offered destinations such as Bayonne, Elizabeth and even Lincoln, New Jersey, was a man I knew and recognized starting from a long time ago in the days I could first remember. He wore a long wool coat, gray pants, and shiny black shoes, as I did. His style of hair was impeccably the same as mine but greyer and the distinct characteristics of his demeanor, including the length of his earlobes, was incredibly similar. It was me twenty years from now. He slowly turned around.
"Dad?"

I walked towards him. I looked around to see if anyone else was with us or even watching. We were alone.

"La bendición. What's going on?"

"Hey! Dios de bendiga." He responded.

"What are you doing here? How do you know those guys? I don't get it." I was confused. We both turned and started to walk towards the outside because there was a slight echo from within and also because it was less confrontational. I really believe it was because we were each looking for a bench to sit on. I could hear a flutist street performer playing what sounded to me like a Jethro Tull tune. The acoustics in the building were amazing.

"Sal and I go back a long way. Back when things were much different than what they are now." He started to explain.

"We never talked about the way things were before I was born. I just know that you were in the Navy and went to St. Bridget's located Downtown and then went to Lincoln High School." I confirmed.

"There's a lot of history and a lot of things you don't know about yet."

A small crowd came and went, most likely tourists from a Liberty tour, but we weren't overly concerned with exposing national secrets. The flutist stopped playing because the passengers must have gone their ways, I guessed. We hadn't made it outside yet although the sounds of a few pigeons cooing reminded me of Mr. Feliciano. I then heard the soft sound of the flute whose melody was exactly that of Ravel's *Bolero*.

"So, what happened to Tio Felix?" I mildly demanded.

"I'm sorry about him. He married your mother's sister a long time ago."

"Dad?"

"'Felix the Cat', your uncle Felix, was being tailed by the Feds not only from one of his customers, Ralphie, who was an undercover agent and had so much evidence on him that he would be going away for life but also for a murder he committed of a government official a while back. They arrested Felix's attorney who enjoyed snorting an eight ball a weekend, and also turned on him. It was just a matter of time before they would close down on him and then close in on you." He tried to explain.

"But I don't do that stuff." I interrupted.

"You used to. You think I don't know about the hustles, your late-night sneak-outs, Starlight? You're just lucky you didn't get caught by the cops, or even Red Beard!" he said.

But I wasn't out of the game. I eventually sold all of my leftover coke stash to Tio Felix, and before I left his stash apartment in a hurry, I grabbed the duffel bag that was in his oven which was where he kept his stuff, and now it's in the trunk of my car back at Rita & Joe's.

"How do you know all of this?" I asked my father.

"Things are not what they seem. Certain truths have been hidden throughout societies to protect people. To protect you. It's like people believing that the earth is round, or that we landed on the moon."

"Wait. What?"

"You're an artist. You know what I mean. You have an open mind. You never dropped the ball, but instead, you push outside the limits. I am extremely proud of you!" he shouted. "Don't you have a show coming up?"

"Tonight, actually." I looked down at my wrist watch.

I didn't consider myself to be solely an artist since I have delved in many things and am many things to different people, and I am not quite sure what my true vocation or destiny is yet, but whenever it fruitions I'm sure I'll be ready for it. For now, it seems, I am my father's son.

I don't know how, but a clarinet joined in on the medley as the sun hit our faces exposing it to the light and at this point, I wasn't really sure if the sun existed or if we lived in an elaborate dome.

We found a bench near the water and unbuttoned our coats before we sat. I remembered when he used to hold me up to look out the viewfinders along the waterfront. After all, this was my father, one of only two people I have ever trusted, with my mother being the other. *What does mom know? How does she fit in all of this?*

By now I had gotten over the shock of my uncle's death or maybe just distracted by the sudden revelations. Throughout my youth, I had been to almost every one of our family's wakes or funerals. I had been exposed to death so much that I had already accepted it as a part of life. We are born to live, then die, I suppose, but I became so numb at the idea that I started to stray from the notion of feeling sadness or rage anymore. I had understood that it was a fact of life that we must all face at one point in our lives or another. Because of my empathy, I had developed the power to comfort people in times of sorrow and death, but as I sat with my dad, I returned to that feeling of gratefulness of being surrounded by meaning, purpose, and love.

Carmine walked over from the car to ensure that we were all right and unharmed, and to let us know that he would be leaving. I told him that I would catch a ride with my father, so he continued his ride back to where he was needed. My dad also signaled that it was ok.
"We'll go to the gallery together," he assured me.

"Thank you, and mom, for teaching me the keys to success. You both have always helped to show me the path to righteousness, but I guess I ultimately wanted to learn those lesson on my own. You've made it too easy to have known the correct course but I felt like it was cheating my life. Maybe I like doing things the hard way. My own way. How do I get back on course?" I asked.

"Where do I start?" he asked me.
"How about when you were born? I want to know all about it, but I want to know the truth."
"I'll reveal what I can." He said me as we started to walk away. And so continued on the flutist, the clarinet player and a guy playing harmonica to complete the crescendo of Bolero as it could only be played by three musicians in this unique and diverse Jersey City...with hustle and pride.